"Braunbeck is much more than a superbly-skilled storyteller. Popular fiction doesn't get any better than this."
—William F. Nolan, Author of *Nightworlds*

"Braunbeck is one of the brightest talents working in the field."
—Thomas Monteleone, Author of *The Blood of the Lamb*

"A phenomenally talented writer who never seems to make a misstep."
—*Shocklines*

"Gary A. Braunbeck is simply one of the finest writers to come along in years."
—Ray Garton, Author of *Ravenous*

"Braunbeck's power is that he can see our fear and our pain, and he can bring it to life in a way that can be both terrible and beautiful at the same time. But he can also see light in the darkness, and his stories and novels, no matter how bleak they may become, also contain a kernel of hope, of humanity."
—*Horror World*

"Gary A. Braunbeck is one of the new breed of horror writers, writing dark noir that will have readers back with the lights on and jumping out of their skin."
—*Midwest Book Review*

"Braunbeck's impeccable skills as an author are a great example of all that horror fiction should be."
—Dread Central

THE GHOSTLY PROCESSION

Charlie Smeds and Eugene Talley watched, dumbstruck, as an ancient, rickety, horse-drawn wooden wagon made its way down the street, the driver's face hidden by a thick kerchief covering his nose and mouth.

The wagon was filled with dead bodies and unearthed tombstones. Some of the bodies were so badly decomposed that bits and pieces of flesh, loosened by exhumation as well as the rattling of the wagon wheels, fell off and were carried away by a nonexistent breeze, vanishing into dust before they reached as high as the lowest streetlight. Many of the bodies—the freshest ones—were still bloated, some slightly, some severely; all were discolored, a few were desiccated, and some were more bone than flesh.

Charlie began to say, "What in the holy *hell*—" but the rest died in his throat when yet another wagon, this one much older than the first, came into view just as the other was swallowed in shadow. This new wagon also carried bodies, but these corpses, despite the sick-making color of their skin, looked *fresh*....

GARY A. BRAUNBECK

COFFIN COUNTY

LEISURE BOOKS NEW YORK CITY

A LEISURE BOOK®

June 2008

Published by

Dorchester Publishing Co., Inc.
200 Madison Avenue
New York, NY 10016

ISBN 10: 0-8439-6050-7
ISBN 13: 978-0-8439-6050-1

The name "Leisure Books" and the stylized "L" with design are trademarks of Dorchester Publishing Co., Inc.

Printed in the United States of America.

10 9 8 7 6 5 4 3 2 1

Visit us on the web at www.dorchesterpub.com.

For Lucy.

I wish I had something romantic or funny to say here, but having you in my life often leaves me speechless.

COFFIN COUNTY

"*Regarding my actions in this world, I care little in the existence of a heaven or hell; self-respect does not allow me to guide my acts with an eye toward heavenly salvation or hellish punishment. I pursue the good because it is beautiful and attracts me, and shun the bad because it is ugly and repulsive. All our acts should originate from the spring of unselfish love, whether there be continuation after death or not.*"

—Heinrich Hein, *Das Bader von Lucca*

"*Someday will be the perfect day,*
a day among dogwoods and fir trees,
sun splashing over his face, far
from school, from brothers
and sisters, from the soiled world
of man . . ."

—Christopher Conlon, "Charlie's Vision,"
Starkweather Dreams

"*The devil has the farthest perspectives for God—that is why he stays so far away from him. The devil, in other words, is the oldest friend of insight.*"

—Friedrich Nietzsche, *Beyond Good and Evil*

"*Madness is the first step towards unselfishness.*"

—Kahlil Gibran

University of Texas

San Ysidro

Columbine

Virginia Tech

1

"My quiver is once again empty . . ."

2

This may seem a bit helter-skelter at first, jumping around like water on a hot griddle, rolling like leaves across an autumn sidewalk, tumbling about like a paper cup caught in the wind; but just as the millions of meaningless individual dots in a newspaper photograph will merge into a single, identifiable image when viewed as a whole, everything will gradually be connected. It has to be. The dead demand it of us. And they must not be ignored.

They *will not* be ignored. That's been tried before. Didn't exactly work out.

3

Around here I'm know as "The Reverend," and I need for you to come along with me for a while.

Admittedly, that doesn't quite have the poetic punch of such classic attention-grabbers as, say, "Call me Ishmael," or "My name is Arthur Gordon Pym," or "I am by birth a Genevese, and my family is one of the most distinguished of that republic," so let's establish right off the bat that I *know* it's not what you'd call a literary stunner, my introduction, but you work with what you've got.

So. *Ahem*.

Around here I'm known as "The Reverend." I run the Cedar Hill Open Shelter on East Main Street, just over the bridge that leads into the area known as "Coffin County." It wasn't always called that, just as I wasn't always called "The Reverend." Both it and I had another name at one time—in my case, I've had several names, at least one of which you'll learn in a little while—but before I tell you about that, and before we step through the gap to experience the night of an appalling slaughter that took place in this town that likes to call itself a city, we need to look a little closer at the place itself; for, like sins of omission, it shares a measure of responsibility.

There was a book written by a man named Geoff Conover, who once lived here, albeit briefly, and in this book—presented ostensibly as fiction, but we who call this place home and who have read it know better—he offers what is to my mind the most accurate description of Cedar Hill that one could possibly hope to find. Not being foolish enough to try to improve upon precision, I submit that description to you now:

> If it is possible to characterize this place by melting down all of its inhabitants and pouring them into a mold so as to produce one definitive citizen, you will see a person who is, more likely than not, a laborer who never made it past the eleventh grade but who has managed through hard work and good solid horse sense to build the foundation of a decent middle-class existence; who works to keep a roof over his family's head and sets aside a little extra money each month to fix up the house, maybe repair that old backdoor screen or add a workroom; who has one or two children who aren't exactly gifted but do well enough in school that their parents don't go to bed at night worrying that they've sired morons.
>
> Perhaps this person drinks a few beers on the weekend—not as much as some of their rowdier friends, but enough to be social. They've got their eye on some property out past the county line. They hope to buy a new color television set. They usually go to church on Sundays, not necessarily because they want to but because, well, you never know, do you?
>
> This is the person you would be facing.
>
> This is the person who would smile at you, shake your hand, and behave in a neighborly fashion.

But never ask them about anything that lies beyond the next paycheck. Take care not to discuss anything more than work or favorite television shows or an article from this morning's paper. Complain about the cost of living, yes; inquire about their family, by all means; ask if they've got time to grab a quick sandwich, sure; but never delve too far beneath the surface, for if you do the smile will fade, that handshake will loosen, and their friendliness will become tinged with caution.

Because this is a person who feels inadequate and does not want you to know it, who for a good long while now has suspected that his life will never be anything more than mediocre. He feels alone, abandoned, insufficient, foolish, and inept, and the only thing that keeps him going is a thought that makes him both smile and cringe: that maybe one of *his* children will decide for themselves, *Hey, Dad's life isn't so bad, this 'burg isn't such a hole in the ground, so, yeah, maybe I'll just stick around here and see what I can make of things.*

And what if they do? How long until they start to walk with a workman's stoop, until they're buying beer by the case and watching their skin turn into one big nicotine stain? How long until they start using the same excuses he's used on himself to justify a mediocre life?

Bills, you know. Not as young as I used to be. Too damn tired all the time. Work'll by God take it out of you.

Ah, well . . . at least there's that property out past the county line for him to keep his eye on, and there's still that new color television set he might just up and buy. . . .

This is the person who would look back at you, whose expression would betray that they'd gotten a little lost in their own thoughts for a second there.

It happens sometimes.

So they'll blink, apologize for taking up so much of your time, wish you a good day, and head on home because the family will be waiting supper. It sure was nice talking to you, though.

Meet Cedar Hill, Ohio.

It is a place that you would immediately recognize and then just as quickly forget as you drive through it on your way to someplace more vibrant, more exciting, or even just a little more *interesting*. It is filled with houses like every other house, on streets like every other street, and if you lived here, and if you could, you'd burn rubber on your way out, making damn sure the tires threw up enough smoke to hide any sight of the place should you cave and glance in the rearview for a last nostalgic look at this seemingly unremarkable white-bread Midwestern town.

However, as you'll realize quickly enough, this place is far from unremarkable; in fact, we have a local saying that often draws chuckles from visitors passing through, but isn't nearly as tongue-in-cheek as these outsiders think: "This is Cedar Hill. Weird shit happens here. Get used to it."

We'll come back to that soon enough, you and I. Right now, we need to look at some things; the pages, ghosts, people, places, what-ifs, wherefores, and whys that make up what is known for lack of a more accurate term as "history": imagine all of this history as being the light trapped by early cameras, the illumination carried to obscuras where chemicals in trays will summon forth the scenes, the memories, the moments, the forgotten

faces, the locations once treasured by those long gone
that are now empty lots of dust and detritus where children sometimes play in the noonday sun, all of it sur-
facing out of time and memory to meet us where we
are now, on this page, in this paragraph, at this sentence
where these things are once again given life, given an
identity, given back the warm flesh and bright sparkle
in the eyes that sang of life and hope and meaning;
and perhaps if all goes well, these phantoms will fully
emerge to find their voices once again, still waiting in
the place where they spoke their final words, and these
spirits will whisper: *Here is our story, the story of how
it all began; if you listen carefully, at the end, you'll be
someone else. . . .*

4

From *A Visitor's Guide To Cedar Hill; Spencer-Waters Press, January 1969,* page 36:

. . . Old Towne East is considered by many to be *the* feather in Cedar Hill's cap. A popular area with both residents and visitors, Old Towne East features perhaps the widest range of our city's attractions. Here you will find the original site, still open to the public, of the Licking County Pioneer, Historical, and Antiquarian Society (who have since opened a second and larger facility near the Buckingham House after changing their name in 1947 to simply Licking County Historical Society); there are also art galleries, movie theaters, dancing and nightclubs such as the famous Talley's Hideaway, restaurants specializing in international cuisine, and countless curiosity shops, to name only a handful of the establishments which have helped garner Old Towne East its glittering reputation. A bronze plaque which hangs by the entrance to the Legend Restaurant and Grille proudly proclaims: "Where Clark Gable ate 'The best damned broiled steak I've ever had!' " Inside the restaurant, diners can see the same words, written by Mr. Gable's own hand, on a framed photograph showing the movie star standing with the kitchen and managerial staff.

Such amazing finds are typical of the discoveries waiting for you when you visit Old Towne East, the heart of Cedar Hill culture and nightlife. . . .

5

On the night of August 14, 1969, most of the citizens of Cedar Hill, Ohio, were of the firm opinion that the whole sad-ass world was going straight to hell on greased rails; it didn't matter if you listened to Walter Cronkite, *The Huntley-Brinkley Report*, Eric Sevareid, or even God-bless-him Billy Graham—all the news was lousy: Kissinger and Xuan Thuy were in the middle of Vietnam peace negotiations that were laying goose eggs left and right; members of some psycho cult led by a guy named Manson had butchered Sharon Tate and three other people in Los Angeles, and then turned around the next night and killed Leo and Rosemary LaBianca; the Soviet Union and China were getting into some serious border clashes that everyone just *knew* was going to end up with bright nuclear mushroom clouds lighting up the Commie skies; British troops had been deployed in Northern Ireland to deal with the violence between the Protestants and Catholics after Jack Lynch eloquently pleaded with the U.N. to get involved; and as if that weren't enough, as if a decent, church-going, hard-working, law-abiding, tax-paying middle-class, just-keeping-their-heads-above-water American *still* didn't have enough to make them shake their heads in despair, some farmer named Max Yasgur in Bethel, New York, who should've known better, had agreed to allow a rock festival to take place on his land, and "Woodstock," as the kids were calling it, had parents and police losing sleep over how it was all going to turn out.

Nosiree, no damned doubt about it; everything was on the verge of being flushed right down the crapper.

And knowing all of this, Charlie Smeds, decorated veteran of WWII and Korea, now night watchman at the Franklin Beaumont Casket Factory in Old Towne East, was *still* the happiest man in the world.

Because in three days his son, Robert, was coming home from Vietnam. Yes, okay, right, the boy was now missing his left leg, both Charlie and Ethel had wept more than a few tears after getting that news, but Bobby was by God *alive,* he'd made it out—and after that bloody business at the Battle of Hué, his son's survival qualified in Charlie's eyes as an indisputable miracle: three understrength marine battalions, less than 2,500 men, had fought against over 10,000 soldiers from the People's Army of Vietnam and the Vietcong who, still fired up from the Tet Offensive less than a month before, attacked the airbase at Phu Bai where Bobby was stationed. Bobby was injured late in the second week of the battle when a PAVN B-40 rocket was fired into the fuel depot less than fifty yards from the storage shed he and a dozen of his fellow marines were using for temporary cover; Bobby'd taken some metal in the shoulder and lost partial (and *temporary,* thank God again for all blessings) use of his right arm, but that didn't stop Bobby or the other men from fighting their way out. The longest and bloodiest battle of the war so far, and Bobby survived with minor injuries. "I feel like me and the rest of the guys are invincible after getting through that," he'd written to Charlie and Ethel in his last letter, fourteen months ago. Then added: "Knock wood."

And after all of that, after surviving one of the most terrible battles of the war—if not *the* most terrible battle, period—he lost his leg on a routine patrol because he'd stopped to pet a damn dog and in the process stepped on a land mine. The dog of course emerged uninjured. Charlie imagined that Bobby was going to make a lot of tasteless jokes about that, being a cat lover like his mom. If *he* didn't make the jokes, then Charlie would be obligated to. Bobby would expect nothing less from his old man.

So on this August night, three weeks into the worst drought central Ohio had experienced in nearly forty years, the temperature finally bottoming out at eighty-seven degrees as Charlie arrived at work at nine P.M., the rest of the world might be going down the tubes, but Charlie Smeds's world was as bright and cheerful as a child's favorite storybook; say, *And to Think That I Saw It on Mulberry Street*, *The Wind in the Willows*, or *The Story of Ferdinand*. A happier man you couldn't find.

Charlie entered the small but comfortable office that served as his HQ on the west side of the ground floor, turned on the lights, set his lunch pail and thermos of coffee on the desk, checked his pocket watch to make sure the time matched that on the wall clock, and then fired up the ham radio to check in with the sheriff's department. Franklin Beaumont required that all watchmen check in with the sheriff's department every two hours to let them know everything was fine. Charlie had been going through this routine for nearly twenty-five years, and it was now second nature to him—but not something that he took lightly. Too many guys who worked a job like this got careless and sloppy, thought it was okay to sit on their asses and read magazines or listen to music on the radio or catch forty winks or pick their nose to see if anything interesting had gotten lodged up there when they weren't paying attention. It was too easy to get lazy when you worked alone and unsupervised. But there was no slacking on the job for Charlie—except of course on his dinner break. He rarely took his break at his desk, it felt too lonely, so he went outside, weather permitting, and ate his dinner on the bench facing the corner of Cedar Crest Avenue and East Main, giving him a nice view of the stairs leading up to Talley's Hideaway; afterward, he'd tamp some tobacco into his pipe and have a nice, relaxing smoke.

But that was for later. Right now, he had a job to do, and Charlie Smeds, grabbing the high-beam flashlight from its hook on the wall, unlocked the office door that led out onto the main floor of the factory and set about the business of making an honest living.

Charlie had his routine down to an art form; first, check that all the stairway doors were locked and secured; next, do a sweep of the front-most area of the main floor to make sure all the machinery had been properly shut down at the end of the shift; then it was on to the four elevators used by employees to access the top three floors, checking that the doors were open and the power was off; after that—and this was something Charlie had come up with on his own, much to Mr. Beaumont's approval—he used the wall-mounted phone in the employee lunchroom to dial the numbers of the lunchroom phones on floors #2, #3, and #4 to make certain no one had accidentally gotten locked in when the place was shut down for the night (this because a young woman who worked on #3 had one night been sick and in the bathroom when everyone left, securing everything behind them; the doors could only be unlocked from outside, so if for some reason you didn't make it out with everyone else, you were stuck for the night . . . as that young woman would have been had not Charlie, on a whim, decided to call the upper floors); the last part of Charlie's routine involved going into the display/sales area of the building, where dozens of caskets were arranged in neat rows for funeral home directors to peruse before placing their orders. The craftsmanship that went into a Beaumont casket was known all over the country, and it wasn't unusual to have funeral home directors fly up from as far away as California to make purchases.

The building itself was immense, taking up nearly two-thirds of the block, and a single pass from his office to the display area took Charlie the better part of two hours, giving him just enough time to get back to the office and radio in to the sheriff's department, maybe have a quick cup of coffee or rest his feet for five minutes before starting the whole process once more. Here, there, and back again; lather, rinse, repeat. To watch Charlie Smeds make his rounds, you'd think you were watching a workingman's ballet, it was so well-choreographed; and on this night, knowing that he was less than seventy-two hours from embracing his son again, Charlie practically *did* dance through his rounds. He even whistled, something he almost never did on the job.

At one thirty A.M. Charlie let himself out the door facing Cedar Crest Avenue and took his usual place on the bench. The night was still unbearably hot and dry, but he didn't mind in the least. He had a nice view of the street, of the darkened clubs and shops and galleries, and—best of all—of the glittering night sky. The stars were out in full force tonight, and as Charlie dug into his enormous meat loaf sandwich on rye—*nobody* made meat loaf like his Ethel, just one of a thousand reasons he was the luckiest man in the world that she permitted him to be her husband—he watched the stars and remembered all those times that Bobby as a child had talked about being a spaceman, this being a dream born from watching those old science-fiction

movies that Channel 10 always showed on Saturday af-
ternoons. Charlie wondered if Bobby and the rest of his
buddies over in Vietnam had been able to watch last
month when Apollo 11 landed on the moon and Neil
Armstrong had done the impossible—set foot on a
place other than Earth. Yessir, things weren't nearly as
awful as most folks thought, not if the human race
could actually put a *man on the moon.* Miracles, meat
loaf, and starlight were Charlie's companions on the
bench that night, a good woman was waiting for him
back home, and his son would soon again be sleeping
under the roof of the home where he was born. A man
would be a fool to ask for more.

At the top of the stairs leading into Talley's Hideaway,
the door opened and out onto the landing stepped
Eugene Talley, son of William "Bill-to-My-Friends-and-
Customers" Isaac Talley, who'd opened the doors to his
club way back in the 1920s. Eugene had his father's
onyx complexion, massive shoulders, and childlike
grin, as well as a booming, musical, rich baritone voice
that always reminded Charlie of the late Dr. Martin
Luther King, God rest his gallant, embattled soul.

"Fine evening, isn't it?" said Eugene.

"It was until you decided to come out and ruin the
quiet."

"As opposed to the way you ruin my perfectly good
view of an empty bench? The high point of my day is
coming out here after closing down and looking at that
bench. It's a splendid bench, as benches go. The *Mona
Lisa* of benches, one might even say. But what do I get?
I get to look at you sitting there, instead. By the way, I
think I saw a pigeon take a shit on it earlier, 'bout at the
spot where you parked your bony butt."

Charlie smiled. "You're in a rare mood tonight, Gene,
if I do say so."

Eugene returned the smile. "Sorry I couldn't get out

here sooner, Charlie. Couldn't get the receipts to balance out. Do my eyes deceive me, or is that one of Ethel's amazing meat loaf sandwiches you're eating?"

"No, it's *half* a meat loaf sandwich. The other half's still wrapped up with your name on it, if you don't mind sitting in pigeon shit with me."

Eugene spread his arms in front of him. "Now how am I supposed to turn down such a charming invitation?" As he made his way down the stairway—Eugene had arthritis in one knee, and so took the stairs a bit slower than most folks—he said, "Any word about your boy yet?"

Charlie beamed. "I was wondering how long it was gonna take you to ask. Ethel and me got the word this morning. Bobby's coming home in three days."

Now Eugene's smile became wide and radiant. "Oh, Charlie, isn't that just *fine?* That is by far the best news I've heard in a while. *Damn* fine news, my friend. *Damn* fine." He reached out and shook Charlie's hand as he reached the bench. "Please tell Ethel that I am so happy for all three of you."

"I sure will," said Charlie, handing Eugene the other half of the sandwich, which Ethel had purposefully made twice as big as Charlie could have possibly eaten on his own, knowing how he liked to share with Eugene on his break.

"I'll tell you what," said Eugene, unwrapping his half of the sandwich and giving it a good, deep, appreciative smell, "when Bobby gets himself settled, you bring him and Ethel down here one weekend and I'll make sure you get the best table in the house. Their dinners and drinks are on me."

Charlie blinked. "What about *my* dinner and drinks?"

"Did you make this meat loaf sandwich?"

"I did not."

"You just spend two years in Southeast Asia and get yourself wounded twice?"

"I couldn't very well be sitting here with you if I did, now, could I?"

"Then you pay. I am a generous soul, not a rube to be taken advantage of."

"That just warms me right down to my hemorrhoids, Eugene."

"If you'd unclench your skinny behind once in a while, maybe you wouldn't *have* any hemorrhoids to complain about. Ever consider that?"

"Why do I put up with you?"

"Because you and I are the only people in this town who can appreciate the aesthetic value of benches. Damn, this sandwich sure is something. Tell Ethel she really outdid herself this time."

"She does live for your praise."

"Hell, buddy, if it weren't for you and Ethel, most nights I'd have to settle for fried eggs and—what is *that?*"

Charlie sat up a little straighter. "You mean that noise?"

"No, the piece of cake you think I can't see under your napkin—*yes,* that noise."

The two men sat in silence for a moment, listening as the sound grew closer.

"If I didn't know better," whispered Eugene, "I'd swear that was the sound of a—"

"—holy shit," said Charlie, pointing toward the corner of Cedar Crest and East Main. "*Tell* me that ain't what I think it is."

Eugene, as stunned as Charlie, could only shake his head.

Charlie made the sign of the cross. A few moments later, as both men realized they weren't imagining things, Eugene did the same.

6

From *A Visitor's Guide To Cedar Hill*, pages 59–60:

". . . has voted to make a plot of the grounds and graves in the Old Graveyard at the Eastern section, taking care to protect and preserve the tombstones as they and those whose final resting place they mark are transported to a less neglected site," wrote the mayor in his 1902 proclamation.

And so the bodies which had lain undisturbed for nearly one hundred years were the first to be exhumed and transported to the expanded grounds of Cedar Hill Cemetery, now the county's oldest and most famous burial site.

With tongue firmly in cheek, one citizen at the time of the Old Graveyard exhumations wrote a snippet of verse that remains popular to this day:

The first cemetery was Beckwith's backyard
Where formerly Murphy sold eggs, bread, and lard.
The next was the corner of Cedar Crest and East Main;

Where now the Museum stands amid sunshine
and rain.
Later they moved it to Cedar Hill North,
So Old Adam dug up his wives and set forth,
And through Cedar Hill streets both the wide and
the narrow
Trundled their bones in an ancient wheelbarrow.

One mystery that has persisted concerning the
remains of the Old Graveyard is the mound and
lone stone by Cedar Crest Avenue. All sorts of
tales have been passed around about it, the most
popular being that a man and his horse are en-
tombed there as symbols of those who were once
buried in the area. (It is perhaps from the early
Welsh settlers that this originated.)

Why the stone was not removed is not known,
nor does anyone know why the mound still stands.
It is probable that there are still bodies buried in
the area, under the sidewalks and alleyways, because the 1902 proclamation did not stipulate the
removal of all corpses buried there, due to the fact
that so many settlers perished during the Great
Cholera Epidemic of 1805 that locating and removing all bodies would be nearly impossible.
Many of those bodies are now most probably
buried beneath the foundations of homes and
businesses, with a particularly high concentration
in the Old Towne East area. But with the continued expansion of the Cedar Hill population, it is
expected that the city's government will be seek-
ing yet more land over the next few decades, and
perhaps some of the still-buried forgotten dead
can at last be exhumed and moved to a proper
place of final rest. . . .

7

Charlie Smeds and Eugene Talley watched, dumb-struck, as an ancient, rickety, horse-drawn wooden wagon made its way down the street, the driver's face hidden by a thick kerchief covering his nose and mouth.

The wagon was filled with dead bodies and unearthed tombstones. Some of the bodies were so badly decomposed that bits and pieces of flesh, loosened by exhumation as well as the rattling of the wagon wheels, fell off and were carried away by a nonexistent breeze, vanishing into dust before they reached as high as the lowest streetlight. Many of the bodies—the freshest ones—were still bloated, some slightly, some severely; all were discolored, a few were desiccated, and some were more bone than flesh.

The *clop-clop-clop* of the horse's hooves echoed much more loudly than it should have, not because it was a still, dry evening, but because as Charlie and Eugene watched, the shadow cast by the horse and wagon turned the asphalt street around and beneath it into cobblestone.

Charlie began to say, "What in the holy *hell*—" but the rest died in his throat when yet another wagon, this one much older than the first, came into view just as the other was swallowed in shadow. This new wagon also carried bodies, but these corpses, despite the sickening color of their skin, looked *fresh,* as if death had claimed them only mere hours ago. There were two people in the front of this wagon; both had their noses and mouths covered with heavy winter scarves, and both wore thick gloves as well as heavy overcoats. The sound of the horse's hooves hitting the cobblestones was muffled because of the snow blanketing the areas of the street where the wagon's shadow fell. Behind this wagon, leaving footprints in the snow cast by their own shadows, marched a procession of people of varying ages: the elderly being assisted by the younger and stronger, the middle-aged who walked arm in arm or sometimes alone, and, at last, several children, all dressed in winter clothing over one hundred years out of date, all of them trying to look brave as they fought back the tears that sometimes won out, and then froze to their faces before getting halfway down their cheeks.

At the end of this procession walked one little girl, far too thin and pale, completely alone, hugging a tattered, handmade doll to her chest. The frozen tears on her face did not stop her from crying even harder. Her eyes were the saddest that either Eugene or Charlie had ever seen. As the wagon and procession moved farther down the street and into the darkness, the little girl stopped, staring down at her feet and wiping her nose on the sleeve of her coat, which Charlie realized was far too light for the winter weather.

She exhaled, her breath misting into the air, squeezed her doll tighter, wiped her nose once more, and then simply stood there, staring at Charlie and Eugene.

"My daddy told me about this when I was a kid," said Eugene, gripping Charlie's arm, his voice a whisper as if he were afraid that if he spoke too loudly, the spell would be broken. "I didn't believe him until I saw it for myself one night."

Not looking at his friend, Charlie gave a slow nod of his head. "They're all ghosts, ain't they?"

"To *us* they're ghosts. To them, they're still alive in whatever time it is they lived in. If that little girl can see us, we probably look like ghosts to her."

"What should we do, Eugene?"

"I vote for just staying put like this until everything's finished passing by."

The little girl held out her doll and said, "My mommy made this for me. But she's in Heaven now with Daddy. They both got *real sick* and . . . and they went to sleep last night and they never woke up."

Without thinking, Charlie said, "Are they in the wagon?"

The little girl nodded. "Yes, sir. We have to come along so we can say a prayer over everybody's grave. Everyone left in town is going to be there." She looked up the street, toward the shadows where the wagons and procession had vanished. "I'm tired, sir. I don't feel good. It's so *cold*. Could you maybe . . . maybe take me there? I won't be a bother, truly, I won't."

Charlie pulled his arm from Eugene's grip and walked out into the street toward her, reaching out with both hands to give her a hug and pick her up, but just as his hands touched her shoulders, she exhaled again and her eyes fell into their sockets, disappearing into the darkness within her skull; and then in a series of soft, dry sounds, her entire head began collapsing inward, her flesh crumbling and flaking away, becoming dust as her face sank back, split in half, and dissolved, vanished in a puff of winter mist. Charlie nearly lost his balance, not only because of the shock of what he'd just seen, but also because he'd been readying himself to pick up the extra weight.

Eugene made another sign of the cross. "You all right, Charlie?"

"Hell, I don't know." The lost, hopeless expression on the little girl's face was still burned into his memory, where he imagined it would remain for the rest of his days. "Dammit, Eugene—why didn't I think to ask her name?"

Eugene sighed and shook his head. "What good would it have done?"

"I . . . I don't know. It just seems like it would've been the proper thing to do, you know? Good God—I ain't seen a body just *fall apart* like that since my division liberated the camps at Strubing and Gunskirken Lager."

Eugene sat back down and gestured for Charlie to join him. As soon as Charlie, now shaking, took his usual place on the bench, Eugene patted his friend's shoulder and said: "Back in the Prohibition days, Dad had a fellah by the name of Granger who made rum runs for him. Those days, Dad got most of his hooch from Kentucky, and Granger was always the one who made the payoffs and the pickups. Well, one night, just as he's getting back into Cedar Hill, Granger runs into some Prohibition boys who didn't take too kindly to his 'uppity' attitude—that's what one of them called him, 'uppity.' That's all the excuse they needed to pull out their pistols and start firing. Some uppity nigger in a Minerva full of booze gave them good target practice. But Granger, he was strong and he was big and he was fast. Made them Prohibition boys chase him all over hell's half acre before they shot out his tires and he had to take it on foot. You know what those bastards did? They shot him in the back of both his knees and he dropped like a sack of wet cement. But that wasn't enough, not for them and not back then, oh, no. *Then* they turned their dogs loose on him. After that, they tied him to the back of their car and dragged him all the way to the downtown square where they strung what was left of him up by the neck so the birds could have a little snack. Papers back then, they said he was still alive when they hanged him. He stayed there for damn near two days before some regulars from the place come to cut him down. Daddy was one of the men who helped do it.

"One time, after I come home from school crying because some other kid called me a 'coon' and the rest of the kids laughed, Dad said to me, 'Yeah, that's pretty terrible, them calling you such an awful name, and I'm sorry it upset you, but if that's the worst that ever happens to you on account of you being the color you are, count yourself lucky.'

"Then he told me the story about Granger, and said that on some nights, some real dark nights, if you're down on the square around two in the morning, you can see the ghosts of the Prohibition boys as they string up poor Granger. I didn't believe him, so one night he wakes me up about one thirty, and we drive downtown to the spot where it happened, and . . ." Eugene shook his head. ". . . and I'll be *damned* if I didn't stand there next to the car and watch it happen all over again. Dad, he couldn't look at it for too long—me, I couldn't look away. I mean, I've seen photos in old books about some of the things done to black folks over the years, but I never thought about it too much beyond just what I saw in the picture, right? That night I had no choice, because even though it was two in the morning, the whole goddamn thing played out in front of my eyes clear as day. I could even hear the Prohibition boys laughing and calling Granger these foul, *vile* names, and then shouting up at him to kick harder after they strung him up from the streetlight . . . God, Charlie, I'd never heard a man choke to death before, and Granger, he was in *so much pain*. I still have nightmares about it sometimes."

"I never much believed in ghosts," said Charlie. "At

least, not like in this way. Far as I was concerned, I figured ghosts were just, y'know, something dreamed up by a guilty conscience."

"Well, now you know better."

Charlie gave a quick nod. "Damn straight I know better now." He looked at Eugene. "How do you—I mean, I know you still have the nightmares—but how do you . . . how do you go about your day-to-day stuff, knowing that stuff like this actually exists?"

Eugene grinned. "As much as it terrified me, the more I got to thinking about it, the more I decided that these ghosts, like the ones we just saw, regardless of what time in the past they come from, I decided that these ghosts are proof that God exists. I figure it's His way of reminding us of what's come before, and also maybe His way of warning us to make sure we take care that it never happens again."

"Does that make it easier for you?"

"Most days, yes."

"And on them days it *don't* make it better?"

Eugene shrugged. "I go to the movies or something—anything to distract my thoughts. But you know what I think, Charlie? I think once a man gets to be our age, when fifty is getting to be more and more of a distant memory and sixty's so close you can make out its features, it's kind of like a gift, witnessing something like this, even if it's as terrible as what I saw with Granger. It's a gift because it proves to guys our age that there are still great mysteries in this here sad old world, and I don't know about you, but I like that right down to the ground. Yes, I certainly do."

"You never try to figure out *why* this happens?"

Eugene shook his head. "I gave up trying to find an explanation a long time ago, my friend. I don't think there is one . . . and I'm not sure I'd want to know even if it turned out there was."

They sat in silence for a minute or two, both staring at the spot where the wagons and procession had passed by, but especially at the spot where the little girl had stopped to speak to them. The street was once again dark, smooth asphalt, with no traces of the snow both men had seen.

Eugene looked at his watch. "Damn, Charlie, I hate to do this, but I still got some work to do before I can head home."

Charlie checked the time on his own watch. "Shit, it's three minutes after two. I'm late checking back in." He began gathering up his lunch pail and coffee thermos. "The sheriff's department figures, y'know, that maybe some nights I go to the bathroom after I take my break, so they give me an extra fifteen minutes before someone calls."

"Then why the rush?"

"I hate being late. Goes against my nature." He saw the piece of cake under the extra napkin in his lunch pail and took it out. "Piece of cake for the road?"

"And here I'd thought you were going to hog it all for yourself." He took it from Charlie. "Give my compliments to Ethel, and make sure you tell her and Bobby about the free dinner and such for all three of you. Be an honor to serve your fine lady and veterans like your son and yourself."

"Thanks, Eugene." Charlie shook the other man's hand—which was so big Charlie probably could have sat in it—and then watched as Eugene made his way back up the stairs and into the Hideaway. Now assured that his friend was safely inside, Charlie let himself back into the factory.

Locking the door behind him, Charlie took a few extra seconds to lean his forehead against the cool steel door and steady both his breathing and the beating of his heart. Ethel was never going to believe this, not in a million years. *Hey, hon, guess what happened at work tonight? I saw a bunch of ghosts walking down the street. One of 'em even talked to me.*

That's nice, Charlie. Now, if you'll just sit here real quiet, I have to go make a couple of phone calls, okay? Don't panic if you hear sirens in a couple of minutes, all right? Here, have another piece of cake while you're waiting. Use the plastic *fork, please.*

Forcing himself to laugh, Charlie decided to chalk this one up as a Mystery, thank you very much, Eugene. So it was a night for meat loaf, miracles, and mysteries. Men well past the age of fifty needed some mysteries in life, to keep it interesting. Like Eugene, Charlie had heard stories all his life about strange things happening here, but had dismissed them as local folklore or just plain old bullshit. Never again.

Exhaling, Charlie checked to make sure his hands were steady, lifted up his head, and turned to face the area of the main work floor that faced Glenn Carroll.

Eyes growing wide, breath catching in his chest, arms shaking again and his hands losing all of their strength, Charlie Smeds didn't hear it when his lunch pail hit the floor with a loud, metallic clang and burst open, spilling its contents and shattering the inside of the coffee thermos that until this moment had lasted him nearly twenty-five years. All he could think of was Ethel's face, her smile, her kiss, the feel of her hand in his own, the way the warmth of her body comforted him in the night whenever he awoke with night terrors, and how very much he wished he were back home with her right this second, the two of them making Big Plans for Bobby's homecoming.

He stared at the thing a few yards away from him, and wondered if Eugene would call this a Mystery, as well, or if he'd be scared right down to the marrow of his bones. Charlie thought that maybe, just *maybe*, if he closed his eyes and didn't move, the thing would be gone when he opened them again, and if that were the case, he'd put in for an early vacation like Ethel had been asking him to do. So he closed his eyes, pictured his wife and son, pulled in and released a slow breath, and then opened his eyes again; this time a sound did escape him when he saw what still stood less than fifteen feet away: Charlie Smeds gasped. Had anyone else been there to hear it, they would have known that it wasn't just a simple gasp, it was more the precursor to a much more forceful and terrified sound, the kind of sound you wouldn't expect to hear from a man who'd fought in two wars and had seen enough brutality and death and horror to last three lifetimes.

Without realizing it, Charlie pressed one of his hands against his mouth to prevent such a sound from escaping him. There very well might be mysteries and miracles in the starry night on the other side of the door behind him, but this . . . *this* . . .

8

From *A Visitor's Guide To Cedar Hill*, pages 47–48:

In the early days of Cedar Hill, when the Irish and Welsh immigrants still worked peaceably with the Delaware Indians to establish shipping lanes through Black Hand Gorge, the North Fork of the Licking River marked the eastern boundary of the community—an area later inhabited by the Shawnee and Wyandot Indians. Across the river and to the east, however, lay a place that was sole territory of the *Lenni Lenape,* who claimed it was cursed: *M'wa'Ka-ne-pay-oo-ta'rtai:* Dog Town.

It was given its name by a settler named Elias Hughes who, while on a hunting expedition, wandered into uncharted territory on the far side of the Licking River. He came upon a large *pop-ho'kus*—a cedar tree—that had a massive crack in its center which expanded and contracted at regular intervals. In short, the tree was breathing. Hughes took an ax and began chopping at the tree, which is said to have covered him in blood from head to foot. As he was pulling back to swing once again, Hughes froze with horror when the tree uprooted itself and fell forward, the large crack in its center issuing forth, as a woman giving birth to a child, a creature that was, as he wrote, ". . . an evil, godless abomination of Nature and all she holds dear. Before me lay a demon that was well surpassing nine feet in height. It turned toward me, and with astonished eyes did I watch its gaping, bloody wounds, inflicted by mine own ax, moisten and move, hideously quivering as they healed over as if by miracle. The abomination rose and whispered, *'Ta'lee!'* ('Remember!') before bounding over the hill behind it. I followed to the crest, where mine eyes were offended with an even more terrible sight. Below were hundreds of monstrosities who in form and behavior were identical to the creature I had wounded, excepting in size. These were the height of a normal man. So deeply affected was I by this I dropped all that I carried and ran. May God be merciful and abrogate their blasphemous images from my mind, and may He see fit to keep mankind from ever encountering these devils again."

Over the years the legend has gone through various oral revisions—some believed the creatures were indeed dogs, others thought them to be coyotes, still others claimed they were wolves or perhaps even members of the *Tūk'sit:* the Wolf Clan of the *Lenni Lenape,* adorned in their ceremonial costumes; others believed them to be nothing more than the ghosts of the dead, and that the sight of them caused Hughes, in an obvious state of hysteria, to hallucinate the image of so-called "monstrosities."

Regardless of the truth—which we shall never know—the legend and the place never failed to engage the imaginations of young and old alike—but especially the young, who often went there to camp and tell ghost stories with their friends under the cold autumn moon. No boy in his right mind could resist a chance to spend the night in Dog Town. Some of the more imaginative young people even claimed to have seen the "Breathing Tree" appear in various locations around the county, its limbs still bearing the marks left by Hughes's ax, and still bleeding.

Yet another interesting variation on this legend claims that, from deep inside the "breathing" gash in the center of the tree, there is often seen . . .

9

Were you listening? When Eugene Talley said to Charlie: *"I gave up trying to find an explanation a long time ago, my friend. I don't think there is one . . . and I'm not sure I'd want to know even if it turned out there was,"* did his words perhaps strike a chord of curiosity within you? Did you yourself wonder?

There *is* an explanation for the odd, disturbing, frightening, and (at the very least) peculiar occurrences that have been part of Cedar Hill's history—even before it *was* Cedar Hill.

Physicists think of the universe as a four-dimensional/four-layered sheet; three existing in space, one in time, with the possibilities of other disconnected sheets (composing the unknown quantity of the multiverse); they do not regard time as a sequence of events that simply *happen;* instead, all of the past and future are simply *there,* and time extends in either direction from any given moment in much the same way space stretches away from any given location. So the "there" that physicists refer to, we call the present: a simple point on the four-dimensional sheet of the universe—a dot in the middle of a page.

In simpler terms, there are places in this world—odd,

forgotten, banal, and sometimes ruined places—where the corners of the finite and infinite aren't quite squared, so it's easy for a small piece of the past, the future, or even an alternate reality to slip through the cracks; when that happens, people usually start throwing around terms like *unexplained phenomena* or *hallucination* or *miracles*.

The word they're actually looking for is *palimpsest.*

When copying Biblical texts, ancient monks were often forced to erase pictures and words from previously used sheets of parchment because they lacked sufficient supplies of paper. As the ink from these newly created pages began to dry, the impressions left on the parchment from what had been there before began to show through. View these pages in their modern-day museum homes and it's easy to see where the original drawings and text "ghost" through, creating two simultaneous pages on one sheet; past and present merging into one: the former bleeding into the latter, overlapping to create a hybrid but no less sentient reality: palimpsest.

Cedar Hill is one of those areas—sometimes referred to as "places of power"—where the corners of the finite and infinite don't quite come together as they should, and on nights like this, nights that find people like Charlie Smeds and Eugene Talley witnessing—and even interacting with—events that took place hundreds of years ago, the cracks open a little wider, the holes get a little bigger, and the scrim separating this reality from whatever waits on the other side becomes all the more weaker. Cedar Hill is a border town, and such a place, as you can well imagine, requires a guardian, a sentinel, a gatekeeper. But I'm getting ahead of myself.

If you require further proof that what I'm saying is true, if for you seeing is believing, then I suggest we turn our attention back to Charlie. Take a good look at his face. Remember the light in his eyes. Summon back, if you can, the sound of his laugh, the timbre of his voice, the quality of his character. And look with him at the thing that has bled through from the page beneath.

10

It was the tallest, ugliest, thickest, most unnaturally twisted-looking cedar tree Charlie had ever seen, and it was standing dead center on the main floor as if it had been planted there two hundred years ago and the factory had somehow grown around it. Its dense, broad roots disappeared into the concrete floor as smoothly as a finger into water; there were no cracks, no gaps, no damaged bark; roots and floor were perfectly sculpted together.

Charlie took a few tentative steps toward the tree, his eyes focusing on one of the lower branches where something thick, wet, and dark was dripping from a deep gash that had to have been made by an ax. The closer he got to the tree, the more Charlie saw that it bore the marks of several ax strikes, and not particularly skilled strikes, either; the wounds—and *wounds* they were, because every jagged score was bleeding—had begun to scab over in a few places, but not enough to prevent Charlie from seeing that, beneath the bark, instead of cedar wood, the tree was made of soggy red tissue and tightly wound sinew.

And it sounded like the damned thing was breathing.

Charlie knelt down at the point where the nearest

root vanished into the floor and, surprising himself, touched it. It was real, all right, no doubt about that; it felt like the bark of any other tree, except for the warmth radiating to the surface, as if the thing were running a serious fever. Charlie pulled away his hand and looked at the palm; even under the low-wattage security lighting he could see that it was covered in glistening sweat—only could something this gummy be called sweat?

Wiping his hand on the side of his pants, Charlie rose to his feet and backed away, holding his breath. The sound of someone—or *something*—else breathing was louder now, but it was also strained, wheezing, filled with phlegm.

Okay, he thought to himself, *there are options here: you can go over to Talley's and drag Eugene down here so somebody else'll see it, but there's no guarantee that it'll still be here when you get back; you could go radio the sheriff's department and tell them that a breathing, bleeding, feverish cedar tree has broken into the place and see how long it takes for them to haul your ass to the nuthouse; or you could just take Eugene's advice and look at this as being a gift of Mystery, a little present from God to remind folks that He's still paying attention.*

Charlie could feel himself sweating underneath his shirt. Taking off his hat, he saw that the inside of the rim was soaked in perspiration. *Why* was it getting so hot in here? Maybe Ethel was right, maybe he was coming down with some bug. *You've been worrying over Bobby ever since we got the news, hon. You said yourself that your sleep's been off. A man your age, that can be enough to make him sick.*

Charlie thought that the best thing for him to do was go back into the office, check in with the sheriff's department, and then call Don Fortney, the weekend watchman, and see if he'd cover the rest of Charlie's hours tonight. Don had been saying just the other day that he could use some extra hours during the week. *Yes, sir, that's what you ought to do, Charlie Smeds. That's what a smart man would do, no doubt about it.*

So of course he continued to stand there and stare at the breathing tree. Try as he did, Charlie couldn't look away. The more he stared, the easier it became to see how the center of the tree was expanding and contracting with each deep, painful breath. Blood from the ax wounds dribbled down onto the floor, each drop hissing as it struck the surface. Charlie wiped his face on his sleeve, and then unbuttoned the top three buttons of his shirt. His mouth was dry, his throat raw and parched. He couldn't look away from the yawning vertical gash that was opening in the center of the tree. Hot—*Jesus,* it was so hot in here. Maybe that light had something to do with it, that silvery light slipping through the quivering slick pink meat inside the vertical gash. For a moment, Charlie wondered what Eugene would make of this, if he could maybe explain what kind of Mystery gift from God this was supposed to be. Charlie started working his tongue in and out of his mouth in an effort to produce some spit, but it did no good. It was too hot and too dry; even the sweat on his skin seemed to evaporate as soon as it reached the surface. His eyes were starting to hurt, he needed to blink, to produce some tears so the damned things wouldn't just dry up and fall back into their sockets, like with that poor little girl, sad little ghost-girl following the wagon filled with bodies, holding her dolly to her chest as if it were something alive, something that could both receive and return love, and Charlie almost laughed at the thought as he pictured his own head collapsing inward, its flesh crumbling apart and flaking away, becoming dust as his face sank back, split in half, and dissolved; only here, right now, it'd dissolve with a hiss,

just like the blood spattering down from the tree's
branches, hitting the searing floor and—*poof!*—all over,
all gone, bye-bye, and Charlie pulled in a deep, scorch-
ing breath, a breath like sucking down invisible fire, but
his lungs welcomed it, nonetheless, welcomed the heat
and the pain because that meant the body was still functioning, was still able to move, to react, and that meant
he wasn't crazy yet, nosiree, not him, not Charlie, the
sweltering temperature wasn't sizzling his brains like it
did those British soldiers he'd seen in the VA hospital,
guys who'd been over in North Africa with General
O'Connor fighting Rommel's goddamned Panzers under a merciless sun; some of those poor guys'd had their
brains actually *boiled* inside their skulls, the heat was so
intense, but Charlie, right here, right now, he was holding his own, even though he could feel the skin on the
bottoms of his feet blistering against the increasing intensity of the heat emanating from the floor, surrounding him in radiating waves that made everything
shimmer as the silver light from inside the moist shuddering meat of the tree grew brighter, beckoning him,
so Charlie moved to step forward, to let the light embrace him—

—*One small step for Man*—

—but his feet were weighted down and it took damn
near everything he had just to lift his right foot off the
floor; when he looked down he saw that the sole of his
right boot had melted into this long, stringy, thick, black
glop that was gluing him to the spot, and from the smell
of it, from the stink of burning flesh that now filled his
nose, Charlie knew that his left boot and foot must be in
the same sad shape, and shouldn't he be screaming or
something, what with the skin being seared off the bottoms of his feet—and there was no mistaking the smell
of broiled, burned, seared flesh, not for him, he'd gotten
a gutful of that horrible smell when his division liberated

the concentration camps and he'd had to help shovel the remains of bodies out of the ovens—but he had to keep moving, he had to get to that beautiful silver light before it went away and left him behind, so Charlie squatted down, making sure that his knees didn't touch the floor, and began untying the laces of his boots, but now even the bootlaces were smoldering from the heat and Charlie felt the skin on his fingertips singe against the laces, but he kept at it because if you had a job to do, you did it to the best of your abilities, and it took the better part of thirty seconds and most of the skin from his thumbs and index fingers, but Charlie pulled his smoking feet free of the disintegrating boots and was just starting in on his socks when the beautiful, wet, engorged lips of the tree parted and sent a ray of near-blinding radiance shooting upward and to the left like the directed beam of a spotlight, the radiance whispering his name, calling his name, *singing* his name, and so Charlie moved, stepping forward onto the nearest root of the tree, the *cool, so cool, thank-You-God-so-cool* root, so cool and soothing beneath his ruined, agonized feet, and he was so grateful that he didn't even mind hearing the whimpers, the cries, the screams, the terrified, sickened, horror-struck groans of the unseen ghosts he knew were moving forward from within the light to enter this world for whatever reason, for however long—he'd know soon enough, he suspected—but for now, right now, his ears ringing with the shrieks of unbearable suffering, he wanted only to stand here and rejoice in the sensations as the scorched, liquefying flesh of his feet melted like candle wax into the ruts, grooves, and furrows of the bark, but as he began to lean toward the lustrous, distending lips the light began to weaken, and he looked up to the branch ten feet over his head where the fading beam illuminated a black-hooded body hanging by its neck, lifeless arms slack, its pants stained and sopping with the contents of evacuated bowels, and Charlie began turning away as the stench of the dead man's piss, vomit, and shit assaulted his senses—

—God, Charlie, I'd never heard a man choke to death before, and Granger, he was in so much pain. I still have nightmares about it—

—the hooded body shuddered and twisted to the side and kicked out, its left arm shooting forward, its hand grabbing Charlie's left wrist as another hand, this one drenched in the same clear, viscous substance Charlie had earlier wiped on the leg of his pants, pushed against the brightly veined membranous sac forming in the center of the saturated lips of the tree, clawing its way out and grabbing Charlie's other wrist, the combined force of the hands' struggle wrenching Charlie upward, tearing what flesh remained from the bottoms of his feet as his arms were pulled apart and he threw back his head to scream but couldn't because now he knew who and what these two men were, and they in turn knew the same of him, and as the three merged for the moment into a single being of a single mind filled with layers upon layers of memories, the lips of the tree parted as the figure trapped inside began shredding the remains of the birth sac while the black-hooded figure raised its free arm to grip the rope of the cattle halter and began pulling itself up . . . and Charlie Smeds, his mouth twisted open in a silent scream, thought of his wife's smile, of his friend Eugene's generosity, of his son Bobby's courage, and begged God to be merciful and let him live to see them again in the bright light of day—hell, even in the murky, rainy, gloomy light of day, he wouldn't be picky, Lord, truly he wouldn't . . .

. . . and the sheet beneath bled through to the sheet above . . .

. . . and Charlie Smeds heard a dim, terrible voice say a single word, one he himself had heard more than a few times as a child . . .

" . . . *Hoopsticks* . . ."

11

From *A Visitor's Guide to Cedar Hill*, page 31:

... grislier legends connected with certain areas of downtown Cedar Hill are those of a man named Green, who murdered several people and threw their bodies into the sewage system, which is said to have for a time caused all the water in the area to run red, and that of a character said to have roamed the streets of Cedar Hill during the 1920s, "Hoopsticks." Said to be an umbrella repairman, he was the dread of children everywhere, for mothers would warn their children that if they misbehaved, "Hoopsticks" would carry them off to a large black box near Raccoon Creek, which was both his home and the terrible factory where he turned children into umbrellas, using their bones and their skin for raw materials. The "Hoopsticks" legend lives to this day, though his name often changes, as does the location of his crimes, but always, it seems, the stories take place somewhere around downtown, near midnight, or in the darker hours that follow. . . .

12

"My quiver is once again empty, and that, I'm afraid, simply will not do . . ."

13

At 2:07 A.M., in the small dining room of a house located three blocks from the Beaumont Casket Factory, Don Fortney, age forty-six, a day-shift sheet-metal press operator at the Roper Manufacturing plant Monday through Friday, and night watchman at the Beaumont Casket Factory on the weekends, was sitting at the table eating a bologna, onion, and ketchup sandwich and drinking the third glass of water he'd had since getting out of bed twenty minutes ago. His right leg was bouncing up and down—a nervous habit that was now so much a part of his waking hours that he no longer noticed it—and he just knew that if he didn't pee pretty soon, he was going to have to wake his wife, Margaret, and have her drive him over to the ER so someone could run a catheter up into his bladder and relieve the goddamn pain and pressure.

"Let me guess," said Margaret from the doorway. "You didn't call Dr. Bishop and make an appointment, did you?"

Don shook his head. "No, I didn't."

Margaret came over and stood behind him, massaging his shoulders. "Don, honey, you've got to have this bladder infection treated, and soon. You haven't had a decent night's sleep in over a week."

"You think I don't know that?"

"There's no reason to snap at me."

He reached back and squeezed one of her hands. "I know, and I'm sorry. It's just, this . . . this isn't the kind of thing a fellah can easily talk about with another guy."

"Paul Bishop has been our doctor for over twenty years, dum-dum. There isn't a part of either of our bodies, inside or out, that he hasn't seen up close." She bent down and kissed the top of his head. "I love you, but you're being stubborn and stupid. You can't keep going like this."

Don only nodded, then took another bite of his sandwich.

"Yeech," said Margaret, coming around and sitting in the chair across from her husband. "I don't know how you can stand to eat something like that in the middle of the night."

Don shrugged. "It's cheap, and it fills you up." He finished off his glass of water, decided to have one more, began to rise from his chair, and almost doubled over from the surge of sharp pressure just above his groin. *"Goddammit!"*

Margaret grabbed his hand and squeezed it. "Okay, John Wayne, that's it. We're getting dressed and I'm driving your sorry ass to the emergency room."

Don gave a slight nod of his head once again. "Okay but could—*ow!*—could you at least let me try to go on my own one more time?" He looked up at her. "Please, hon? I promise you, if I can go, then first thing in the morning I'll call Dr. Bishop and tell him it's urgent."

Margaret pressed her hand against his cheek. "If you don't, I will."

"Deal." He accepted her offer to help him get to his feet, which hurt like nobody's business and caused him to cry out a couple of times, but once they managed to return him to the upright position, it got a bit easier.

"And if I can't go," he said, "then we'll drive over to the ER. I just hope whoever shoves that thing up inside of me has had more than two hours of sleep."

"You're finally talking sense," said Margaret. "Now I *know* you're sick."

They both laughed—Margaret harder than Don, because even laughing hurt. Both of them were almost out of the dining room when Don stopped and said, "Wait a second, hon. I gotta turn off the lights."

"You picked one hell of a time to think about our household budget. You stand right here, I'll do it." Margaret leaned him against the doorway and began turning back. "You worry too much about the bills."

"Well . . . so do you. So there."

"Don't change the subject. Just, next time, do me a favor and—"

Don reached out and gripped her arm. "Did you hear that?"

"Hear what?" She reached over to gently pull his hand from her arm. "Honestly, hon, I think maybe losing so much sleep is causing you to—"

She never finished the sentence; just as she pulled his hand from her arm, the wall and picture window facing the dining-room table blew apart in a thunderous, deafening blast of plaster, wood, bricks, and countless shards of flying broken glass, shaking the entire house as if someone had detonated a case of TNT right on their porch. Don threw Margaret to the floor and then flung himself on top of her, holding her in a powerful grip and pressing his weight down against her. Both of them screamed, but the earsplitting volume of the explosion drowned out any sounds they made. Both remained on the floor, their shuddering bodies pressed together, feeling each other's heartbeat trip-hammer against ribs, frozen with dread, shock, and panic, their eyes pressed tightly closed. Don was thinking: *If one of us has to die, let it be me.* Margaret was thinking: *If one of us has to die, let it be me.* (They would never tell each other that after it was all over; but in a way, each of them knew.)

Not daring to move until he was certain it was all over, Don listened as the last bits of wood snapped and fell, but even then he didn't roll off of his wife; it wasn't until he heard the final crackles of falling glass shards at last fall to silence that he released his breath and his grip on his wife's body and rolled to the side.

"Oh, my God, Don," said Margaret, blinking against the dust, smoke, and tears in her eyes. "What just . . . are we . . . did . . . oh, honey—are you all right?"

Don pushed up on his elbows and kissed her forehead. "I think so. What about you?"

Margaret closed her eyes again, taking a silent inventory. "I think all my working parts are in order." She struggled up into something resembling a sitting position, then helped Don to do the same.

"You sure you're all right?" she asked again.

"I'm good, hon, really. I think I'm okay."

"That's a relief." And she slapped him across the face with such force he damn near slammed the back of his head into a large section of the oak dining table that had landed less than a foot away.

"What the hell was that for?" he shouted.

Margaret's eyes were filled with more anger than he'd ever seen before. She reached out, grabbed the neck of his T-shirt, and pulled his face close to hers. "Don't you ever, *ever* do something like that again. You might have been killed."

Rubbing the side of his face that she'd struck—and, damn, she could hit *hard*—Don shrugged his shoulders. "What was I supposed to do, just hit the floor on my own and hope you'd have enough sense to do the same?"

"Yes!"

"No way. No way in hell. Sorry, but if that's the way it's gonna be, you'll be slapping me around like some red-headed stepchild."

She cupped his face in her hands and kissed him. "I might have lost you."

"And I didn't want to lose *you*."

For a moment they looked into each other's eyes; what they saw there made any more words unnecessary, excepting three.

"I love you," said Don.

"I love *you*. Now . . ." She looked into the demolished dining room. "What the hell happened?"

She and Don got to their feet and, holding hands, made their way toward the middle of the wreckage. A streetlight outside had been hit so hard that it now bent backward nearly all the way to the sidewalk, but the light itself was still functioning, which was a blessing in disguise; the power was now out in the house and the streetlight provided the only illumination.

Don entered the disaster area first, shaking his head. "Well, at least now we get to see if all that insurance we've been paying on is worth the paper it's . . ." His voice trailed off.

"What is it?"

Wordlessly, Don pointed to the far end of the dining room. Margaret first looked at his face, saw the color drain from his cheeks, and then turned her gaze in the direction he was pointing.

An oak coffin was embedded in the far wall. Half of it stuck out like some weird piece of art that had been purposefully placed there. The other half was buried in the brick, wood, plaster, and mortar.

They looked at one another, then at the demolished wall.

"Do you realize," said Don, "that if we hadn't gotten up when we did, we'd both—"

"Shh, honey, please. Please don't say it." Margaret made the sign of the cross. "Please don't."

"Okay."

They stared at the half of the coffin that was visible.

Don said: "Isn't the downstairs bathroom on the other side of that wall?"

Margaret nodded. "Guess it was a good thing you never made it there, huh?"

"Yeah, about that, hon . . . we don't need to go to the ER after all."

Margaret looked at him. "But you—oh, hey, wait a minute. *Oh, honey* . . . you wet yourself, didn't you?"

"My bladder hasn't felt this empty in weeks. I'm sorry about the carpeting."

Margaret leaned in and kissed him. "That's okay." Then: "I think I peed myself, too."

Don burst out laughing, as did Margaret. For nearly a minute they stood there, howling with laughter. After that had run its course, they walked nearer to the coffin, then looked outside.

"Son-of-a-*bitch*," whispered Don as he saw that the wreckage wasn't limited to just the streetlight and their dining room.

Margaret nodded. "Couldn't have said it better myself."

They stood staring in silence until the sounds of the first sirens began wailing in the distance.

Outside, for as far as they could see along the smoky street, coffins or pieces of coffins were everywhere; on lawns and rooftops, through the windshields of parked cars or the living-room windows of nearby houses, scattered in large pieces all over the street; a few had even landed in one piece against trees and were standing upright. It would have been almost funny in a gallows-humor kind of way if not for the bright orange-red mushroom cloud of fire a few blocks over, rising higher and higher with each smaller distant explosion, hovering over the roofs of the neighborhood like hell's own hammer, ready to slam down and smash everything into rubble.

"Oh, Christ," said Don. "Oh, *shit!*" He looked at Margaret. *"Charlie. Charlie Smeds!"*

Margaret put her hand against her mouth. "Oh, honey . . . *oh, no. . . ."*

Both of them made the sign of the cross and sent out a prayer for Charlie's safety. If God was listening, He gave them no indication. . . .

14

. . . nor had He given Charlie any indication that He'd heard the man's prayers, but Charlie knew that didn't mean the prayers *weren't* heard.

It was almost fifteen minutes after two and he was fading fast. The two figures from the tree were still playing tug-of-war with him, but the pain from his ruined feet had long ago reached a pitch where everything suddenly went numb. Charlie could no longer feel the flesh sluicing off his feet and legs. If he turned his head and looked down, he could *see* the liquefied skin dribbling down to the floor and hissing as it came into contact with the surface . . . but *feel* it? Not so much. And maybe *that* was the answer to his prayers.

The hooded figure disengaged itself from the cattle halter and, letting go of Charlie's wrist, dropped down onto the factory floor. Charlie wondered why the hooded man didn't start screaming from the heat. It didn't even look like his shoes were affected.

Charlie swung to the side. The other figure, the one coming out the tree's birth sac, caught him in both its arms and laid him across a bigger, thicker root. Looking up, Charlie tried to make out the features of the figure's face, but this close, it was nothing but a blur. He was getting tired, so tired . . . sorry, Ethel, I'm beat, give Bobby a hug from his old man, would you?

Charlie's head flopped to the side. He was facing the hooded figure that now stood less than six feet away. At this distance, Charlie could see him pretty clearly. *Huh, you were right, honey; I need glasses.*

The figure reached up and tore the hood from its head, tossing it to the floor where it immediately caught fire and burned instantly away into ashes. The figure's head lay to the side at an odd angle, and Charlie realized that was because its neck had been broken from the hanging. The Resurrected Man pressed his hands against the sides of his head, moved it back into its proper position, and with a quick, hard flick of both wrists, snapped his neck back into place.

"Whoo-doggie—to quote the immortal Jed Clampett— I am going to have *such* a headache," he said. "But that's a small price to pay, wouldn't you agree, my brother?"

The figure born from the tree said, "How many times do I have to tell you not to call me that?"

"Was I supposed to be keeping track? Oh, my, my, my." Crossing one arm across his midsection so that the other could rest on it vertically, the Resurrected Man rested his head in the palm of his upright hand, drumming fingers on the side of his face as if in deep contemplation. After a moment he dropped both arms and shrugged. "Nope. Sorry. Thought I might be able to come up with a number if I thought about it for a moment, but it appears I was mistaken."

"A lot of that going around."

"Indeed." He took a few steps toward Charlie, tilting his head to get a better look in his eyes. "I'm afraid this one's a lost cause, *brother.*"

Charlie tried to say, *I ain't dead yet, you smug bastard,* but all that emerged was a faint squeak. He felt the figure from the tree tighten its grip on his body. He wondered if the man, or angel, or demon, or whatever he/it was had a name. *Mr. Tree,* thought Charlie with a smile, remembering the name of a favorite character from a children's show he used to watch with Bobby, before his son grew up and swapped children's shows for rifles, napalm, and land mines.

"I told you," said Mr. Tree, "stop calling me—"

"Well, then, what *should* I call you? Ah, I have it! How about I address you by your *real name?*"

"How about I address you by *yours?*"

For a moment the Resurrected Man was silent; then, in the petulant tone of a spoiled child, said: "Then what fun would any of this be?"

"This is supposed to be *fun?*" said Mr. Tree. "I must have missed that memo."

"Well," said the Resurrected Man, "I suppose that can be overlooked, seeing as how many other, more important things you've missed in the past. You know, appointments in Samarra, hillside gatherings, things like that."

Mr. Tree sighed and shook his head. "Do whatever it is you plan on doing."

"Are you really so impatient for this to begin?"

"No, I just want you to shut the fuck up and go away."

The Resurrected Man considered this. "All right, then. Oh—in case I don't see you for a while, it's been a thrill, as always. *Dear brother.* And remember—the count always starts at zero, so we've got our work cut out for us." His eyes began to glow a bright silver, and he thrust out a fist, his arm twitching and trembling, his hair rising on end as if he'd touched some gigantic Van der Graaf generator. Closing his eyes, he spoke two words—"*Ta'lee,* motherfuckers!"—before opening his fist to release what looked like either a butterfly or a large moth; Charlie couldn't tell, everything was getting dark around the edges; even the butterfly looked black; he'd never seen something like a black butterfly before. Huh.

The butterfly—Charlie decided it was a butterfly and not a moth—bounced around for a few seconds as if it were dancing among bright flowers in a brighter field under the brightest summer sun ever imagined, and then it began to ascend, rising gracefully toward the ceiling beams and pipes, and Charlie couldn't help but admire the beauty of its movements, wishing that Ethel could see this, she always loved butterflies, and she'd love this one, he was sure of it, the way it flowed so light and free and its wings suddenly bright like gold, like a splash of gold, like—

—like fire.

As soon as the butterfly landed on one of the ceiling beams, it burst open like a water balloon only instead of water, flames spilled out, rolling in all directions across the ceiling and devouring anything in their path; wires melted, cables snapped, and windows exploded, sending thousands of shards of glass flying everywhere.

Mr. Tree bent forward and shielded Charlie's body with his own as the shattered glass rained down, stabbing his back in a hundred different places. Charlie could see a small fireball bloom near the far end of the main production floor, near the display area, churning in place for a few seconds before sweeping both sideways and downward, blistering the paint on the outer wall of the employee break area. Large, molten clumps of flame and liquefied metal dripped down all around them, rupturing into blazing puddles that looked like blue-red-orange-black lava.

Charlie reached up and grabbed Mr. Tree's head, turning it toward him.

". . . the . . . tanks . . ." he managed to get out.

"I know," said the man looking down at him with the kindest eyes Charlie had ever seen.

On the floor above them, *directly* above them, if Charlie's memory served him right—and when *hadn't* it?—was the polishing area where the tanks of oil, varnish, and wood finish were stored.

Flames swept upward, ever upward, their hiss, crackle, and snap gaining volume, building in intensity, growing into a snarl that became a howl and then, at last, a screaming, agonized roar as the ceiling above began to give way.

"Look at me, Charlie," said the man holding him in his arms. In these last moments of life, Charlie no longer thought of him as Mr. Tree.

"*Look at me,* Charlie."

Charlie did as he was told.

"Everything will be fine, Charlie. It will be over in a few seconds. There's no need to be afraid, do you understand?"

". . . are you . . . are you Hoopsticks?"

The man looked so sad. "No, not really."

". . . you . . . you have to get out . . ."

"Shh, Charlie. Save your breath. I won't leave you."

". . . you'll . . . die . . ."

The man actually smiled. "Don't worry about me, Charlie." He placed a hand on Charlie's forehead and began stroking his brow, then, with a touch as soft as a baby's hand gripping your finger for the very first time, closed Charlie's eyes. "Listen to the sound of my voice. *Listen.* Do you know where you are? You're in Talley's Hideaway, sitting at the best table in the joint. You're surrounded by people you love. Do you see them, Charlie? See how they're smiling at you? Ethel looks so happy, doesn't she? So proud of both you and Bobby. The music, can you hear it? The music is so happy and joyous. Makes a man want to grab his lady's hands and dance the night away. And here comes Eugene, just like he promised, making a big deal out of all three of you, and the people are laughing, and the beer is cold, and the food is so fine, isn't it, Charlie?" He leaned closer so that he could whisper in Charlie's ear. "Now give your boy a hug."

Charlie smiled.

The figure from the tree looked up to see that they were alone; the Resurrected Man had made his usual fast, dramatic, messy exit.

The man holding Charlie in his arms turned for a last look at the Breathing Tree. "I'm sorry you had to be the one we chose."

A few moments later the storage tanks one floor above their heads exploded with such force that the entire building was almost instantaneously gutted from top to bottom, the blast slamming downward with such force the Breathing Tree was uprooted and blown forward, snapping at the trunk and falling forward to crush both Charlie Smeds and the man holding him. The man Charlie thought of as Mr. Tree felt one microsecond of blinding, cataclysmic, torturous pain; Charlie felt nothing at all because he wasn't there, he'd left about thirty seconds ago, he was up at Talley's Hideaway, dressed in his best suit—okay, his *only* suit, but it was a nice one— and he was having a wonderful dinner with his family and listening to Eugene tell one of his endless supply of colorful stories. Charlie never knew that the reason he felt no pain in the final moments of his life was because the man holding him had taken it away, taken it into himself, suffering both his and Charlie's physical agony.

This man's last thought was an amused one: Charlie had actually asked him if *he* was Hoopsticks, and that made this man smile. *People and their superstitious legends.*

And then all was—as the saying goes—hellfire and damnation.

15

The entry about Hoopsticks that appears on page 31 of *A Visitor's Guide to Cedar Hill* never fails to make me laugh. It's not that the authors have gotten anything wrong—there was indeed a man named Green (Edward Taylor Green, to be precise) who did murder several people and threw their bodies into the sewer system, causing the water in that area (the north side) to run red for several weeks; so, from a purely factual standpoint, nothing in page 31's entry is incorrect—it's just that, counting from the first time his name is used, the authors devote exactly one hundred words to Hoopsticks's legend, reducing him to little more than a glorified footnote. Considering how long he's been an active part of the town's history—arguably even a guiding force *behind* that history, one filled with more horror and violence than the authors of the *Visitor's Guide* were willing to reveal—I would have preferred they quoted the actual document from which they oh-so-carefully selected their information; however, knowing the contents of that document, I find it hard to begrudge them their decision to censor most of it.

I know the hour is getting late, but I need you to come along with me for just a little longer. If you'll look over here, you'll see one those corners where the finite and infinite don't quite match up; there's a gap, and a rather large one, at that; more than enough space for us to look through together and see:

A gray, rainy, dismal night outside this twenty-four-hour diner; from where we stand, unseen between the raindrops, we can make out only blurred, indistinct shapes on the other side of steam-fogged windows, but then someone inside reaches up with a napkin, presses it against the glass, rubs an ever-widening circle, and like the iris-in of an old silent film, we're given a clear view: we can see that it's warm inside, full of life, buzzing with the music of a dozen or more conversations, the rattle of plates and the ding! *of the short-order cook hitting the bell on the pass-through and shouting "Order up!"*

But then we sense movement behind us, and turn to see a figure in a dark, rain-slicked parka walking toward the diner. A large, mean-looking dog—a black mastiff—accompanies it. The figure's destination is clear, for we can see the light reflected from its eyes as it stares at the diner's front door. Whether or not this figure is a man or a woman we cannot tell, for the shadows cast by the hood of the parka obscures all its features, excepting, of course, those intense eyes.

Mark this moment, this place, this time, and remember it; this is where we will enter the next part of our story, and you need to be prepared for what follows. Turn away now—you don't want to see any more, not yet. Instead, I want you to think about something said by the man who was holding Charlie Smeds during the last moments of his life. Wasn't it curious, of all the things this man could have said, that he chose to turn toward the cedar tree and say: "I'm sorry you had to be the one we chose"?

In order to explain the reason behind those final words, you need to know more about Hoopsticks;

specifically, you need to know the full contents of
the document that the *Visitor's Guide* authors chose to
censor.

The document is part of the historical society's private archives, and can be accessed only by the organi-
zation's officers and select members. It is untitled, and
its author is unknown; he or she does, however, quote
from the journals of one of Cedar Hill's original found-
ers. And yes, as I promised at the start, this is where
everything starts coming together.

And so:

It had probably always been there, but it wasn't
until the autumn of 1924 that the people of Cedar
Hill gave it a proper name: Hoopsticks. Oh, it had
been, and would be, called other things: Piegger,
Jimmy Goblin-Eyes, the Ghost of County Road #22;
the Delaware Indians even whispered of a hunch-
backed, raven-cloaked Supernatural Being, a Serpent in semihuman form, named *Ya'kwahe,* the
eater of souls who hid within the shadow you cast
at midday; but "Hoopsticks" was the name perma-
nently placed in local legend.

Said to roam the streets of West Cedar Hill and
those of Old Towne East, he was the nightmare
dread of every child: an umbrella repairman
whose deformed twin brother, Gash, grew out of
his back. The two of them wore a quiver slung over
their shoulder, and that quiver was said to be filled
with the severed spinal cords of unruly youngsters.

There was a time, long ago—so goes the
legend—when Hoopsticks and Gash had been
separate, two men, each with two arms and two
legs, but they did something so dreadful, so atro-
cious, something so horrible that even the Devil
was sickened, and so grabbed both of them in his

fiery fist and uttered a terrible curse, melting them together.

Mothers warned their children that if they misbehaved, Hoopsticks would creep into their room some night, whispering, *"My quiver is once again empty, and that, I'm afraid, simply will not do,"* and carry them away to a large black box near Raccoon Creek, which was both his home and the terrible factory where he turned children into umbrellas.

Children asked, *Why does he do that?*

Because, said their mothers, *Hoopsticks knows that no child is rotten to the core, so he steals them away and grinds them down so he can get to their goodness; then he takes each child's goodness and stuffs it into one of his five thousand jars.*

How come? whispered the children, pulling their blankets close around them.

On account of what the Devil said, mothers replied with a grin. *Ol' Scratch declared that if Hoopsticks got himself enough goodness to fill all them jars, then he can mix it all together in a big iron kettle and it'll make a batch of greasy Devil-tallow—and you know what they say about Devil-tallow: It'll turn a farmer's crops to ashes, make a healthy cow birth a six-legged calf, cause the dead to wake up screaming inside their caskets . . . it'll even burn a freak twin brother off old Hoopsticks's back. That's how come. So you just lay here all by yourself in the dark and you think about this, child: Every time you're bad, every time you don't do your chores or disobey or speak ill of someone else, Hoopsticks and his freak twin brother are that much closer to pulling themselves apart. Then there'll be two of them. And if that happens you won't never be safe again.*

They say the first time Hoopsticks appeared in Ohio was the spring of 1798.

Calling himself Mr. Josiah Comstock, he accompanied a group of Welsh, Scotch, and Irish immigrants led by Elias Hughes and Jon Ratcliffe, who came up the Licking River to establish the first white settlement in Delaware/Wyandot territory. They landed at the spot that is now called Cedar Hill.

Seven years passed, during which Cedar Hill became an official township in 1803. The settlers worked peacefully alongside the Delaware, Wyandot, and emerging Shawnee Indians to establish shipping lanes through the Narrows. Over the course of these years some mangled bodies were found floating in the river. Everyone was content to accept Comstock's explanation: "My friends, we must all of us remember that a new and wild territory such as this often harbors many dangers for the traveler who loses his way. Have not we heard the baying of the wolves at night? I put it to you that these unfortunate dead whose names we shall never know fell prey to wolves, perhaps even bears or wild dogs or any number of beasts unseen whose home we have, by our presence, made smaller.

"Let it rest at this; that these nameless dead shall be given a proper Christian burial, and that whenever we speak of them, it will be with piety and humility. If each of us swears to our Lord to do this, then these nameless ones shall not have died unmourned."

Then, on an oddly starless night in August of 1805, the Reverend Samuel Whittsley (from whose journal all this is known) left his small church to pay a visit to the newly arrived Stephanus family.

Elias Hughes and Jon Ratcliffe accompanied him, each bearing a gift of food prepared by their wives and daughters.

It was well known that the Stephanuses' oldest daughter, Sarah, was suffering from a serious fever. Fearing that their daughter's sickness might be contagious, the Stephanuses took a cabin on the outskirts of the township proper so the other families need not worry. It was a lonely location, and Reverend Whittsley made it a point to visit the family at least twice a week. Hughes and Ratcliffe had wished to come along this night in order to offer additional kindnesses and prayers.

As they neared the Stephanus cabin, Reverend Whittsley noted with some alarm that there were no candles burning in the windows. Had the family for some reason given up their vigil at the girl's bedside? She could not have succumbed, for one of the other children would have certainly been sent to fetch him so he might say a few words for Sarah's immortal soul.

Whittsley voiced his concern to Hughes and Ratcliffe, both of whom ran ahead of the older man and knocked on the door—but received no answer.

A muffled shriek sounded from within, of a ". . . singularly puzzling and nervous-making quality" that neither man had before encountered. Ratcliffe, fearing that a wolf or wild dog had gotten into the cabin, forced open the door and took a step inside, raising his lantern. A moment later, he was joined by Hughes and Whittsley.

(**Editor's Note:** The journal gets deliberately vague at this point. Judging by what information Whittsley provides, it's clear that what he saw was too horrifying to describe in detail.)

. . . and that's true; Whittsley couldn't bring himself to describe what he saw in that cabin in detail. But you need to know those details, so steady yourselves a little, and then we'll return to the rest of the document.

A muffled shriek sounded from within, of a singularly puzzling quality that neither man had before encountered. Ratcliffe, fearing that a wolf or wild dog had gotten into the cabin, forced open the door and took one step inside, raising his lantern. The light revealed a scene so foul that Ratcliffe, a man of considerable strength in both mind and body, nearly fainted.

The small cabin was clotted with the bodies of the seven Stephanus family members. Each had been stripped of their clothing, crudely scalped, and their genitalia removed with a bowie knife. The floor was awash with their blood and the evacuated contents of bowels. And in the center of it all, naked and sobbing, covered from head to heel in gore and coursing rivulets of thick liquid feces, knelt Josiah Comstock. Around his neck hung a strip of dried animal hide on which he'd sewn the amputated sexual organs of his victims. Interspersed with these fresh parts were other, older human appendages—tongues, fingers, ears that were so shriveled and desiccated as to be nearly unrecognizable. Comstock opened his eyes and saw Ratcliffe standing in the doorway, then shrieked softly. He was clutching the still-warm scalps in his trembling hands, rubbing them over his fully erect penis. Strings of moist hair and bloody clumps of gore clung to his member like webbing.

"O, Lord, O good Christ save us," whispered Ratcliffe, coughing. The bile that had risen in his throat spluttered out of his mouth and spilled down his chin, staining his shirt. By now, both Elias Hughes and Reverend Whittsley had entered the cabin. The extra light from Hughes's lantern exposed further horrors.

Mixed in with the blood and filth on the floor were looping entrails, teeth, and eyes with the stalks still attached. Josiah Comstock had also mutilated his own body, severing the flesh of his chest so the flaps hung down in a ghastly parody of a woman's breasts.

The soft shrieks issuing from Comstock's throat became the low purr of a cat being gently stroked. "Five hundred days," he whispered. "Five hundred days . . ." His voice cracked on the last word and twisted into an obscene, squealing laugh.

Reverend Whittsley, with tears in his eyes, made the sign of the cross and forced himself to take in everything before him. It was a testament to his composure that he was able to notice what the other men did not.

"S-Sarah," he choked. "I don't see . . . w-where is . . . is Sarah?"

A reptilian smile slithered across Josiah Comstock's face as he tilted his head to the side, indicating the far corner of the cabin. Not moving his gaze from Whittsley's face, Comstock quoted Luke 24:22: " 'Certain women made us astonished.' "

Hughes swung his lantern around and moved toward the corner. Its light like ink from an overturned well spread in front of him, unveiling, one repulsive detail at a time, what had become of the oldest Stephanus child.

Her hands, covered with deep, seeping scratch marks, were folded together as if in prayer. Her wrists had been bound together with rope and tied to the headboard of her bed. Her arms had been broken at the elbows. Part of her forehead had been bludgeoned in with an iron that lay at her side. Her tongue had been ripped out. Her throat was a patchwork of bruises. Her nightgown had been ripped open down the middle. Her breasts had been chewed with such frenzy that little of them remained. Comstock had split her from stomach to pelvis like a gutted deer. Her legs were bent at the knees and spread wide apart as if she were about to give birth. Her ankles had been snapped and tied to the short posts at the end of the bed. Her vagina had been hacked away and gummy ribbons of her killer's seed speckled the surface of her exposed intestines.

But the worst thing of all, the thing that made Elias Hughes drop weeping to one knee and Reverend Whittsley press a fist against his mouth to keep from employing the Lord's name in vain, was the expression on Sarah Stephanus's face. Every appalling moment of her torture was chiseled into her features, and Whittsley knew, as soon as he saw that her startling blue eyes were open and staring out toward the middle of the cabin, that Comstock had made her watch as he slaughtered her family.

She had died last.

"One year," intoned Josiah Comstock, rocking back and forth on his knees, "four months, fifteen days, nine hours, seven minutes, twelve seconds . . ."

Whittsley pulled in a strained breath and, turning his face toward an unseen Heaven with its unseen God, whispered, "It cannot be too severe."

Elias Hughes met the Reverend's gaze and a silent understanding passed between them.

The news spread quickly and before the hour was gone the adult colonists, in horror and fury, dragged Josiah Comstock from the cabin, then beat, kicked, shot, burned, spit upon, and partially skinned him. Toward dawn he was taken, whimpering and still alive, into the dreary depths of the surrounding forest and hanged by his neck from an ancient, twisted, and (some said) evil-looking cedar tree.

His ruined body made one half-turn to the left, then was still.

The colonists buried the Stephanus family, then set fire to their small, lonely cabin, burning it to the ground. The ashes were later gathered, poured into a burlap sack that was tied closed with twine and taken downriver to an unexplored section of the Narrows. The sack was thrown into the river, where it broke against a large rock. It was said by those present that the water turned the color of blood as the ashes were absorbed.

In order to keep their children away from this terrible place, the colonists warned that a wretched monster crouched unseen beneath the water, waiting to carry all disobedient children away to its black cave; the only way to recognize it was by its misshapen back that stood above the surface like a large rock. *If you see it, you must run at once,* they would whisper. *Gaze a second longer, and it will be too late for you.*

Until the time of their deaths, Hughes, Ratcliffe, and the other colonists all wore a special cloak of shame, haunted by the knowledge that each of them shared responsibility for what had been done to Josiah Comstock and, by association, to the Stephanuses and the nameless dead found in the river.

There were other bodies they never found, each one mangled more horribly than the previous, for unbeknownst to Cedar Hill's founding fathers and mothers, Josiah Comstock had been murdering "lost travelers" since the day the first group of immigrants landed on the shores of Licking County. Most of his victims were selected from the work camps that were scattered in a sixty-mile radius around the colony. The workmen—hired to help construct the shipping lanes—and their families had, for a while, provided Josiah Comstock with more than enough gratifying flesh. It was only because the urge came upon him without warning that he made the mistake of choosing a family of fellow colonists to be his next victims.

But Josiah Comstock did not die on that dreadful night in 1805.

A few minutes after twilight, sixteen hours after Hughes and the others had left him, his body made another small half-turn, this time to the right.

Something crawled along the branch from which his body hung.

A stray bit of pale moonlight shone through the leaves and landed on the branch, revealing a black butterfly, each of whose unmoving wings was the size of a man's hand.

Josiah Comstock reached up and gripped the back of the noose. The rope crackled and smoked and blackened as his touch burned through it. He dropped to the ground, tore the noose from around his neck, vomited blood, then cupped his hands and lifted them upward.

The black butterfly vanished from the branch like an image, then instantly reappeared in the cradle formed by Comstock's palms.

He looked in the direction of the settlement and smiled through ruined lips.

"Five hundred days," he croaked. His voice was thick and congealed. He held the black butterfly against his chest.

"I cannot believe the number is so low," came a voice from behind him.

Comstock turned to see Reverend Whittsley standing a few feet away, Bible in hand.

"Let me guess," said Comstock. "You told everyone that, as a man of God, you were duty-bound to come up here and say a few words for my eternal soul?"

"You already know the answer," said Whittsley, dropping the Bible to the ground as Comstock released the black butterfly. Both men watched it flutter up and away into the night.

"Do you ever get tired of this?" whispered Comstock.

Whittsley looked at him. "What choice do we have in the matter?"

"There were choices, earlier. It's just that the wrong ones were made."

Whittsley rubbed his eyes. "So where and when to now? Forward, back, sideways?"

They stood in silence under the silver moon. Then Comstock said: "I kind of like it *here.*"

Whittsley looked around for a few moments, then shrugged. "Good a place as any for the next few hundred years . . . or so."

One last little bit from the document that you might find of interest, this having to do with that section of the Narrows where the ashes of the Stephanus cabin were disposed of:

(**Editor's Note:** I found that section of the Narrows on my last visit to Cedar Hill. Whittsley drew a pretty accurate map in the journal. The locals say that if you stood on the south bank of the river at exactly six thirty P.M., you can see the water turn the color of blood as it flows past that rock. They're right; it looks a *lot* like blood. Do you know what the section is called on the map—not Whittsley's map, but *any* map of Cedar Hill you buy today? "Bloody Run." If ever you find yourself standing there at that time of day, it'll give you the creeps, trust me.)

The legend of Hoopsticks persists to this day. People say he didn't die with Comstock, though. They say he came back. . . .

And I can attest to the truth of that last statement, for he did come back . . .

. . . in June of 1805, as an epidemic of cholera where people were dying so fast the bodies had to be collected in express wagons every eight hours . . .

. . . he did come back . . .

. . . in March of 1840, as a flood that killed fifteen people and left hundreds more without shelter . . .

. . . he did come back . . .

. . . in February of 1876, as an outcast Wyandot warrior named Ictinike who rampaged through five different white settlements, killing dozens of women and children before a posse of lawmen gunned him down . . .

. . . he did come back . . .

. . . in January of 1901, as a ghostly head that was seen hovering inside a covered bridge on County Road #22; it was believed that no fewer than twenty people died of fright or were driven hopelessly insane from encountering it . . .

. . . and, still, he came back . . .

. . . in September of 1915, as a fire that gutted and razed the newly erected Cedar Hill Courthouse, killing the seven people who'd been trapped in the basement, among them Anthony Spencer Ratcliffe, a direct descendant of the same Jon Ratcliffe who was one the first men to see the slaughtered bodies of the Stephanus family . . .

. . . he came back . . .

. . . in the autumn of 1924, as a shadowy figure on the streets of West Cedar Hill who was responsible for the murders of six children and whose name found a permanent place in local folklore . . .

. . . he came back . . .

. . . in October of 1945, as a massive windstorm that passed through five neighboring counties before deciding to vent its wrath on Cedar Hill; houses were blown apart, trees uprooted, power lines snapped, and the spire high atop the Second Presbyterian Church toppled to the ground, crushing and killing the minister, Ronald Gregory Hughes, an amiable man who often boasted that "his people" had been the first religious leaders to settle in the county . . .

. . . he came back . . .

. . . in August of 1969, as a massive fire that destroyed a majority of Old Towne East (to which we will return momentarily) . . .

. . . and he came back again . . .

. . . on July 4 of 1976, as a teenager named Andy Leonard, a typical "All-American" boy who, for reasons that were never known, went on a shooting spree that killed thirty-two people and wounded thirty-six others, making it the worst mass shooting in U.S. history to that date . . .

but he wasn't finished; he came back yet again . . .

. . . in 1994, birthed from a mother's grief and anger at the abduction of her daughter, in the form of a golemlike creature called "Mr. Hands," that for a short while terrorized Cedar Hill with a series of brutal, bloody murders directed at those who would dare harm children . . .

. . . and he came back . . .

. . . in 2005, this time as a rift between one reality and another, wherein a lonely, innocent man named Gil Stewart, powerless to stop his being wrenched back and forth between realities, believed he was being threatened by a group of supernatural beings called the Keepers who possessed the power to turn people into animals and animals into people, all of it culminating in a violent and fiery tragedy . . .

. . . and he would come back a final time, when one survivor of the Leonard Massacre returned to Cedar Hill over thirty years later to at last unearth the truth about Hoopsticks's origin and power (but that is another story, best saved for another time).

But what of the period between 1994 and 2005? Did

Hoopsticks simply shrug away Cedar Hill, deciding that he was bored with it for the time being?

He did not. To quote the Bard: "Therein lies the tale."

You might very well wonder how I know all of this—or perhaps you've already figured it out. Regardless, turn around with me and look back one last time at that horrible night in 1969 when both Charlie Smeds and Eugene Talley lost their lives in the worst fire in the town's history. Just a few more moments, and then I will tell you all about the thirteenth time Hoopsticks returned to Cedar Hill, leaving in his wake a path of violence, death, and grief that made the rest of his visits combined seem like child's play.

16

The Cedar Hill Fire Department arrived at Beaumont Caskets just as the flames reached the stain, oil, and wood polish storage tanks, all of which went up simultaneously in an eighty-foot mushroom cloud that ignited nine other nearby buildings. When it was all over and the fire at last contained (some fifteen hours later), firefighters from three other counties had been called in and most of the buildings in a four-block area were either gutted beyond saving or piles of smoldering cinders.

Besides Beaumont Caskets and Talley's Hideaway, thirteen other businesses were destroyed, and none of them ever reopened their doors. So much debris from the explosion landed in Hopewell Park five blocks away that several of the trees were set aflame, and since it was the middle of August, and the middle of a drought, the grass was brown, dry, and brittle; it didn't take long for the park to be razed (an automobile graveyard is there now).

The explosion scattered caskets and countless sections of caskets around a four-block area in every direction. During the nearly five months of cleanup that went on afterward, one volunteer remarked that the area looked ". . . like a county full of coffins."

This was overheard by Jack Donovan, a reporter/DJ

from WHTH Radio who was there covering the cleanup efforts; the phrase stuck with him, and by the time he made his six P.M. news broadcast that night, he'd pared the volunteer's remark down to—you're way ahead of me, aren't you?—"Coffin County." The *Coffin County Update* became something of an isolated pop-culture phenomenon for about six weeks, especially after a rumor surfaced that Beaumont Caskets had been deliberately burned down by Vietnam protestors because of Franklin Beaumont's supposed ties with Lyndon Johnson (this was neither proven nor disproven).

The area slowly but steadily became a magnet for the so-called "less desirable elements" of Cedar Hill's denizenship—homeless people, drug addicts, alcoholics, thieves, street-corner racists spouting their doctrine of hate to all who passed by, as well as young runaways and those only too happy to exploit their desperation and vulnerability.

Now the buildings that line the streets squat like diseased animals waiting for someone to come along and blast them out of their misery. What few stores remain in the area sell mostly liquor and keep bars on their doors and windows; the clerks who work there are armed well beyond even the most lenient definition of "legally." Most of Cedar Hill sees it as a cancer growth, this area, a breeding ground for violence and anger and despair where the inhabitants accept degradation as a way of life, where brutality is second nature, and where rape, murder, and robbery are looked upon in the same way that most people look upon rush-hour traffic: you put up with it and try to get yourself home in one piece. Everyone has opinions and ideas about what should have been done or what should be done about Coffin County; in the meantime the city officials avoid talking about it, thinking about it, doing anything to improve it, or going anywhere near the area.

Coffin County is a place where the spirit would have to rally in order to reach hopeless. It is a place where the odd and the damaged, the despondent and the discarded, the lost and the shabby come when they reach the end of their rope and life offers no alternative but to crawl into the shadows of poverty and just give up.

But when twilight arrived following the night of the conflagration, when the firefighters were gone and the police had barricaded the area from the press and the curious, when no one was there to gawk at the destruction and smoldering ashes, a certain area near the center of the devastation began to swell, ripple, and then rise and fall as if it were breathing. The ashes began to take shape; had anyone been there to witness this, they would have sworn that the undulating cinders and residue assumed the shape of a human being, one that pulled itself above the surface as if rising from the grave, and then opened its eyes, shaking its head to scatter the ashes from its face. This figure of ash struggled to its feet, looked around, and began stumbling in the direction of the stone wall that was all that remained of Talley's Hideaway. The figure paused there for a moment, wrote a message on it in ash, and then blew the ash away so that it would appear that nothing was written there at all. After that, the ash figure, peeling away large sections of fire-charred flesh to reveal the red, moist, regenerating tissue beneath, made its way into the night to begin its preparations.

I don't mind telling you that it hurt like hell, peeling away that fried flesh, and the regeneration process wasn't exactly what you'd call a party, either. It never is.

I was the figure Charlie thought of at first as "Mr. Tree." I was also the man the original Cedar Hill settlers knew as the Reverend Samuel Whittsley—which is not my real name; the Resurrected Man was of course Josiah Comstock—and that is not his real name, either: whether this information will prove necessary to the rest of this has yet to be determined.

The time has come for us to return to that gap through which we will enter the next part of the story. Don't be afraid, just take a deep breath and step through, it's big enough for all of us; if it helps, close your eyes until you're all the way through and can feel the cold night rain on your face. Then take a deep breath and open your eyes, turn around, and see the figure in the parka who is walking toward the diner. We're close enough now to see that the figure is a man. He wears a watch. The time is 10:45 P.M. He orders the dog—a large, black bull mastiff—to sit, and it obeys. The man reaches out and takes hold of the handle on the door, pulls it open, and we follow him inside. . . .

17

The man in the rain-slicked parka entered the all-night diner a little after 10:45 P.M. Despite the lateness of the hour, the place was packed, due in no small part to the thunderstorm that had moved in an hour before. None of the customers paid him the least bit of attention.

A shift-weary waitress looking fifteen years older than her twenty-nine years glanced up from behind the cash register and smiled at the man, but the hour, the cold rain pounding against the windows from outside, and too many dead hopes prevented her smile from being anything more than hollow and hopeless, an empty expression from the depths of an austere and lonely heart.

Grabbing a menu with ragged edges from the cracked plastic tray hanging beside the register, she brushed a strand of prematurely gray hair from one of her eyes and said, "Is it just yourself tonight, sir?"

The man gave a short, sharp nod of his head.

"Terrible weather tonight, isn't it?" said the waitress, making small talk more out of habit than any real desire to engage in conversation with another human being. "Seems like this storm just came out of nowhere."

"Just like miracles," replied the man in a deep, sepulchral voice.

The waitress stared at him. "I beg your pardon?"

"Haven't you ever heard that expression before?" asked the man. " 'Miracles out of nowhere'?"

The waitress shook her head. "Can't say that I have— but it's sure an interesting phrase. I'll remember that one." She came around the counter and gestured for him to follow her toward a booth in the back.

The man reached out and gently, quickly, with the awestruck tenderness of a parent's hand on a new-born's cheek, touched her shoulder. She stopped, then turned to look at him.

A silver shimmer danced across his gaze as he looked into her eyes. In the millisecond between that flash of silver and the sadness that took root in her chest once it had passed from sight, she felt as if he had called forward, taken in, and come to know everything there was *to* know about her; every little-girl fantasy, every petty jealousy and unspoken desire, all of the goals she'd failed to achieve throughout her now-lonely life, and the people who had, in one way or another, suffered because of those failures.

She tried to pull away from him, to break the grip his gaze had on her, but she knew in a breath it was use-less, that this stranger with the intense eyes and voice like a mournful train whistle at midnight controlled her now just as strongly as did her last husband, whose idea of affection usually manifested itself in black eyes and bruised ribs.

"S-s-sir . . ." she whispered.

"Shhh," he replied. "Just a moment or two more, please."

She remained still as he sifted through the emotional detritus she carried from two failed marriages, count-less bad relationships before that, pushing aside small regrets and little cruelties until he finally came to the one thing she never spoke of with anyone: the lingering, still howling-raw ache from the death of her three-year-old daughter in an automobile crash four years earlier.

"How terrible it must have been for you," he said. Then: "But . . . she didn't suffer. She didn't feel a thing."

He listened to the music she liked, smiled at the movie stars she'd had crushes on over the years, was surprised by the books she'd read and the lies she'd told, yet his silent searching was more satisfying than any lover's touch, finger, or tongue. Every private, complex, contradictory aspect of her character was revealed to him.

They had been standing by the empty booth for less than five seconds.

None of the customers paid them any attention, lost as they were in their own thoughts, their own worries, their own conversations.

The waitress was remembering the day of her daughter's death, remembering how she herself had been so sick but had taken some decongestants, anyway, because her daughter wanted to go to the Fourth of July cookout on the downtown square and the poor little thing had seen so much disappointment already in her life that Mommy couldn't say no, even though she felt terrible. So Mommy took the pills and was driving them downtown and was feeling a little dizzy and closed her eyes for only a second, that was all, just a second, maybe less, just long enough to clear her vision because things were getting a little blurry, then her daughter screamed, *Mommy! Look out for that man in the truck!* And by the time Mommy opened her eyes it was too late, she'd swerved over the center line and the truck came down on them like a curse from heaven and oh, Jesus, hon, I didn't mean for it to happen, I'm so sorry, I miss you so much, it should've been me, it should've been me, it should've been—

—then the man with intense eyes was there, touching her daughter's cheek. "I promise you, Edna—and what a lovely, lovely name that is, you shouldn't be embarrassed by it—I *swear* to you that Karen didn't suffer. There was a single moment of fear, but once the truck hit you, she was gone. There was no pain for her, no pain at all."

And Edna saw Karen smile at her; but for all the love and forgiveness that was in that smile, there was also an infinite amount of regret.

Then in a blink it was gone, and Edna was once again just a shift-weary waitress with less than a high-school education standing on a grimy floor in a cheap all-night diner where the scarred wooden booths and tables were just as raggedy as the edges of the menu in her hand.

She tossed the menu down and nearly lost her balance. The man reached out and steadied her. This attracted the attention of a few people near the back who were waiting for Edna to come around with the coffee pot so they could get refills.

She wiped some sweat from her face and took a few deep breaths to steady herself, and then looked into Miracle Man's eyes once again.

Take me back to her, please. Please take me back to Karen.

His voice again, like satin against her skin. "Do you have anyone else, now that your daughter is gone?"

"I don't know what . . . I mean . . . I . . ."

"A husband, a boyfriend—any friends at all?"

Her eyes began tearing, much to her embarrassment. "Not really. I mean, I know the other girls who wait tables here, and I talk with a lot of the regulars, but I don't know nobody well enough to ask them to, y'know, come visit or go to the movies or nothing. It's just me."

He reached out and touched her cheek. "But you're

more than enough. There's a universe inside you, Edna. You just never realized it. I showed you nothing that wasn't already inside you. You felt nothing that wasn't already there. Karen has always been with you. There's an entire branch of the multiverse where Karen never died, where the two of you are together and happy and you don't have to work these terrible hours and feel so all alone."

"I'm sorry," said Edna. "I guess . . . I guess I don't understand."

"You will," he said, smiling. "I promise you, Edna, *you will.*"

He kissed her cheek, threw open his parka, pulled out a Tec-9 semiautomatic with a 50-shot clip, and opened fire.

Everyone moved at once, running for doors, throwing themselves under tables, grabbing for loved ones who were with them or calling out the names of those loved ones they'd never see again. All were drowned out by the cold, contemptuous crack of continuous rattle-gun racket.

A joyful noise, in its own way, followed by the austere, awestruck silence of those who had just witnessed the coming of a miracle.

Out of nowhere.

18

At the same instant the stranger in the parka walked into the diner, Ben Littlejohn awoke from the best dream he'd had in years. In the dream—in the good part, anyway, the part where he wasn't running and choking—he'd been the one to make the late-night run to the market, not Cheryl; he had been the one standing in line when the three teenagers ran inside brandishing their weapons and screaming for everyone to get down; he'd been the one shot twice when one of the kids panicked and began spraying the front of the store; he—not Cheryl—had died on the floor under the too-bright overhead fluorescent lights; and as he felt the last spark of his life begin to fade away, he was given a glimpse of the future where his wife and unborn son were doing fine; yes, Cheryl missed him terribly, and Ben's son had never known him, but Mommy told him all about the kind of man Daddy had been. It was a nice way to die.

Ben blinked against wakefulness, trying to hold on to the last few hazy images of the dream, but . . . no good. He was awake and alive and Cheryl was still dead and the three fuckers who'd robbed the market and shot five people—only one of whom had died—were still out there, having never been caught.

Looking at the clock on the nightstand, Ben realized that in less than ninety minutes, the third anniversary of his wife and unborn son's murders would begin.

He rose from the too-big bed and shuffled downstairs to the kitchen where he drank some orange juice straight from the carton—something Cheryl would have thrown a fit over. Feeling the twinges and seeing the auras that warned of an oncoming migraine, he took the carton of OJ into the downstairs bathroom and dug a couple of Imitrex tablets from the box in the medicine cabinet. Once the tablets were down and the OJ gone, he went back up to the bedroom and turned on the small reading lamp clamped to his side of the headboard. He stared down at the framed photograph next to the alarm clock; he and Cheryl, on their wedding day. Even now he could still remember every nuance of the moment this picture had been taken; the scent of her perfume, the slant of the light coming in through the church window, the bead of sweat that took so long to crawl down his spine he thought he was going to have a seizure, the aroma of the flowers in her bouquet as well as those on the altar, the way she squeezed his hand—not one long squeeze but a rhythmic series of them, in perfect time with the beating of her heart, now his as well: squeeze *(I Cheryl take thee Benjamin to be my wedded husband)*, release; squeeze *(. . . to love and to cherish, till death . . .)*, release, the two of them exchanging themselves for themselves with each breath, silently and willingly bestowing some part of their being into the other until, at the moment the photograph was taken, they were one: this day, this moment, this breath, this love, till death.

Three years and it still hurt like hell, thinking about what Should Have Been.

God, honey, he thought, staring into her frozen smile. *I miss you so much.*

He looked at his gun in its holster, hanging off the headboard near the clamp-on lamp. Sometimes the presence of that gun was almost too much of a temptation.

I shouldn't have let you go. Or I should have gone with you. Instead of you. Maybe if I'd gone along instead of staying here and acting like a baby because I had that awful cold . . . but you wouldn't hear of it. It was bad enough that I had to sleep on the couch because we didn't want you getting sick, you didn't want me to make it worse by going out for the cold medicine. God, honey, can you ever forgive me?

His chest hitched and his shoulders slumped and his eyes stung as the guilt once again raked iron hooks through his guts. He pressed one hand against his eyes and surprised himself by not crying. But he shook; at first only in his stomach, but it quickly fanned up into his shoulders, then his arms, then his hands. He felt the thin layer of sweat that covered his body and tasted the sudden sourness on his tongue.

He stared at Cheryl's smile again and felt a little better, remembering the way she'd always rub his back when he woke from a bad dream or had a bad day at work. He looked once more at the gun that was too much of a temptation sometimes and shook his head, almost laughing at himself for being such a clichéd, self-pitying, melodramatic jerk. Cheryl would get so *mad* at him if he ever . . .

"Asshole," he whispered to himself. *This is not how you honor the memory of someone's life. Why can't you be grateful for the time you had with her, why can't you treasure that instead of acting like some character from a Clifford Odets play? Only not quite as cheerful.*

He did laugh this time, knowing that Cheryl would have gotten the reference.

He turned off the light and lay back down, rubbing his sore neck for a few moments and trying to summon the memory of Cheryl's fingertips against his skin, and for a moment or two he almost had it, but then he was fully in the grip of the migraine medication and could sense sleep sneaking up, and that was fine by him, because maybe he'd go back to the same happy dream he'd been having before he awoke. It was a nice way to die; it really was.

19

Outside the diner, the black bull mastiff sat immersed in the unreason of the rainy darkness and watched as blood bloomed over the inside of the windows. Eventually, the man in the rain- and blood-slicked parka came back out. The dog looked up at him, its tail wagging. A bloody hand came down to rest on its head and stroke its brow.

"Patience, my friend."

The grieving wail of a train whistle echoed in the distance. The dog whirled around, baring its teeth.

"Easy, boy, easy. No need to get yourself so worked up this early. Turn around—*turn around*. There you go. Now . . . here."

The dog accepted what was placed between its teeth, knowing this was not something to be eaten or played with or worried.

"You're a good boy. You know what to do, yes? Good. Excellent. I'll see you again very soon."

The dog whined, blinked, then looked in the direction of a loud thunderclap. When it turned back, the man had vanished into unreason and the rain. The dog walked over and sat under the awning over the diner's doorway. It wasn't so wet here. The dog liked that.

20

The phone rang at 11:20 P.M. Groggy, sore, and cursing, Ben fumbled for the receiver. Lifting it to his ear, he remembered something his father had drilled into everyone in the family when Ben was a child: *Mark my words—if the phone rings anytime after eleven at night, it's either really bad news or a wrong number. Ain't no in-between.*

"Yeah?" said Ben, his voice clogged with phlegm and weariness.

"Ben Littlejohn?"

It was a voice he didn't recognize. "Who is this?"

"*Detective* Ben Littlejohn?"

"Yes . . . ?"

The caller chuckled. It sounded like the stone doors of some ancient tomb being wrenched open after thousands of years. "Are you familiar with the Moundbuilders Diner?"

"What about it?"

"You might want to get someone out there right away. There's been some sort of terrible shooting."

"Who is this?"

"Edna thought of me as Miracle Man, but you can call me Hoopsticks. Very pretty woman, Edna was. Note the use of past tense."

Click.

Ben pulled the receiver away from his ear and stared at the thing as if expecting it to become a serpent. A scalpel-sharp chill sliced across the back of his shoulders. He quickly shook it away as he called Dispatch.

There's been some sort of terrible shooting.

("Mark my words . . .")

21

only eleven hundred days this time? you're getting a bit unreasonable in your old age, my torturer. they died nobly.

. . . .

   i see. not that nobly.
   and there will be more. there will always be more.
   in the name of unruh and simmons and lepine and huberty and rupert and dahmer and lucas and gacy and sherrill.

. . . .

   you are so right to correct me, my torturer. and also in the names of richland and frontier and bethel and heath and jonesboro and parker and columbine.
   your will be done.

. . . .

   and fuck you, too.
   only eleven hundred days. you can be quite the malicious bastard sometimes.
   i am sorry, my torturer. forgive my outburst. you've forgiven nothing else. dum vita est, spes est.

22

As the sun perched on the horizon like a vulture examining a field of fresh carrion, Ben Littlejohn stood shivering in a corner of the blood-drenched diner sipping bad lukewarm coffee from a plastic travel cup. Streams of bright morning light, intensified by their reflecting off the polished chrome of the shelves behind the counter, lanced into his eyes with almost laser precision. God, was he glad he'd taken the Imitrex last night; if he hadn't, he'd be on the floor right now. He blinked, squinted, then stepped to the side and out of the path of the reflecting light, taking care to remain within the taped boundaries that separated the safe area from the rest of the scene.

Jim Wagner, one of the first two patrol officers on the scene, came over and asked if Ben wanted him and his partner, Tom Sanderson, to accompany the final load of bodies to the morgue.

"No. Ident officer's already there."

Wagner, trying not to let it show too much, was visibly relieved. Ben was too wrung out at the moment to be upset. He'd been a uniform once—not all that long ago, truth be told—and knew the old superstition.

It was a rarely spoken of belief among Cedar Hill

police officers that whoever pulled Freezer Duty—
accompanying bodies to the morgue or dealing with
family members who came to identify the remains or,
worst of all, having to go to someone's home and tell
them that a loved one was dead—would face some
form of death in their own lives before the year was out,
be it their own or that of someone they loved.

Confronted with something as grim as this scene,
Ben couldn't be upset with Wagner for holding on to a
shopworn superstition. Everyone knew cops were a superstitious bunch, anyway, though damned few of them
would ever admit it.

Wagner's face suddenly froze in an expression somewhere between awkwardness and humiliation, as if
he'd just realized that Ben knew the real reason he'd
asked about Freezer Duty.

"Don't look so embarrassed," said Ben. "I'd rub a goddamned rabbit's foot right now if I had one."

"Yessir. Thank you, sir."

"Who's got the dog's body?"

"We do, sir, Tom and me."

"It has to go to the Humane Society shelter. The on-
duty vet will do a quick autopsy to check for drugs and
then dispose of the body."

Wagner left. Ben rubbed his eyes again and then
shook his head to clear away the cobwebs trying to
form in there. He watched as various other uniformed
officers pointed out all possible evidence to the two
CSU team members from Columbus there to process it;
bag, tag, and inventory, everyone moving as smoothly
and efficiently as he'd ever seen—and considering the
arguably pitiful tools at their disposal, that was saying
something.

To an outsider looking in, it would appear that here
was a seasoned crime scene unit functioning at the
peak of efficiency—and they'd be right, at least in part.

Right now that efficiency could be attributed more to the need for continuous movement than to good training. Ben suspected that everyone on scene was grateful for the painstaking detail work that came with a major crime scene, because it made the whole—the blood and the shell casings, the bits of stray human meat still being located, the chalk outlines and the lingering stink of evacuated bowels—something of an abstract. Each element was an entity unto itself and was in no way, for the moment, connected to anything else around you. It was only later, when you were back in more familiar surroundings, when everything would be assembled bit by bit and coalesce into a single Thing, that you could allow yourself to acknowledge the reality of the whole, if still not completely accept it. So for now it was bag, tag, and inventory, all the time being grateful that there *was* such tedious standard operational bullshit because it prevented you from dwelling on the repulsive, gore-sodden, grisly truth of what was right there in your face.

There's been some sort of terrible shooting . . .

Ben took another sip of coffee, winced as it hit his stomach, and reminded himself that he and his partner, Bill Emerson, were in charge until Captain Goldstein arrived. He had to—

—*Edna thought of me as Miracle Man, but you can call me Hoopsticks*—

—keep himself steady.

Shit like this happened in New York or Los Angeles or Chicago but not, repeat *not,* in Cedar Hill, Ohio. Ben had been just out of college back in 1976 when that Leonard kid went on his rampage, and once everyone had recovered from that—if you could call it recovering—there was this sense throughout the community that the Leonard Massacre had been It, the Big Bad Awful, the One Horrible Event, and something like it would never happen here again. But happen again it had, and there would be time for shock and grief and anger and confusion to rear their ugly heads later; but for now, in the abstract, it was bag, tag, and inventory, measure the area and make sketches, collect all blood and tissue samples, then articles of clothing and this time, God help them all, *teeth*—which wasn't even close to being the worst of it.

The CSU photographer was busy with the last series of pictures, photographing everything from one direction, then the opposite direction, setting up his shots like some kind of ghoulish Ansel Adams while the uniforms outside kept the steadily growing crowd of spectators and television news crews under control.

Outside and overhead, the loud rhythmic pounding of the police helicopter's rotary blades slammed in sync with the pulsing in Ben's temples, making him once again glad that he'd taken migraine medication— not only that, but he had thought to bring an extra dose with him, if the need arose. A loud squawk erupted from the chopper's PA system, followed by a voice warning the crowd to stay back behind the barriers.

Another uniformed officer came up to Ben and informed him that Captain Goldstein had just radioed in to say he'd be here in a few more minutes. After that, Ben stepped over to an isolated table near the back of the diner where all of the evidence collected thus far had been placed. No one had been sitting at this table, no one had died near it, and there'd been no blood close to or on it—he'd had the area sprayed with luminol to make certain. A mistake along those same lines had royally fucked up a murder investigation he'd been part of six years ago—though, thankfully, not as the detective in charge; he'd still been a uniform, a good eight months from his detective's exam.

He examined everything on the table and then took

the small digital voice recorder from his coat pocket. Pressing the RECORD button, he began verbally inventorying the items. Ben chose to do it this way because it beat the hell out of having to fumble with a notebook and pen; when your hand started getting tired you started rushing things or were tempted to start skipping over items or using abbreviations that later made no sense. Verbally recording your notes was much more thorough and always guaranteed that you'd overlook nothing, be it the color of a victim's clothing, the position of a car in the parking lot, the location of a jacket, or where a fork had been found in relation to a body and splash or spatter patterns of blood.

The bodies had been examined, counted, and hauled away; the Tec-9, like everything else that had been collected, lay on the table in an evidence bag; and three wallets plus one purse (*which equals four missing bodies,* he reminded himself, as if there were a chance in hell he'd forget it) were neatly arranged on a nearby chair.

Ben stopped talking and stared at the Tec-9. The touch of a hand against his left shoulder startled him and he almost dropped the voice recorder. He turned to see Captain Al Goldstein standing next to him.

"Where the hell were you just then?" asked Goldstein.

"I just suddenly found myself thinking about James Huberty."

"Who?"

"The guy who shot up that McDonald's in San Ysidro back in '84."

"The 'I'm going to hunt humans' guy?"

"Yeah," replied Ben. "I remember seeing this picture of a cop who was kneeling over the bodies of one of the victims, a little boy who was splayed against a bicycle. The thing was—and this just occurred to me for some reason, after all this time—the thing was that the kid's hand was reaching out and you could see the hand of another person just outside camera range reaching *in* toward the kid. I was just wondering if that hand belonged to the little boy's mother, if she'd been trying to get to him in those last few seconds. She didn't make it. Their hands were still an inch or two apart."

"I remember that picture too," said Goldstein. "I think the *New York Post* ran it. The cop was crying, wasn't he?"

Ben rubbed the back of his sore neck. "Can't really blame him, can you?"

Goldstein offered him a cigarette. "Look, Ben, I hate to sound crass but I need for you to be on your A-game here. I need you focused. I know, *believe me* I know how son-of-a-bitching awful this has to have been for you, having the bastard call you and then walking into all of this, and I'm sorry I couldn't get here sooner, but the mayor and the chief and the safety director and everyone down to the janitorial staff at city hall have been reaming my ass over not having enough quote qualified personnel unquote to put on this. The chief wasn't exactly overjoyed that I called the Columbus CSU in before clearing it with him. When I politely reminded everyone about the budget cuts they gave me a collective 'So what?' and then sat there looking at me like I was supposed to whip out the yarmulke and chant secret words from the Aggadic statements of the Talmud or something to materialize extra and *non-salaried* Homicide personnel from thin air."

"So what's the word from on high?"

"For the next seventy-two hours I've got carte blanche and a blank check to do whatever I deem necessary. And you and Bill are running the investigation."

"I'll bet the chief loved hearing that."

"I thought for a moment that he might do a little dance, but the mayor sided with me, Sheriff Jackson

offered to put his entire department at our disposal—I
didn't even have to ask—and the safety director kept a
nice brown sheen on his nose by backing the mayor,
so for the next seventy-two hours . . . well, sixty-eight
now . . . it's up to me, you, and Bill. Where is he, anyway?"

"In the back going over tapes from the security cameras."

Goldstein looked surprised. "This place has security
cameras?"

Ben nodded. "Shocked the shit out of me, as well,
but, yeah—three of them, in fact." He pointed the first
one out to Goldstein and was about to show the captain
the locations of the other two when Goldstein stopped
him.

Stepping in front of Ben, his eyes serious and unblinking, Goldstein said, "I have to ask you this next
question, Ben, and I don't want you to take it the wrong
way."

Ben thought: *Oh, good—here it comes.*

What he said was: "Yes, sir?"

"Can you handle this? I don't mean the logistics, co-
ordinating personnel and paperwork and all that happy
horseshit—you're a wizard at that, always have been—I
mean the . . . the *stress* factor involved here. I *know*
what today is, so does Bill, so does everyone at the department." Goldstein put a hand on Ben's forearm. "I'm
sorry as hell about what happened to Cheryl, Ben, you
knew it then, you know it now. She was a wonderful
person and it makes me sick that she's no longer a part
of this world but those three wastes of carbon who
killed her are still breathing and aboveground. A situation like this is bad enough without the added pressure
of a lousy, *lousy* anniversary. So I need to know right
here and now if you can handle this, if it's going to bring
up any . . . any . . ."

" 'Emotional difficulties' was a favorite term of my former psychiatrist's."

"You're not making this easy."

"I apologize, Captain. Is the mayor and everyone else worried that I'm going to flip out because of what happened to my wife and child and let this bastard get away?"

"Let's just say that there are Well-Pressed Suits who are not convinced you're psychologically prepared to head up this investigation, even with Bill Emerson and me watching your back."

Ben swallowed. Once. Very hard. "Was any kind of alternative offered?"

"It was suggested—not by me—that either Bill could run this on his own, or that Robbery or Narcotics could be put in charge with a decent chance of success. I then suggested that we could call in the city hall maintenance crew to run the show because I can at least *depend* on them. That went over like a fart at a funeral. I've got permission to pull any or all personnel from any division to assist you and, if necessary, take over. I have no intention of doing that last one, but I need for you to look me in the eyes and tell me you can handle this. I'm not asking because I have any doubts; I'm asking because I gave the mayor and the chief my word that I would ask. So, for the last time, please—can you handle this?"

Ben looked down at his hands and thought about his job. Six times out of ten, homicides in Cedar Hill resulted from a domestic dispute that took a fast ugly turn, while four times out of ten occurred when someone had too much to drink or toke or toot and decided they wanted to teach someone a lesson. Ben and Bill Emerson had yet to deal with a homicide case where the victim and killer didn't know each other in some capacity. Last year had seen a record number of homicides here: sixteen. Arrests and convictions had been made in all but one, and that was only because the suspect—a drug dealer who worked out of Coffin County—had blown his own head off before the police arrived to bring him in.

Ben looked up at Goldstein. "Sir, for over five years Bill Emerson and I have been the sum total of the Homicide Division, and in all that time I have not once, *not once,* screwed up an investigation by allowing my 'emotional difficulties' to enter the picture. I admit that I had a fairly serious meltdown right after Cheryl's death but with all due respect, who the hell wouldn't have?

"The answer to your question is yes. I feel that I am more than capable of heading up this investigation with Bill and keeping it separate in my mind from what happened to my wife and son, despite what day this is."

Goldstein gave a tight smile and a quick, decisive nod of his head. "Good answer. I liked it a lot."

Captain Albert Goldstein was not known for ruling with an iron fist. His detectives, according to detractors, were a bit too fast and loose with proper procedure when expediency was called for—but somehow their ability to adhere precisely to procedure when, like now, it was absolutely necessary was somehow conveniently overlooked when higher-ups wanted to complain about "Captain SuperJew." If it weren't for the enviably high conviction records his divisions consistently maintained, Goldstein would have probably been busted back down to patrol status by now, which would not have exactly broken the hearts of those Well-Pressed Suits who still harbored their share of anti-Semitic sentiments (never on the record, of course; open bigotry was simply not the central Ohio way). But there was one point on which even his most vindictive critics couldn't argue; that Al Goldstein's officers and detectives were fiercely, passionately—and in some cases almost evangelically—loyal to him.

Ben thought once again how fortunate the Cedar Hill Police Department was to have a man of the captain's qualities on the force.

Goldstein lit a cigarette and began to toss the used match into an ashtray on a nearby table.

"No disrespect," said Ben, "but you know better than that, sir. Not at a crime scene."

"Shit, yes—sorry." Goldstein tossed the match into the portable flip-lid ashtray that Ben produced from one of his coat's many pockets. After taking one deep drag, he crushed out the cigarette, as well. "Oddly enough, not functioning on a lot of sleep."

"So we have seventy-two hours?"

"I think we should only count on forty-eight. The chief didn't like losing out to me, and my money's on the mayor giving in to him a little so there aren't any hard feelings. So call it forty-eight." He shook his head. "Nothing like trying to function under conditions of complete trust and faith. Does wonders for the colon."

The burst of a camera flash near the front re-emphasized the presence of reporters who had been outside for the last four hours, snapping photos, video-taping the exterior of the diner and the victims' cars as they were hauled away, scrambling to get interviews with anyone who went into or came out of the place, and now some television crews were broadcasting live from the scene for the early-bird breakfast crowd. None of them had yet been allowed closer than fifty feet to the front door, and the new uniforms arriving on the scene were going to make sure it stayed that way.

Goldstein glanced out at the growing crowd of non-media spectators. "I heard something about a dog?"

"It had a note in its mouth. It walked up to the first two uniforms on the scene and dropped it at their feet."

"Which unit?"

"Sanderson and Wagner. After it dropped the note, it

lunged for Sanderson's throat and they had to shoot it. They left about ten minutes ago. The dog's body is bagged and in the trunk of their cruiser."

"Let me see the note."

Ben handed Goldstein the note, which was still sealed inside its clear plastic evidence bag.

Goldstein fished through the pockets of his own coat for a few seconds, then grunted in exasperation. "Dammit! I left my glasses in the car." He handed back the note. "Would you mind?"

"You're going to love this," said Ben, then began to read: " 'Hannibal crossed the Alps with one of the greatest armies in history. He arrived at the outer gates of Rome, and Rome was all but in his hands. At the outer gates he stopped, turned around, and went back. What made him stop?' "

"Is that it?"

"No. On the other side are the lyrics to 'Don't Get Around Much Anymore,' and he signed it 'Hoopsticks,' and you haven't asked me about the bodies yet."

"How many were there?"

"That depends. The killer took the time to lay a piece of correct identification on each adult victim, and all IDs check out. There were nine bodies in here; five men, four women, and an infant."

"Good God."

Ben pointed to the wallets and purse. "The thing is, we have no bodies to go with these. There are IDs in all of them, so we know who they're supposed to belong to, but . . . no bodies have turned up yet. Bill and I have sent uniforms out to search the periphery three times now, widening the circle each time. Nothing has turned up yet. So the total body count is either nine or thirteen—going on the assumption that the four missing people are dead."

"And you put out—"

"—APBs on all four, just in case that assumption is wrong."

Goldstein stuck a fresh smoke between his lips but did not light it. "I think you're right, they're probably dead. I mean, *look* at this place. How could they not be?"

Ben felt his hands starting to tremble. He took a deep breath and steadied himself. "No one was shot in the head, Captain. *No one.* The killer walked in here and sprayed the place with a Tec-9, even stopped to reload and spray the place again to make sure everyone was dead, and not one person is shot in the head—or even *grazed* there, for that matter. Complete chaos in here, people running around, crawling, thrashing on the floor while he keeps firing at random, and yet no one gets shot any higher than the center of the chest."

"You think it was on purpose." It was not a question.

Ben nodded. "It had to be. He didn't want to damage any of the faces. He *wanted* us to be able to identify the bodies immediately."

"Prints?"

"He left prints on the weapon and both magazines, as well as every shell casing. I ran out of lift cards and had to beg for more from the Columbus CSU guys. We have thumb, index, and middle-finger prints from the note, and he left two handprints—*handprints,* for chrissakes!—on the glass of the front door."

Goldstein shook his head. "Come on, Ben—there must have been dozens of prints on that glass. I'll bet everyone who walks in and out of here opens the door by—"

"He wiped the glass clean on both the inside and outside, then pressed his left hand on the inside window and his right on the outside."

Goldstein rubbed his eyes. "He's either a supreme idiot or is just fucking with us because he thinks he can.

Are you sure those prints don't belong to one of the missing bodies—uh, people?"

"Not a hundred percent, no. But I'm positive they didn't belong to any of the bodies we found inside—the medical examiner and CSU guys helped us determine that by process of elimination. We used the left and right thumbprints from all the victims and made a visual comparison to the prints on the door. The victims all had plain whorl patterns on their thumbs, two deltas each, normal. The thumbprints from the door are accidentals. Each has three deltas, and that's rare. None of the victims' prints matched, everyone here knows better than to touch glass, and we're going on the assumption that the four missing people are dead, so unless he can make a corpse stand upright, do windows, and then walk out of here under its own power, the prints on the glass belong to the killer."

"They're *that* clear?"

"Yes."

"Have you sent any prints along to our lab?"

Ben nodded. "When I went through the lift cards the CSU guys gave to me, I sent one of the units out for more. I also sent along a set of the handprints. I figured those would be enough to keep Stan busy for a while."

"What time was that?"

"Four forty-five this morning. I called Stan and got him out of bed and told him to wheel his ass over to the lab. He said he'd be there to meet the unit and then called me a bunch of names."

"He's a charmer."

Ben took another sip of the now-cold coffee, moved back into the middle of the safe area, and finally lit the cigarette Goldstein had given to him. "It shouldn't be this easy."

Goldstein, lighting up as well, said, "It reminds me of that old Gordon Lightfoot song."

Ben stared at him. "Afraid you've stumped the band, sir."

" 'Too Many Clues in This Room.' "

"That about says it."

Both men fell silent for a moment, watching as a pair of uniformed officers were forced to physically move a cameraman away from the side of the diner. Neither the cameraman nor the reporter with him looked particularly happy about it. They'd have to make due with shots of the still-growing crowd of spectators.

Ben rubbed his eyes and exhaled.

"You're not back in San Ysidro–land again, are you?" asked Goldstein.

Ben blinked and gave his head a quick shake. "No . . . no, sir. I was just . . . sorry. It's been kind of a long night." He downed the rest of the coffee. When he spoke again his voice was thin and hollow sounding and the words came out in a rapid, deadly cadence: "He tore out every last one of the victims' eyes. We looked, for the better part of three hours I had five uniforms on it, but we couldn't find them anywhere. He jammed coins into the empty sockets and then stapled everyone's eyelids to their foreheads. I can just imagine what the photos are going to look like. You should have seen it, sir, all of those bodies with wide silver eyes staring up at the ceiling, reflecting the light. If I live to be a hundred, I don't think I'll ever get that image out of my head."

"I'll bet I can top it," said a voice from behind him. Ben and Goldstein turned to see Ben's partner, Bill Emerson, standing in the doorway leading to the cramped offices in the back.

"I wasn't aware there was some sort of contest going on here," said Ben.

"Let's not discuss the exhaustive inventory concerning those things of which you are not aware, especially after having consumed that sludge you claimed was coffee," replied Emerson. Bill Emerson stood a little over five foot seven and had a head of thick gray hair, sad blue eyes, and a heavy, wide gray mustache. He was also a solid slab of beef from head to toe and could have easily been mistaken for a prizefighter, until one looked at his hands; Bill Emerson's hands were disparately dainty when compared to the rest of him: hairless and smooth of skin, with long, thin, delicate fingers, they looked outright feminine—something about which he received no end of grief and joking from his fellow department members. It also didn't help his case that he occasionally worked for a Columbus ad agency as a hand model for magazine and television advertisements, the money from which he donated to the Cedar Hill Police Department's Hardship Fund. "Detective Hand Model," as he was called, was a twenty-plus-year veteran of the force, known for his thoroughness, perceptive eye, and sometimes macabre sense of humor— the latter of which had been on fierce display throughout the night, helping to keep everyone's nerves and emotions steady.

Ben Littlejohn knew that Bill, more than anyone else at the crime scene, was probably the most soul sick and heartbroken of them all when confronting this particular crime; Bill and his wife, Eunice, had lost their seven-year-old nephew and three-year-old niece to the Leonard Massacre in 1976 when Andy Leonard, after wiping out nearly his entire family, had driven to Moundbuilders Park and opened fire on the families gathered there to watch the Fourth of July fireworks. If anyone didn't need to see something like this twice in a lifetime, it was Bill Emerson—and yet his sometimes-questionable humor was the one thing that was helping everyone here hold it all together.

Emerson waited for a response, then sighed and shook his head. "You ought to see the expression on your faces. Bo-Bo the Dog-Faced Boy looked more alert."

"Good morning to you, as well," said Goldstein.

"I don't suppose you brought any decent coffee with you, did you, Captain?"

"I did, but Bo-Bo drank it all before I got here."

Emerson nodded. "I deserved that."

"Yes, you did."

Standing to the side, Emerson gestured for Ben and Goldstein to come into the back. They went through the kitchen to a pair of swinging metal doors near the walk-in freezer, then left into the manager's office. A uniformed patrolman was seated at the metal desk, staring at three small television monitors, all of which were filled for the moment with static.

"Got everything set up?" asked Emerson.

"Yessir," replied the officer, whose name tag identified him as B. CASSELL.

Emerson gestured for Cassell to vacate the chair. "Excellent. Now scram for a while, okay? In fact—" He reached into his pocket and pulled out a ten-dollar bill. "—it would serve the progress of this investigation to no end were you to take this money, drive over to the Dunkin' Donuts, and pick up some fresh coffee and crullers. Crullers work for everyone? I don't really care, I'm paying, so crullers it shall be." He shoved the bill into Cassell's hand. "If it costs more than that, I'll cover it when you get back. Get yourself some, as well. Yes, I'm a peach of a human being, you needn't sing my praises any more. Why are you still here?"

Shaking his head and giving everyone a weary but seemingly genuine smile, Cassell left the office, closing the door behind him.

Goldstein pulled up a metal folding chair and sat next to Emerson. Ben sat on the desk behind them, looking down at the monitors. Beneath the monitors was a cheap particleboard cabinet, its doors opened to reveal the trio of VCRs inside. Bill Emerson picked up the remote control for the center unit. "This is the tape from the camera that's behind the mirror over the entrance. You can see almost the entire customer area from this angle. This is right after the guy came in, at ten forty-five." Emerson hit PLAY.

Goldstein stared at the images on the center monitor, and then leaned forward, squinting. "Dammit to hell, this is doing me no good. Without my glasses the guy's face looks like a smudge."

"It's not you, Captain," said Emerson, pausing the tape. "Lean back a little and look again."

Goldstein did so. "It still looks like—hey, whoa, no it doesn't. The waitress, the cook behind the pass-through, that couple in the booth on the left . . . I can make out their faces just fine. But the killer, he . . . why in the—?"

"Look at his hands," said Ben. "They're the same way, just bright silver smudges. Kind of looks like a photograph where someone moved just as the picture was being taken, doesn't it? A goddamn blur."

Goldstein looked at Emerson. "How do you suppose he did it? Some kind of special mask and gloves?"

"I considered something like that," said Emerson, starting the tape again and pointing at the waitress. "But watch her. See the way she looked at him? I mean, yeah, she looks tired as hell but her smile's friendly enough."

Goldstein shrugged. "Part of her job is being friendly to the customers."

"Yes, but don't you think she'd be a *little* nervous if he'd been wearing a mask and gloves? I mean, it was late and she was the only waitress on duty."

"Plus," said Ben, "the rest of the customers aren't paying a damned bit of attention to him. A bad night like this, some guy walks in with . . ." His voice trailed off.

Goldstein looked at him. "What is it?"

"I once dated this girl who did a lot of shows with the Cedar Hill Players—this was a few years before I . . . I met Cheryl . . . anyway—stop the tape again, will you?"

Emerson paused the video. "Let me guess—you think the guy might have been wearing some kind of special makeup?"

Ben nodded. "Yeah. This girl I dated, Beth Boorman, she talked me into helping out with CCP's production of *Pippin*. I remember that they used a special kind of combination greasepaint and pancake mix that looked pretty cool under regular theater lighting, but when they hit it with colored-gel lighting, the makeup became really luminous, like a neon sign."

"But there aren't any kind of special lights in the diner," said Goldstein.

"It doesn't matter," replied Ben. "When the cast gathered for a group photo after opening night, still in makeup and costume, any cast member who wore that special makeup didn't photograph worth a damn under regular lights. They came out looking . . . well, like *that*." He pointed toward the shimmering blur where the killer's face should have been.

Goldstein looked at the monitor, then at Ben and Emerson. "That might be something to check out, see if any theatrical supply stores in Columbus have sold any greasepaint in the last few days."

"Good call," said Emerson to Ben. "Now, maybe you can offer some ideas about this next bit of video." He turned off the center monitor and switched to the one on the right, activating the other VCR's remote. "This camera is located behind a mirror over the kitchen's pass-through. It's also the only camera that has audio." He turned up the volume on the monitor. "Listen to this."

"Terrible weather tonight, isn't it?" said the waitress. "Seems like this storm just came out of nowhere."

The killer gave a blurry nod of his head.

The waitress said: "I beg your pardon?"

The killer's silver smudge of a head leaned a little closer to her.

The waitress shook her head. "Can't say that I have—but it's sure an interesting phrase. I'll remember that one."

"Hold it," said Goldstein, and Emerson paused the tape.

"Rewind that, will you?"

Emerson did so, and then played it again.

"Terrible weather tonight, isn't it?" said the waitress. "Seems like this storm just came out of nowhere."

The killer gave a blurry nod of his head.

The waitress said: "I beg your pardon?"

The killer's silver smudge of a head leaned a little closer to her.

The waitress shook her head. "Can't say that I have—but it's sure an interesting phrase. I'll remember that one."

"Stop it," said Goldstein. "He didn't say anything."

"Yes, he did," said Ben, who'd been watching and listening closely the second time through. "She asked him a question—'I beg your pardon?'—in response to something he just said to her, and then he asked a question of his own and she answered it—'Can't say that I have . . . ' "

Goldstein rubbed the back of his neck. "Well at least my hearing's not going out on me like I was afraid. *Her* voice is clear as a bell. Why didn't it pick up his voice? They're both standing in the same place."

Emerson looked at Ben, who shrugged and said, "I got nothing."

"Your makeup idea might hold up," said Emerson, "but then how do we explain the audio? I can't think of anything he could have done to either edit out his voice or alter it to a pitch or frequency where it can't be recorded. And you can hear the *other* customers' voices underneath, you can even hear the cook drop a metal utensil on the floor of the kitchen. This conversation between the two of them lasts about another twenty, thirty seconds, and hers is the only voice. If these tapes had been taken out of here and tinkered with in a sound lab, sure, there's hundreds of things that could have been done, but this guy didn't come back here and mess with the tapes after the killings. He didn't even shoot out the cameras until after he loaded the second magazine."

Goldstein parted his hands. "Do *you* have any ideas, Bill?"

"I thought I did . . . and then *this* happened."

They watched as the killer reached out with one shimmering hand and touched the waitress's cheek; as soon as his hand made contact with her, her face too became a bright silver blur.

Goldstein told Emerson to turn everything off, and for a few moments all three men remained in silence.

Goldstein crushed out his cigarette. "Does the last camera show anything different?"

Emerson shook his head. "Nope, just the same thing from a different angle."

"Even if he was wearing some kind of special makeup on his face and hands," said Goldstein to the other men, "he would've only transferred a small bit of it to her when he touched her face. It wouldn't have . . . spread like that."

Ben shook his head. "No, it wouldn't have."

Emerson leaned back in his chair and crossed his arms over his chest. "May I now officially introduce the term 'weird' into the investigation?"

"No you may not," snapped Goldstein. "Unless you're leading up to something. *Are* you leading up to something? Tell me you're leading up to something."

"I'm leading up to something."

Ben sighed. "And that would be . . . ?"

Emerson put on a pair of disposable latex gloves, ejected all three surveillance tapes, and sealed each into a separate clear evidence bag. As he began marking the labels on each bag, he said, "You told Ben that the Well-Pressed Suits gave us seventy-two hours to come up with something, right?"

"Yes, and I—how did you know that?"

Emerson gestured toward the monitors. "The same way I know you told him that those seventy-two will probably be cut down to forty-eight. I eavesdropped. I'm annoying that way."

Ben almost laughed. Almost.

"Where are you going with this?" asked Goldstein.

Emerson tossed the first bagged-and-labeled tape onto the desk. "These tapes can be that 'something.' Only for the time being we keep their existence between the three of us and Cassell. The Columbus CSU guys don't know about them yet, and they don't have to. We wait until a few hours before the forty-eight-hour deadline and then lay these on the mayor and the chief—and that's assuming that, being our usual Keystone Cops selves, we haven't come up with anything else before then."

After a moment, Goldstein said, in a soft but intense voice, "You know, don't you, Bill, that I could hang your ass out to dry from ten different directions for even *suggesting* something like that?"

"Yes, sir, I do. But I also think that you're curious enough to want to know *why* I'd make a suggestion like that."

Goldstein folded his arms across his chest. "I am all at attention."

Emerson held up the second bagged-and-labeled tape. "Because here's what will happen if we let the Well-

Pressed Suits know about the existence of these tapes right now. The first thing they'll do is call a meeting so everyone can watch them. All four of us will have to be there. Knowing as you do, Captain, how decisively our city leaders lurch, heave, and wobble into action, we're talking at least two to three hours from now before such a meeting will start."

"Which is also two to three hours counted against our deadline," said Ben.

"One conspirator at a time, please," said Goldstein.

Emerson put the third tape on the desk. "But he's right, Captain. Scratch three hours off until the meeting, and then keep counting the clock that tells the time while the WPS all scratch their heads and cracks before asking each of us individually what we think. We'll have to repeat our less-than-watertight theories one more time, and then probably once more again. By the time the WPS decide that the tapes need to be analyzed, we've lost five to six hours at the inside, and *that's* if the WPS agree to have the analysis done here and not sent to the Columbus Crime Lab. The technicians will spend another five to eight hours copying the tapes, blowing up frames, re-recording the audio track, and running everything through the analysis equipment. *Then* they'll scratch their heads and cracks and call at least one of us down there to repeat the same lame theories that couldn't tread water the first time through. After that, the tapes will be sent to the Columbus Crime Lab because the CCL isn't in the ICU suffering from budget cuts and *have* the state-of-the-art equipment to do a proper job—and that proper job will begin with their repeating the exact same things *our* lab did. After that, they'll get around to playing everything through visual filters and voice synthesizers, first at half-speed, then normal speed, then twice-speed, and while we're all looking at our retirement packages and wondering if it's time for another prostate exam, they'll run half a dozen spectrographic analyses and probably put the tapes frame-by-frame through that snooty new digital imaging processor they have—and not necessarily because they *need to*. They'll do it just to show us they can—after all, we're the *Cedar Hill* Police Department, we pick our teeth with our toenail clippings, clean our guns with bacon grease, and look at chicken innards for ways to catch a break in a case. Looking further into our bright future, while a priest is giving one of us last rites as the other two are loaded into the nursing-home van so they can attend the funeral, the Columbus Crime Lab will send the WPS a bill that amounts to more than all our yearly salaries combined, along with a report that will tell the WPS nothing more than the three of us know at this very moment. Let's be charitable and say that all of this will take the CCL thirty hours from receipt of the tapes to delivery of the bill and report. The WPS will read the report, see the bill, shit their pants, and count it all against our deadline.

"But if we keep these tapes between us for now, we can use them to buy more time when the deadline gets close. Still want to hang my ass out to dry for suggesting this?"

"Yes," said Goldstein. "Except that mine would be right beside it. Can you trust that patrolman who was in here before, what was his name?"

"Cassell," said Emerson. "And, yes, he'll keep it to himself. I already asked him to, in fact."

Goldstein nodded. "And *I'll* remind him when he gets back here with the coffee and crullers." The captain pinched the bridge of his nose between his thumb and index finger. "Just so we're clear on this, you're asking me to go along with a lie that could lose all of us our jobs and pensions, you know that?"

"No," said Emerson. "I'm asking you to go along with

my temporarily restructuring the facts to create a more useful truth."

"I'll remember that at our arraignment." Goldstein picked up the tapes. "You guys have the right idea. If this doesn't work, then we'll all go down together."

"That's downright macho, coming from you, sir."

"Well, they don't call me 'Captain SuperJew' for nothing." Goldstein looked at Ben. "I'll be out here. See me when the two of you are done in here."

Emerson seemed surprised. "Sir, how did you know—?"

"I have many powers that you mere mortals cannot comprehend. I'm not completely dim, Bill." And with that, Goldstein left them alone.

Ben looked at his partner. "What was *that* about?"

"It's about our good captain being more perceptive than even I, the most perceptive among us, gave him credit for. Don't bother looking for the holes in that logic or you'll succumb to that migraine you think I don't know you've been fighting all night."

"Truly impressive syntax."

"Thank you." Emerson stared at Ben. "We haven't really had a chance to talk since I got here."

Ben patted down his pockets in search of smokes, then remembered that Goldstein had the cigarettes, not him. "The last eight hours or so haven't exactly been rife with opportunities for small talk."

"Asking my partner how he's doing on this day of all days doesn't qualify as small talk to my mind. Are you okay?"

"The captain wondered the same thing."

"Well?"

"*Hell,* no, I'm not all right! Three years ago today my wife was gunned down by some crankheads who got away with one hundred and forty-three dollars. I'm *lousy.* But it's not going to affect how I conduct this investigation with you, okay?" Ben was shocked by how loud his voice sounded in the tight confines of the small office.

"Feel better now?" asked Emerson. "I mean, I should think that you would. After all, yelling at me because I'm concerned, that makes it all better, right?"

Ben gave him the finger.

"Eloquent as always."

"I'm sorry, Bill."

"I'm not asking because I'm worried that I'll need to have a Plan B to cover my butt if you crack up. I'm asking because you're my partner and my friend and something like *this* was the last goddamn thing you needed to deal with today."

Ben smiled at Emerson. "And what about you, of the sexy model's hands? You planning on sitting there and telling me that you're doing just peachy keen and that none of this is bringing back—"

Emerson raised a hand. "Not the 'L' name, Ben. Not right now. And, no, I didn't plan on telling you that because it'd be bullshit and we'd both know it. I just know that Eunice is going to be upset by all of this, and my sister . . . my sister will probably be a wreck when she hears the news." He shook his head. "I feel like an idiot. I'd actually begun to think that nothing like this could ever happen in the same place twice. Lucky me, I get to be around for both mop-ups—and you get the satisfaction of knowing that you can still sidetrack me. By the way, you and Eunice are the only two people who can lay claim to that."

Ben shrugged. "It's a gift."

"Shut up and pay attention because we've got a couple of lousy days ahead of us and I want to say this now. If at any time today—or tomorrow or the next day or the day after that—I think you're getting the gist of this—you need to talk to me about what's going on inside you, I will stop whatever I'm doing and I will listen. We both know that regardless of how much progress we make in the next forty-eight hours, the governor is going to force the mayor to call in the feds because it's an election year and nobody respects the Cedar Hill Police, anyway. I'm your friend for life. You can always count on that. I miss Cheryl like hell, too, you know? So does Eunice."

"I know," whispered Ben. "Thank you."

"All right, then," said Emerson. "Now, leave me to the oiling of the machinations to our newborn conspiracy and go see the captain. I'll be at least another fifteen or twenty minutes."

Ben cleared his throat. "Listen, Bill—"

"*Why* are you still here? Should you not be awaiting the arrival of our precious coffee and crullers?"

Ben just shook his head, flipped off his partner once more, and left the office. Once back out in the diner, he watched as Goldstein took the tray of coffees and bag of crullers from Officer Cassell, the two of them having a no-nonsense conversation where they reached a quick agreement. Cassell stood back and gave Goldstein a salute, which Goldstein returned before shaking the officer's hand and sending him outside to help with crowd control. Goldstein saw Ben and, abandoning the coffees and crullers, walked over to join him.

"Officer Cassell seems to have some grasp," said the captain.

Ben started to respond, but then saw that even though the crowd of onlookers had been moved farther back, several reporters had managed to get closer to the door and windows. "Goddammit, why hasn't someone—?"

Goldstein put a hand on his shoulder. "Don't worry about it. I'll finish up out here and talk to the reporters. Give me your digital recorder and I'll have someone at the station transcribe your notes. You can go over them later. Right now, I'm ordering you to go home, take a shower, get some food in you, and rest up. Ninety minutes. I want you in my office at nine thirty."

"Captain, we can't afford for any of us to waste even a few minutes of time, let alone—"

"What we can't afford is for one of the two detectives in charge to lose his fight against a migraine. By the way, you dropped these." Goldstein handed him a foil of three Imitrex tablets. "I can't use that stuff myself. It doubles my heart rate and sends my blood pressure through the ceiling."

Ben took the tablets and slipped them into his coat pocket, and then nodded toward the abandoned goodies. "I was looking forward to the coffee and crullers."

"How sad. Look in my eyes, Ben. Can't you see the tears welling, I'm so sad? *Go home*. I told you once already, I need your A-game, and I'm not going to get it if you make yourself sick. Bill and I can finish up here. You—home, shower, food, meds or a quick nap. My office. Nine thirty."

Ben handed over his voice recorder and started toward the doors.

"Big Mac Massacre," said Goldstein.

Ben turned around. "I beg your pardon?"

Goldstein tapped a finger against his temple. "I just remembered. That was the headline the *Post* ran above the picture of that cop and the little boy. Big Mac Massacre."

Ben stared at him.

"You know what else I remembered?" said Goldstein. "The day after Huberty's rampage, the four McDonald's in this city had their busiest day of the year."

"Go figure," said Ben.

23

tell me, my torturer, i've never asked but find my curiosity nags me to do so: did you ever think i would last this long?

....

of course not.
i wonder how they would react if they knew the truth.

....

oh well. the traditor papilio *waits. it's time i began in earnest.*

24

Some said that even the seasons were afraid to enter Coffin County, because once they did, they were as trapped as the people who lived there. While most of the mid-November snow in Cedar Hill had now mostly melted away, leaving only soggy lawns and cold air, once you crossed over the wrong side of Main Street Bridge it looked as if winter had arrived in full force.

Until a few nights ago a half foot of old crusty snow had been covering the ground since the first of the month, a month that was filled with days and nights of dry cold that had aged the snow, turning it to the color of damp ash, mottled here and there with candy wrappers, empty cigarette packs, broken hypodermic needles, jagged brown glass from broken liquor bottles, used condoms, the occasional disposable diaper, and countless beer cans. The recent rains and temperatures rising slowly into the high thirties had managed to wash away about half of the snow, and what mounds of it remained looked like the bodies of winos who'd passed out in the wrong place and frozen to death during the night.

One such mound, larger than the others, was heaped at the edge of a junk-littered field across the street from what used to be the Garfield, one of the four hotels in the city to be named after an Ohio-born U.S. president—in this case, James Abram Garfield, the twentieth president. The Garfield was less than a block away from the Beaumont Casket Factory, and was one of the many businesses in the area that fell to the '69 fire. (Another hotel, the Harrison—named after William Henry Harrison, the ninth president—was located a little farther away; though it, too, had caught fire, the damage was not quite as extensive as that suffered by the Garfield; a half-hearted attempt to rebuild was begun and then just as quickly abandoned. Most of the Harrison had been torn down, but the main lobby area and basement remained in acceptable condition and were, at very little cost to the city, turned into the Cedar Hill Open Shelter—possibly the only homeless shelter in the country to sport Italian marble tiles on its floor, and a classic ballroom ceiling, complete with chandelier.)

On this morning, just as most of the state was waking up to news of the Cedar Hill shootings, five young boys bounded one at a time over the snow mound across from the Garfield and ran toward the jungle of trash. They were skipping school (not that any of their parents would care if they'd known) and had decided to spend their day building a makeshift fort out of whatever materials they could find buried among the garbage. It took them a little while but when it was done, they'd amassed a wonderful cache of treasure; several large cardboard boxes, five empty metal barrels, dozens of old tires, part of an old backyard swing set that could still stand upright, a pile of long wooden boards, and—the most fantastic treasure of them all— an intact section of a fire escape that took all five of them the better part of half an hour to drag into place, but in the end, it was *so* worth it: their finished fort was a radiant example of state-of-the-art junkyard-fort technology, complete with secret entrances and an imposing lookout tower from which each of them could take a turn at sentry, keeping their eyes peeled for danger.

"It looks like a castle!" one of them shouted.

And indeed it was—in their eyes, at least. A castle fit for a king, and they the noble knights who kept diligent watch, for the world was filled with dark and evil creatures that crept from the enchanted forest at night to wreak their terrible havoc on an unsuspecting world.

Whilst one knight kept vigil atop the tower, the other four gathered rocks and bricks to throw at the windshields of the abandoned cars that sat, rusted and ugly, all along the street. The knights knew these things were not cars at all but clever demons and ogres in disguise. It was up to them, as brave knights, to keep the monsters at bay.

One of the knights cocked back his arm, readying to throw a section of pipe. He imagined that it was not a pipe at all but a golden lance, one blessed by the queen's personal wizard, and he would be heroic for his queen, his aim would be true, and—

—he froze when a saw a face, a dim, terrible face, peer out from behind one of the few rooms in the Garfield that still had curtains. The face looked at him for only a moment, but that was all the longer it took for the boy to not only sense but *feel* something unseen and awful emerge from behind those shadowy and dreadful eyes, something like . . . like . . . like a thin laser beam the supervillains always used against the heroes in comic books; he felt it come through the window and follow the wind's direction right down to his face, drilling between his eyes and soaking into his brain. He dropped the pipe and stood staring at the Garfield. The dim, terrible face vanished as the curtain was dropped back into place.

"What'cha doin'?" shouted one of the other knights.

The boy stood there, not moving, wide-eyed and slack-jawed, staring at the Garfield.

It looks like a dinosaur, he thought. *A dinosaur sinking into a tar pit.*

Even though he wasn't a particularly bright child and never would be, even though he couldn't imagine what something looked like without first seeing a picture or an image of it on television or movie screen, even though his grasp of anything abstract was nonexistent, the boy knew that the image of a sinking dinosaur was not something *he* had come up with; he knew that the unseen thing behind that dim and terrible face inside the Garfield had put that image in his mind.

He watched the dinosaur sink, and as he did the image rippled and snapped like the pages of a comic book being flipped by the wind, and when it stopped, when the comic fell open, he was looking at an image of his stepfather as the man had been on the night he'd killed the boy's dog, Midnight.

Midnight had gotten into a carton of his stepfather's cigarettes and chewed open a pack, and as the boy watched, numbed and terrified, his stepfather grabbed Midnight by his back legs and yanked him off the floor, screaming, *"This is the last goddamn time this dog costs me money!"*

"No," whispered the boy from the time and place he stood now, feeling his heart break all over again because he knew what was coming. ". . . please, *please* don't. . . ."

But his plea was ignored. His stepfather swung Midnight by his back legs and slammed the dog's head into the wall, knocking out several of his teeth and dislocating his jaw, and Midnight was making the most awful noises, yelping and howling in pain, and the boy's stepfather swung the dog again, harder this time, snapping something between Midnight's eyes and sending a spray of blood spitting from his ears when his head connected, but Midnight still wasn't dead, he was still struggling to get free, but he was too weak and in too much pain, and the boy's stepfather continued swinging and slamming Midnight's head against the wall until the dog stopped making any noise and its body went limp and its head was smashed into a bloody glop of meat and dark fur. And then the boy's stepfather swung the dog's dead and broken body into the wall one more time before dropping it to the floor where it landed with a sickening wet thump.

Now the boy, oblivious to his friends, dropped his chin down against his chest and sobbed, just like he'd done for three days after Midnight had been beaten to death, sobbed until his stepfather took a belt to his back, buckle first.

The boy could never understand why his stepfather had gotten so angry about the money he'd spent on cigarettes, it wasn't like he worked for the money or anything, all he did was take some of the food stamps he got in the mail each month and sell them to the black guy who lived a few houses down the street. (*"You don't call 'em blacks or African Americans or anything like that, not in my house,"* his stepfather always said. *"They're all just niggers—unless they can help me out with some cash. Then you can call 'em 'colored' but that's as far as it goes. Now get off your fat, lazy ass, woman, and fetch me a beer!"*)

All of this and more flashed through the boy's mind as the other knights kept yelling for his attention, but he just kept staring at the Garfield, thinking that it looked like a tar-sunk dinosaur.

And then a voice, one that was too old-sounding to belong to any of his friends, a voice as dim and terrible as the face he'd seen in the window, whispered, *And*

where is that great, hulking beast now, the mighty di-
nosaur that once ruled the earth? Gone to rot and dust
and oil. It's a fossil now, just like everyone and every-
thing in your life will someday be.

Had the boy been older, had he possessed a stronger
sense of self or even a shred of the inner resolve that in
adulthood manifests itself as cynicism, then maybe he
could have shrugged it all away as just his imagination;
but he wasn't older, he didn't have the resolve, he
wasn't prepared, and so it was a simple thing for that
terrible voice to open a door in the back of the boy's
mind and let loose something terrible that had, until
now, been locked away.

A wide, almost radiant smile crossed the boy's face as
he listened to what this terrible thing said to him, reminded him of, pulling it out of the darkness where the
boy had hidden it away, denying its existence; now it
was fully in the light and there was no turning away. The
boy walked away from the junkyard. A few of the
knights tried to stop him but he was now too big and
too strong for them; he was Sir Fossil, Protector and
Avenger, and none would stand in his way.

The terrible thing had reminded the boy not only of
his stepfather's actions, but those of his mother, as well;
Mom, who didn't do or say anything about the way his
stepfather would go into the room where the boy's
older sister slept and stay there for hours, making her
do things she didn't want to do, warm, moist things,
calling her names, telling her to roll over and raise that
sweet little ass in the air, it was time for a doggie-ride,
and she'd better moan nice and loud for him because
that made him happy and oh, yeah, sweet, that's it, dar-
lin', keep it up like this and maybe later I'll let you suck
on something nice.

Mom always turned up the volume on the radio or
television when this happened, sometimes making it so

loud the boy got headaches that caused everything to glow and shimmer and made him sick to his stomach. Sometimes he'd go into the basement and cram himself into the crawl space beneath the stairs where he always kept two pillows and a blanket inside a trash bag; he'd wrap himself in the blanket and sandwich his head between the pillows, blocking out as much of the sound and light as he could. It didn't matter that the basement was damp and mostly dark, there was still a little bit of light that got in through one of the ground-level windows, and any light at all made the hurting and the sick-feeling ten times worse.

His sister was always real quiet after their stepfather visited her. Sometimes he left bruises and cuts that Mom would help to clean, all the time saying things like *Now, hon, you know he didn't mean to hurt you* or *I think you must be exaggerating, young lady, he wouldn't do such filthy things to you* or *He's not like that at all, you'll see, he loves us all very much and I'm sure as soon as he finds himself another job and we move to a better neighborhood things'll get a lot better—just as long as you don't upset him, you know I'd get a job myself but he won't let me so I don't think you ought to complain if he maybe hugs and kisses you more than you'd like, there are kids whose parents never hug or kiss them and that makes you lucky. . . .*

The boy, now the brave knight Sir Fossil, he would make it all better; he would take away the hurting and the crying and make everything better for his sister and for Midnight, they'd all see when Midnight came back, when he crawled up through the oil and rot and dust and bit the boy's stepfather on the leg—no, *in the throat,* that was it, Midnight would rip the man's throat right out and then drag his body down into the tar pit where the mighty dinosaur would roar and finish the job and they'd all love it when they were fossils because that's what everyone and everything was, just fossils, future fossils that hadn't been sucked under the tar yet. . . .

Brave Sir Fossil—today Brave Sir Fossil, the Avenger—stooped down to grab a thick, sharp, sickle-shaped piece of broken window glass from a pile of trash in front of one of the many abandoned, rotting buildings that marked his path home. A few blocks later he found an equally thick cardboard tube that he slid over one end of the sharp glass sickle, creating a makeshift handle and hilt, and it was no longer a piece of glass and cardboard, it was a great, magical crystal sword that a noble knight would use to slay his enemies.

The boy was so filled with what the unseen thing had given to him that he had to share it with someone *right now* or he'd burst open, so he slowed down as he neared the corner, stopping in front of a small market. He stood staring through the window at the man behind the cash register. It took a moment because the man was talking to someone else but eventually he looked up and met the boy's gaze.

I'll make it all better; I'll make it all go away, thought the boy, and just as the unseen thing that the terrible face in the Garfield had flown down on the wind and drilled between his eyes, the boy sent that thought to the man behind the cash register. He could see that the man felt it enter him, and that made the boy happy—so happy, in fact, that he sang a happy tune to himself as he made his way down the street, a song about not getting around much, anymore. The words were funny—he'd never heard the song before until it just appeared in his head like this, but he *liked* it, he liked it a lot.

Two blocks away from his house, the boy saw a partially used roll of duct tape mixed in with more sidewalk garbage, and his smile grew even brighter. Digging the roll out of the pile (there was a lot of old, stinking food in there), he used the tape to wrap the handle firmly in place, and then twisted the tape around, stick-side up, so he could tape the handle and hilt to his hand; it wouldn't do for a gallant knight to drop his sword in the heat of battle, enemies could not be struck down if you were unarmed, and today there were enemies to smite, demons that could disguise themselves not only as cars but also as a man who said he loved you and your mother and your sister (especially your sister) but all he really wanted was someone to yell at, hit and make bleed, and do filthy, wet things to in the middle of the night.

He slid his sword underneath his coat as he walked toward the steps leading into his house—well, the half of the house where his family lived, anyway. Brave Sir Fossil entering the monster's lair. Even from out here by the mailbox he could hear his stepfather screaming. That meant he wasn't drunk. When he was drunk he could hardly form words. He only screamed when he was sober, like it hurt too much not to be drunk.

One hand grabbing the wooden railing that ran alongside the steps of the front porch, the other clasping the handle of his crystal sword, Sir Fossil made his way up the stairs, wondering if Midnight would be happy to see him again and whether or not his mother and sister were going to like being in the tar with the dinosaurs. He didn't care if his stepfather liked it or not.

25

In the center room of the sixth floor on the front side of the Garfield Hotel a moldy curtain was dropped back in place by a sad-eyed man whose long gray hair was tied in a ponytail. He shook his head wearily and sank to the floor, reaching into one of his jacket pockets and removing a Mauser HSc Super .32 semiautomatic pistol.

He looked down at the gun and caught sight of his reflection in a broken piece of nickel-backed mirror that lay nearby. He laughed at the sight; it was the sound of a terminal cancer patient chuckling at a tumor joke. The face he saw was a patchwork quilt of deep lines, windburns, and scars in various stages of healing. It was a face he had grown to despise.

He leaned his head against the wall and, remembering the look on the little boy's face a few moments ago, wondered: it might be true that energy, like matter, was not infinitely subdivisable and could exist only as quanta—but that didn't mean it couldn't be manipulated. Electrons swirled in the electromagnetic field of the atomic nucleus, planets spun in the gravitational field of the sun, and everything in the universe could be reduced to nothing more than a series of standing wave fronts—especially thought, which was the most easily accessible form of quanta in the spectra. It was only a matter of directing your own energy and knowing how much manipulation it would take to achieve the desired results. You simply homed in on the chosen thought/wave pattern and, like a beam of radiation passing through an interferometer, split the wave down the center, led each of the halves along separate but accurately determined paths, then recombined them to create an interference pattern. Since the boy was so young and so full of undirected energy, the rest of it wouldn't take long. Like a continuously branching bolt of lightning, the interference waves would home in on the thought patterns of another person, skewing their consciousness; they, in turn, would pass the interference on to another and another and so on, the irreversible chain reaction continuing as the frail foundation of each individual psyche crumbled, leaving madness in its wake.

Madness . . .

. . . then confusion . . .

. . . violence . . .

. . . destruction . . .

. . . Chaos.

The man released a long, desolate sigh. There was in his mind an image of butterfly wings; still, dark butterfly wings.

He shoved the business end of the pistol into his mouth and squeezed the trigger. The back of his head opened up like a blossoming flower. Wide splashes of blood, chunks of skull, and wriggling, gore-sopped bits of sluglike tissue splattered over the wall behind him. His body fell to the side, limbs shuddering in a final grotesque seizure. The hand holding the pistol flexed open and stilled, the weapon sliding from his grip and clattering against the floorboards. For several minutes there was only a murky, stained silence as the man, without flesh, without bone, without cells or blood or resonance, found himself swirling among the countless bits of human thought that collectively and unconsciously gave systematic order to the universe. He drifted across the whole cosmic panorama, gathering stray bits of intelligible signals—snatches of old conversations, ideas that had been flicked around from mind to mind but were never acted upon, memories of myths and myths buried in humanity's collective memory—and arranged them into a neat, orderly whole, one that was alive with human thought: he saw eukaryotic thought, singularities of thought, metazoans and huge interlacing coral shoals of thought wherein all true history was hidden, and in this surging psychic sea of perpetually collapsing probability waves he found the one that held a part of his own perceived history and submerged himself in it . . .

. . . to find that his torturer was waiting for him there, as well.

how many more times? he wondered. *how many more times do you, i, and dear brother have to go through this to appease you, my torturer?*

He remembered all the faces he'd worn, the places he'd visited, the ever-increasing body counts; the screams, the blood, voices begging for mercy, children cowering in corners, stacks upon stacks of corpses, over and over, death coating his tongue and spirit . . .

. . . he had come back so many times . . .

. . . and he would come back so many more times; but for now, here he was again, this time as a Miracle Man who'd walked into a diner one rainy night and pulled a Tec-9 from underneath his parka; who stared out from a window of the Garfield Hotel in Coffin County; who sent a bolt of psychic static into the mind of a little boy who was, by now, passing it on to others; a Miracle Man who had pumped a bullet through the back of his own skull and whose body now lay on the filthy floor as something small and corrupt scuttled through the walls—

—then the silence returned—

—and became a poem as a beam of sunlight, alive with dancing dust, seeped through the tears in the curtains and cast a soft morning glow on the index finger of the man's gun hand.

The finger twitched; then the middle finger and thumb; the man's wrist bent to the side as his arm trembled. His eyes blinked. A deep groan crawled up from the center of his chest. He rolled over into a half-sitting position. A globule of blood dripped from his nose and vanished before splashing on the floor. He rubbed his neck—as if he could ever forget that particular pain—and then reached around to touch the back of his head: there was no bullet-blown chasm there anymore, only soft hair tied in a ponytail.

He pulled himself to his feet, inhaling deeply and choking on the stench of his renewed existence. He snatched the Mauser from the floor and shoved it in his jacket pocket, then walked over to the window, ripped down the curtains, and stood bathing himself in the dirty, dispirited sunlight.

"Dum vista est, spes est," he whispered.

Then: "Can't blame a guy for trying."

And then, after another moment: "Oh, *right* . . . yes you can. My bad."

26

According to its detractors, the Cedar Hill Police Department didn't have a lot going for it; most of the divisions were housed in an ancient brown Richardsonian Romanesque building that looked like some dreary, forgotten mansion from a gothic horror film. The building was still standing only because the Licking County Historical Society had managed to get it declared a historical landmark and secured funds from private donors to update and repair the electrical and plumbing systems. The building was well cared for, and funds were always at hand for any repairs, if needed. The same, unfortunately, could not be said of the police department's budget; it was understaffed, underequipped, and those who worked there were almost woefully underpaid. The chief of police was often more concerned with PR than anything else, the safety director couldn't make a decision on his own if his life depended on it, and yet—despite massive budget cuts over the past five years—the city council demonstrated its faith in the department by finding the money for the construction of a shiny new city building, rather than allotting money to hire more trained officers and other law enforcement personnel. This didn't exactly have the underpaid and overcriticized department dancing the Charleston in the middle of the downtown square.

No, God knew it didn't have a lot going in its favor; but one thing it did have was Stanley Roth, who was not only the best latents expert in the tristate area, but arguably one of the ten best in the country. It was because of Roth's reputation that, when both the state and local budgets did a belly flop into the red, leaving numerous smaller police departments in the Buckeye State temporarily unable to procure the necessary equipment to establish their own AFIS (Automated Fingerprint Identification System) network, the FBI chose Cedar Hill as one of the test sites for its experimental EXCEL Project. EXCEL stood for Examination of Catalogued Evidence of Latent Prints, and the project's goal was to at long last establish a nationwide latent cognizant network. In theory, EXCEL would enable any police department in the U.S. to quickly access a large part of, and ideally *all*, of the FBI's criminal database, allowing those departments with the proper clearance and necessary equipment to search through every fingerprint file in the country in a matter of a few days, possibly even twelve hours or less if the search was narrowed to specifics regions; if the search consisted of one state looking through the records of another specific state—say, New Jersey searching the fingerprints in Utah's database—it would be a question of minutes.

Cedar Hill was an ideal location for the FBI to make a test run of this new system; it was not a large city (population 47,000), and its police department was functioning with only the basic equipment needed to get the job done. The city was a Class-A, Red, White, and Blue, #1, Mom, Dad, and Apple Pie *typical* small American city. The police department was small enough to meet the FBI's criteria, and the city itself was just financially depressed enough to have a higher than usual crime rate for its location.

Since a large number of states had already implemented their own AFIS systems—and since each these systems was different and thus unable to "talk" to one another or tie into the FBI's AFIS system—a bastard child of AFIS, called DIM, was born. DIM (Dissimilar Interface Module) was—once again, in theory—a Holy Grail of electronic criminal detection.

When the burden of explaining DIM and EXCEL fell on Stan Roth's shoulders, he rolled his wheelchair up in front of the Well-Pressed Suits and put it like this: "Somewhere in Washington there is a nondescript house or building, and somewhere in that nondescript house or building there is a door that can only be opened with a programmed card key. Behind that door is an elevator that goes several hundred feet beneath the surface of the city and opens its doors to reveal a long corridor. At the end of this corridor is another door that requires a different card key. In the room behind this door is a vault. In that vault is a box. In that box is a compartment. And in that compartment, there are twelve computer chips. In the center of each chip is a microchip, and this microchip is the proverbial 'keys to the kingdom'—the kingdom in this case being any computer network with its own AFIS. With this chip we can, in theory, gain access to any other system or network without it even knowing we're doing it, if we want to be really sneaky, which we won't have to be. In short, this 'X-chip,' as they're calling it, can instantly gain access to every criminal database in the country and 'talk' between AFIS systems—which is something even AFIS can't do. Add to this that we will also be *given* our own AFIS network, and when used in tandem with EXCEL and DIM will enable us to gather and compare latents information in record time, thus making it possible for us to catch the criminals sooner. The FBI wishes to give us one of these chips. I think we should accept their offer."

And so they did. It took five days for the new equipment to arrive and be installed and then checked, double-checked, and triple-checked before it began downloading information and codes. Stan remained in his office the entire time, sleeping on an old army-issue cot and sending out for food.

Astoundingly, it worked, often much quicker than had been predicted. And it was just the thing that one of the ten best fingerprint experts in the country needed in order to Do His Thing.

Except that, right now, Stan Roth didn't feel like one of the ten best experts in the country; in fact, he felt rather doofuslike as he sat back in his chair, began chewing on his right thumbnail, and stared at the second of three forty-inch flat-screen monitors arranged on top of his massive work station.

" 'He who doubts from what he sees/Will ne'er believe, do what you please,' " he whispered to himself, never moving his gaze from the monitor. He drummed the fingers of his left hand against the side of his keyboard; after a moment he stopped, raised his hand, and examined it. Then he looked at the screen again. Then his hand. Then the screen once more. He thought about opening the locked desk drawer where he kept a secret stash of one-pint Jack Daniel's Green Label.

"No, you'd better be a good droid," he said aloud. Then he looked at his hand. And then the screen. Then his hand once more. (He'd reversed the order this time because he didn't want to fall into a rut.)

He made his hand into a fist and began tapping it against his bearded chin.

And then he stared at the screen some more. No doubt about it; he was definitely in a rut.

" 'If the Sun and Moon should doubt/They'd immediately go out.' Tell me, Stan, doesn't it worry you that you've started talking to yourself like this, quoting William Blake and such?—Why, yes, yes it does."

He groaned in frustration and leaned back a little farther, covered his face with both hands, blew an exasperated breath through them, and then ran his fingers up into his hair and mussed it around a little in order to get the blood flowing back to his brain.

A voice from behind him said, "Aren't you embarrassed by these little pep talks you give yourself?"

Stan turned his wheelchair around to see Maureen Cahill, his personal assistant, standing in the doorway of his office. "Don't bother to knock or anything, just come right on in and make yourself at home."

Maureen pushed the door closed and walked over to stand behind him. She looked at the image on the screen, and then put her hands on Stan's shoulders. "Jesus, Stan! I could chop meat on these things. A little tense, are we?"

"What is it with this 'we' shit? And please remove your hands from my person or I'm going to run upstairs and file a sexual harassment complaint against you."

"Uh-huh. I don't know if anyone's pointed a couple things out to you lately, but, technically I'm employed by you, not the department—even though it lists me as being 'auxiliary personnel' because you insisted—so were you to call my bluff and try to file any charges against me, odds are the folks upstairs would just laugh and say, 'You should be so lucky.' And the other thing, call it the elephant in the living room, is that your days of running anywhere are a thing of the past."

Stan put his arms down, grabbed the wheels of his chair, and spun around. "Is *this* what it's come down to? Handicap jokes?"

"Don't get all sensitive and self-righteous with me. You get all the good parking spaces."

"Right," said Stan, snapping his fingers. "*That's* why I stepped on that Bouncing Betty in Vietnam—*good parking spaces!* And all it cost me was the use of my legs. What would I do without you here to keep me humble?"

Maureen covered her mouth as she yawned, then smiled at him. "Well, for starters, you wouldn't've had someone to give you a ride here at five in the morning."

"I have already apologized for calling you at that god-awful hour."

"I know, but you're fun to pick on."

Stan shook his head and started turning his wheel-chair back around, then stopped halfway and said, "You are an evil, shameless, wanton strumpet."

"Your words capture my heart and bind its wings. What's going on, anyway?"

Stan turned back to the console. "*This*," he said, pointing at the monitor.

Maureen leaned closer, adjusting her round, wire-rimmed glasses. "Are you still on the thumbprints?"

"Three guesses."

She smacked his arm, but not at all hard. "Don't be mean. Your nostrils flare and it's kind of creepy."

He almost said something in reply but decided against it. During the seven years Maureen had been working with him, Stan had never been able to keep pace with her when it came to wisecracks, but that was one of the reasons he liked her so much—probably *too* much, if he were to be honest with himself. The two of them not only spent a lot of time together on the job but outside of work, as well. It was all mundane stuff—dinner out once a week, a movie or concert a couple times a month, shopping out at Indian Mound Mall; your run-of-the-mill, nothing-to-see-here, we're just-good-friends type of things—but lately Stan was discovering that he had deeper feelings for Maureen, and that scared him. She was basically the only true friend he had in his life and he didn't want to ruin that.

He realized that he was staring into her eyes and felt a warm blush of embarrassment spread across his face. Maureen must have caught it, because she looked away for a moment and cleared her throat, as if making that sound would rid the room of the sudden awkwardness.

"So," she said, pulling up a stool and sitting next to him. "Are you going to tell me about this or should I just put in a preorder for the paperback?"

Back to business, then.

Thank God, thought Stan.

Handing Maureen the lift card with the thumbprint on it, he said, "When Ben called this morning he made it clear that he'd rather I not run the initial series through DIM. I'm guessing he and Bill want to get as much done on their own as possible before the feds are called in on this—and the feds *will* be called in once I run this through DIM because when I do . . . oh, boy, the red flags that will fly."

"Take me through it."

He explained to her how he'd begun by photographing the latent of the left thumb lifted from the glass on the door of the diner. He'd then enlarged the photo five times, traced the print with black ink on white tracing paper, took a photo of the tracing, reduced it to a one-on-one size, scanned it into the computer, and manually set the crosshair references on the core and axis of the print. Once that was taken care of, the computer rotated the print fifteen degrees left and right of the axis, searching for outstanding characteristics—a scar, a ridge, a dot or a whorl—and then plotting such markings as points of identification.

"I figured there wouldn't be much of a problem since the print was an accidental—and before you ask, that's a print that doesn't fall into any of the regular classifications. I pulled up the accidental files for Ohio that were downloaded from the FBI's database when all of this was initially set up. The print is running against them as we speak." He pressed a key and the image was enlarged. Stan rolled his wheelchair back and then turned it sideways so as to give Maureen an unobstructed view. He pulled a small collapsible pointer from his shirt pocket, opened it to its full length, and used it to indicate the areas in question.

"There are ten points of identification on this thing. Going clockwise from the extreme left delta—" He pointed to the first solitary semicurved groove. "—to the extreme right delta, we've got Delta Number One, then a short ridge, a dot, this inverted V-shape break in the flow is the bifurcation point, then Delta Number Two, then a trifurcation point—the three branches right there—and the ridge ending.

"Now right here," he said, tapping the tip of the pointer against the screen, "is what makes the latent an accidental—Delta Number Three."

"Huh," said Maureen. "I don't think I've ever seen one of those before—not that I understand all the minutiae of what you do. I get the big-picture stuff and some of the details, but the really complicated stuff flummoxes me. I'm guessing that this third delta is kind of rare?"

"Make that *very* rare. Some prints will have less than two deltas, which isn't that big of a deal, but *this* . . . notice anything about it?"

Maureen leaned closer to the screen, studying the print. God, she had amazing eyes.

"It's near the core in a central pocket loop whorl," she said.

Stan was pleased that she'd been able to identify it; that meant he'd actually taught her something. Nodding his head, he squeezed her hand and said, "Right. Can you tell me what that means?"

Maureen shrugged. "It's a meeting trace. So what?"

"So this is *extremely* rare. Not quite unique in the dictionary sense of the word, but close enough for rock 'n' roll. This didn't bother me much at first because, taken by itself, a whorl like this is not impossible." He pointed to the extreme left and right deltas. "But then I noticed that the tracing between these guys fell within two ridges—"

"—another meeting trace whorl," said Maureen who, from the look on her face, was starting to understand.

"Yes!" said Stan, a bit more loudly than he'd intended. "And that means that Delta Number Three in the central pocket loop whorl should be either an inner or an outer trace . . . but it's neither, and *that* is impossible. You cannot have two separate meeting traces and two different types of whorls in the same goddamn fingerprint."

"Then it's a forgery. Someone took two dissimilar prints and layered them together. Maybe the CSU guys accidentally touched a couple of lift cards together. From what I hear, the diner was a horrible mess."

"And CSU is trained to function in the middle of horrible messes. No, I don't buy it. Columbus loves to make Cedar Hill look like Hicktown, U.S.A., every chance they get, which is why they sent their best CSU guys. The evidence sent to me has been as carefully and professionally processed as any I've ever seen."

Maureen shook her head. "Okay, then. If it's not a forgery, and it isn't the result of human error, then . . . ?"

Stan drew circles in the air around the print. "Then there's a third species of human being walking around out there that we don't know about."

Maureen stared at him.

Retracting the pointer and slipping it back into his pocket, Stan returned her stare and said, "If you've got a better explanation, I'm all ears."

"You're not *serious?* A third species of human being?"

"You're the one who just started studying forensic anthropology; are you going to deny it's a possibility? If so, then enlighten me with another alternative."

"Don't make fun of me, Stan."

"I'm not and I never would, I swear . . . but I think you may have lost track of one pertinent piece of data."

"That being?"

He gestured toward the monitor. "That thumbprint wasn't isolated. It came off the print of an entire hand."

Maureen's eyes grew a little wider. "Oh, yeah . . . right. Have you run the other prints taken from the hand?"

"I'm running them individually and the hand as a whole. I'm only using the downloaded data already in our system. I'm hoping I can find a match there." He looked down at his right hand, balled it into a fist, and then relaxed it. "You know, I've always thought that the hands were the sexiest part of the human body. Don't ask me why, but it's such an amazing device, the hand. One of the few things God got right about people. 'See! how she leans her cheek upon her hand: O! that I were a glove upon that hand/That I might touch that cheek.' " He gave a small laugh. "I hate winter. People wear gloves in winter. Gloves are an obscenity."

Maureen reached over, grasping his fingers. " 'First time he kissed me, he but only kissed/The fingers of this hand wherewith I write; And ever since—' "

" '—it grew more clean and white,' " said Stan.

"Good God," said Maureen, a smile both on her face and in her voice. "Who would've thought there was a classical Romantic hiding in you?"

Stan felt himself blushing again. "Any sixth-grader with half a brain can memorize a little Shakespeare and Browning."

"Be still my heart."

"Now *you're* making fun of *me*."

"No, I'm not. And you just go ahead pretending that

I'm wrong, that there isn't a Donne or Yeats lurking inside you. Go ahead. But remember—I know your secret."

Stan shrugged his shoulders and moved his wheelchair back in front of the monitor. "Don't take this the wrong way—or, on second thought, do—but was there a specific reason you came in here?"

"Yes. I'm going to run over to the Sparta for some food. You want anything?"

"Whatever you're having is fine with me."

Maureen began to leave the office. Stan looked over his shoulder and said, "Hey."

"Hey what?"

"Thank you for the ride this morning, and for agreeing to help me out here today. I know this was supposed to be one of your days off. I really appreciate your listening to me prattle on."

"You're an interesting guy, Stan Roth. You'd think after working with you over the past seven years I would've run out of new things to discover about you, but it hasn't happened yet. I like being your assistant, but I like being your friend even more. I just sometimes worry that you spend too much time looking at peoples' hands and not enough time looking at their faces. Back in a few minutes." And with that, she was gone. The room hummed with her absence.

Stan rubbed his eyes and began reciting another snippet of verse to himself. " 'There was an old lady from Nantucket . . .' "

Then he turned back toward the computer as it beeped and the words MATCH FOUND appeared on the monitor.

27

Brave Sir Fossil pulled the blade of his crystal sword from his stepfather's throat but did not turn away fast enough to avoid the spurting blood that spattered across the right side of his face and shirt. A few yards away, in the kitchen, his sister and mother lay in a red, soggy heap, both their necks parted from side to side in a glistening, moist smile. Sir Fossil wiped the blood from his right eye and then stood, his foot planted firmly on the chest of the dead man on the floor. He held his sword high and watched as a beam of sunlight swept in through the window, landing directly on the edge of the blade, releasing a mosaic of colors that danced across the shiny gore that crept down the length of the blade, pooled at the hilt, and then spilled over to run down his hand and wrist.

The monster had been slain, but this monster, like all dragons and ogres and fiends, could be a trickster. A true knight would make certain that his enemy was indeed smote, for the princess would require proof of Sir Fossil's victory. So Brave Sir Fossil stepped over the body of the beast beneath his shoe and moved into the kitchen, nearly slipping in the ever-widening puddles of blood that were crawling across the tile. He crossed to the kitchen counter and pulled the wooden block of knives toward him. The handle of each knife rose out of the wood as if they were a dozen tiny Excaliburs jutting forth from a dozen tiny anvils, awaiting the arrival of the one noble enough to free them all. Sir Fossil grabbed the handle of the largest carving knife and *Whosoever Pulleth This Sword From This Stone and Anvil is the True-Born King* and heard thousands cheer as he slipped it free with no effort, and then held it high over his head. This was a fine blade, but it was not up to the task at hand. Placing the knife on the kitchen counter, Sir Fossil began rummaging through the drawers until he found the cutlery, and from this drawer he pulled forth the strongest blade of them all: the meat cleaver.

It had quite a heft to it, but what needed to be done required a weapon with heft. He ran his thumb along the edge of the cleaver and was pleased to feel the sharp pain and see the blood slide all the way down to the handle. He turned toward the sunlight and held the cleaver above his head while he heard the deafening roars and cheers from the thousands of people who were swarming around him, singing songs of thanks and praise, proclaiming him to be triumphant, and he made his march of glory from the kitchen to the living room, where he knelt beside the body of the slain monster that had disguised itself as his stepfather and grabbed a handful of the thing's long hair because a real knight always carried the severed heads of his enemies back to his king and princess, that made it all right for the dinosaurs to rise up from the tar of history and give back Midnight to his loving master who so missed his best friend in the world, his dog, good dog, good boy, good boy, that's it, just pull back so the smiling neck is tight and slam down with the cleaver, just like Mom used to do with the fresh chickens from the market, just take a deep breath and bring down the blade

with all your strength, and he did, Brave Sir Fossil called
upon all his reserves of strength as he swung down the
blade and felt it break through tissue and bone, spattering more blood in all directions, but the first strike
hadn't been—

—*holding Midnight by his back legs and slamming
his head into wall over and over and there's so much
blood and the dog was peeing and pooping as it cried
out*—

—enough, another would be needed, so he worked
the cleaver free of something that had lodged against it
deep inside the monster's neck, and once the blade
was removed he rose to his feet, this time clutching the
handle in both hands, took a deep breath, leaped into
the air, and came down on the monster with unbound
fury, chopping all the way through meat and bone until
he saw the head separate from the body and once that
was done, once he had proof that his enemy was indeed smote, he pulled his stepfather's hair together and
tied it into a long taut ponytail so he could swing it and
that's what he did next, rose to his feet and, holding the
ponytail with both hands, swung the decapitated head
through the air and right into the wall, the same wall
where Midnight had been killed, and he heard the
bones shatter in his stepfather's head, felt the meat of
the monster's face burst into pulp, rejoiced in the sensation as bits of skull and chunks of sodden tissue covered his arms and heard the screams for mercy that
were drowned out because—

—*crying over that goddamned dog again you little
piece of queer bait you think you feel bad now you don't
know nothin' about feeling bad little prick little fag little
piece of shit bend your ass over and if you scream once
I'll shove this belt down your throat instead of hitting you
with it*—

—the blood was pounding in his ears as he laughed and danced and sang his happy song, spinning around once, twice, three times to make sure he had enough momentum before smashing the monster's face into the wall again and again and again, loving the way the patterns on the wall kept growing bigger and wider, speckled with bits and pieces of ruined human meat that, as far as Sir Fossil was concerned, looked as if someone had squashed the world's biggest tomato against it but he still didn't stop, he swung the head one more time and then just let it drop to the floor; it landed with a sopping, satisfying smack.

Dipping his finger into the monster's blood, Brave Sir Fossil rewarded himself with a few games of tic-tac-toe on a clean area of another wall. After that, he went into the bedroom where the monster had slept with Sir Fossil's mother and used the meat cleaver to smash through the locked wooden drawer on the nightstand. He slid his hand and part of his forearm inside and grabbed the only thing in there: the monster's handgun, a Heckler & Koch 9mm Parabellum. The clip was full, but Sir Fossil remembered there was an extra one, so he reached into the nightstand again and, his hand flopping around like a freshly caught fish on the deck of a boat, eventually located the clip way back in the corner. He put the extra clip into his pants pocket, shoved the 9mm through the front of his belt, retrieved the meat cleaver, and went back into the kitchen.

His mother and sister didn't take nearly as long as the monster, and a few minutes later he had everyone's hair wound and tied into firm ponytails that he looped through his belt and then tied off in strong knots. His mother's head hung from his right side, his sister's from his left, and the monster's head hung straight down, what was left of its face pressing against Sir Fossil's groin.

He tapped the top of the monster's skull, smiling at the muffled, drumlike sound it made. "If you behave yourself," he said to it, "then maybe later I'll let you suck on something nice. Do you remember saying that to her?"

The monster made no reply. Sir Fossil retrieved his crystal sword and moved toward the front door, smiling and giggling as he felt the heads bouncing against him with every step. His was a good and true smile from a handsome fossil face. A moment before he walked out onto the porch, a voice as dim and terrible as the face in the Garfield's window whispered, *"Three weeks, five days, twenty-one hours, fifty-eight minutes, thirteen seconds."*

Sir Fossil glided into the world outside, closing the door behind him, unaware that, instead of tic-tac-toe, he'd scrawled the same word over and over: hoopsticks hoopsticks hoopsticks hoopsticks hoopsticks hoopsticks hoopsticks hoopsticks.

The dim and terrible voice told him what must be done next. Sir Fossil climbed over the waist-high wooden partition that separated the two front porches (taking care not to bang the heads around too much), walked up to the door on the other side of the duplex, knocked, and then waited patiently for someone to answer.

A woman in her late thirties opened the door, looked down at what dangled from Sir Fossil's belt, and pulled in a breath that would have been released as a terrified scream, but the crystal sword was buried up to its hilt in her throat before any sound emerged. Sir Fossil pushed her bleeding body back into the house, closing the door behind him. A few moments later, a heavy thud shook a small area of the front porch. Someone grunted. A splash of blood hit the front window from inside the house. A moment later, a child's hand reached over and pulled down the shade.

Above the porch, poised on the edge of the roof gutter, a large black butterfly fluttered—but did not flap—its wings.

28

Instead of his house—it was no longer his *home*, not with Cheryl gone, no; it was just a place he slept and ate—Ben went to the cemetery by the old County Home to clear his head. It was a sad, pathetic place, but he'd felt a kinship with it since his high-school days when he'd worked part-time as the caretaker's assistant, helping to maintain the grounds and bury the residents or unidentified homeless whose bodies were dumped here by the county. It had been pretty once. He tried to remember that.

The home had burned down in 1969 and the cemetery fell to neglect and decay. Now the bodies were known only by the numbers sloppily engraved on their chipped, broken headstones: 107, 122, 135, and so on. Ben knew that there was a certain morbidity to coming here, but come here he did, if only to remind himself that there were worse things than being a widower and in debt up to your ass at age thirty-six—among other things. A few solitary minutes with the nameless dead and suddenly a lonely house and lonelier bed didn't seem so cataclysmic.

He wandered through the weeds, used condoms, and broken beer bottles, looking at the markers.

76 . . . 85 . . . 93 . . .

There was no need for him to look, though; he knew the layout by heart, could probably even recite the numerical patterns in his sleep. *When* he could sleep.

He stopped to look at one headstone that was so old and worn and beaten by the seasons that its number could no longer be read.

This'll be all of us someday, he thought. Sure, there would be mourners at the end, friends, family, old lovers you thought had forgotten about you, maybe a girl you had a crush on in ninth grade, and they would gather, and they would weep, and they would talk among themselves afterward and say, "I remember the way he used to . . ." Your belongings would be divided, given away, or tossed on a fire, your picture moved to the back of a dusty photo album, and, eventually, those left behind would die too, and no one would be left to remember your face, your middle name, or even the location of your grave. The seasons would change, the elements would set to work, rain and heat and cold and snow would smooth away the inscription on the headstone until it was no longer legible and then, later—days, weeks, decades—someone who happened by would glance down, see the faded words and dates, mutter "I wonder who's buried here," then go on about their business, trying hard to forget that they were part of the same sorrowful cycle of the universe that one day ended with their being just like this. No one would be left to say that this man was important, or this woman was kind, or that anything they strove for was worthwhile. And what happened then? What point, what purpose did any of this have? You dreamed, you loved, you struggled, wept, worked hard, and showed compassion, and all that waited for you in the end was lime and rot and darkness.

He thought then of Cheryl and the lovely spot in

Cedar Hill Cemetery where her grave was. He swallowed twice, very hard, not wanting to remember the night she and their unborn son had died.

(The expressions on Bill and Goldstein's faces when Ben answered the door, the way Bill's eyes seemed to shrink back into his skull when he said, "We need to come in, Ben. Something's happened and . . . oh, God, Ben . . . I don't know how to say this. . . .)

Ben had been thirty-three and just promoted to detective. They were expecting their first baby after three tries that had resulted in miscarriages. It should have been the beginning of a better life for them. Should have been. He wondered how many of the forgotten dead surrounding him had built their life on the unstable foundation of what Should Have Been.

He looked up when he heard the sound of footsteps, and for a moment thought that he saw someone who could have been either Rasputin, Jesus Christ, or Charles Manson walking toward him, then sighed with relief when he saw the clerical collar and realized it was only the Reverend from the Open Shelter.

"Hey, Reverend."

"Ben," replied the Reverend. "And here I thought I was the only one who came out here to lift my spirits."

Ben stared at him. "Is that a joke?"

"Not a very good one but, yes, a joke, nonetheless. How are you, by the way?"

Ben shook his head. "It's been a long night."

The Reverend nodded. "So I gathered from the news this morning. That's not what I meant. I meant, how are you today, on this day?"

Ben leaned his head to the side, studying the other man's face. "You mean—?"

"I mean this is the anniversary of Cheryl's death."

Ben thought for a moment, and couldn't recall ever having told the Reverend about it. But of course it had made the papers, so the man had probably read about it and committed the date to memory. The Reverend was known to have a remarkable memory.

"To tell you the truth, I'm lousy, but there's too much to do today. The captain gave me ninety minutes to rest up and then get back on the job."

"How much longer until you have to be back?"

Ben checked his watch. "About forty minutes."

The Reverend looked around. "So in order to clear your head, you come out *here?*"

Ben shrugged. "Beats drinking myself unconscious."

"True. Listen, I know you're not a particularly religious person, Ben, but if you ever need to talk to someone who's not going to try and bring you back to the church or anything along those lines, all you need to do is come by the shelter. No appointment needed."

"Thanks, Reverend, but I . . . actually, now that I think about it, I might take you up on that sometime."

The Reverend shook Ben's hand. "Look forward to it."

As soon as Ben let go of the Reverend's hand, something occurred to him. "What are *you* doing out here?"

"Saying a prayer over this place and those who're buried here. Their names are never going to be known to anyone, and that breaks what's left of my heart. I keep thinking about something the Greek philosopher Simonides said: 'We die twice when men forget.' " He gestured outward at all the unmarked graves. "If you think about it, the poor souls buried here haven't only died twice, the lack of names on the headstones is a third form of death. If I dwelled on that for too long, it would snap me in half." He stared off in the distance for a few moments at something only he seemed capable of seeing, then snapped out of his melancholy reverie, blinked, and smiled. "I should leave you to your thoughts."

"How did you get all the way out here?" asked Ben.

"I drove the shelter's van. It's parked at the other end of the grounds. I should be getting back, anyway." He reached out and put a hand on Ben's shoulder. "I can't even begin to imagine the horror of what you saw at the diner, but like I said—if you need to talk to someone off the record, someone who knows how to keep things to himself, just drop by, all right?"

"Thanks, Reverend. I appreciate it."

The Reverend turned and walked away. For a minute or so afterward, until the figure of the Reverend was little more than a blur in the distance, Ben watched the man. The Reverend's appearance was a little unnerving sometimes; with his shoulder-length, wavy black hair, dark beard speckled here and there with gray, and intense eyes, he did bare a strong resemblance to Rasputin, Christ, and Manson. It was always hard to maintain eye contact with him during conversation; you always had the feeling that if you met his gaze for too long, he'd be able to see into the deepest, most intimate areas of your soul and psyche. Maybe that's why the mayor and city council never turned him down when he requested anything; they were afraid to look into those eyes.

Ben almost smiled, wishing that the Cedar Hill Police Department warranted that level of fear and respect.

And then he saw it.

A few feet away, perched on the jagged remains of a headstone, was a black butterfly. It wasn't its color that attracted Ben's gaze but its stillness; its wings did not so much as flutter in the breeze. As he knelt down to get a better look (Cheryl had loved butterflies) Ben saw that it wasn't entirely black; a thin strip of white encircled its body at an area just below the antennae. It almost looked like—he chuckled under his breath at the absurdity of the thought—a very tiny animal collar.

He froze a moment. His left eye twitched. He pressed

on it with his finger. It stopped. He leaned closer and blew on the butterfly's wings—

—but they did not move. Not even a fraction of an inch.

He looked at the headstone:

EMILY SUE MODINE

BELOVED WIFE OF HENRY MODINE
MOTHER TO WILLIAM AND PATRICIA
BORN JULY 13, 1960 TAKEN SEPT. 3, 1993

"Where did you come from?" he whispered, feeling cold. "You weren't here last time."

He stared unbelieving, blinked to make sure he wasn't seeing things, then walked the entire cemetery again.

29

Stan Roth cracked his knuckles and looked at the screen of his computer, then the piles of readouts that were scattered across the top of his desk, and decided, *Screw this, I'm going to try it anyway.*

He called up the Panic Hand Program, something he'd designed himself a few years earlier. PHP was his last resort. The program was designed to take whatever information was available from an existing print or set of prints—in this case, the thumbprint from the window and those lifted from the Tec-9—and create a hypothetical visual image of what the rest of the hand looked like. The two-part program had been born out of desperation five years before when, during a nearly botched murder investigation, only two partial prints had been lifted from the victim's body. The system he'd had back then couldn't do jack shit with a partial. So Stan, using his personal modifications of print classifications from the National Crime Information Center, had come up with twelve initial combination equations and ran both partials through, factoring in all the variables such as the angle of the print, points of identification, etc. It had been a nerve-racking experience, leading him up more than a few blind alleys and producing countless dead ends. But it had, eventually, constructed three decent approximations of the suspect's hand. He then made tracings of the approximates, photographed them, reduced them, ran them against the files, and had come up with a dozen possible suspects. He passed the information along. The police rounded the suspects up for questioning, and #4 turned out to be the killer.

Stan had been incredibly smug for months afterward—but not so much that he didn't spend his off-hours working out the bugs in his program.

"Feet, don't fail me now," he whispered to himself, then chuckled.

He began feeding in the points of identification as they'd been mapped out in the initial print scan. Along with each point came its NCIC code: P for plain whorl, PI for a plain whorl with an inner trace, X for accidental, XO for an accidental with an outer trace. D for a double loop whorl, DI for a double loop whorl with an inner trace, AA for arch, and TT for a tented arch. After that came the radial and ulnar listings: ulnar 12 (for its twelve ridges), radial 63 (for its thirteen ridges plus 50).

Before doing the first run, Stan automatically removed nine of the twelve equations—they were for something much more linear. The three remaining equations were designed for exploring the relationships of nonlinear nonproportional elements, such as eight different print patterns existing on the same supposed hand. These equations were deliberately crafted to deal with the features you left out when you wanted a fast, clear understanding of what you were dealing with and usually made some kind of sense out of a disorderly stream of data. He hoped.

Once everything had been fed into the program and the code patterns double-checked, Stan affixed each of the nine prints with a primary ID point. In the case of the thumb, he went with the central pocket loop whorl. This would give the computer a point of reference for each print and enable this first sequence to produce a series of points as it traced a hypothetically continuous path. A number and a letter (or letters) would represent each path from each equation in the readout.

The first scan with equation #1 came up as 0-CM.

The first scan with equation #2 came up as 10-X.

The first scan with equation #3 came up as 0-DI.

"Well, at least you're trying," Stan said, then sat back as the computer went through every possible combination of prints and codes, searching for similarities, no matter how tenuous, that might be hidden in the data.

The codes came up surprisingly quickly. 0-CM, 10-X, 0-DI; 4-P, 12-AA, 0-PI; 9-XO, 20-TT, 0-CM; 16-XO, 36-P, 2-D; 30-PI, 66-C, 7-AA; 54-D, 115-X; 93-TT, 192-DI, 74-CM . . .

Twenty minutes later, he had code designations for over one thousand combinations: eleven hundred and fifteen, to be exact.

Piece of cake.

He told the computer to scan through and reaffix any secondary points of identification that did not coincide with the stream of the three equations. It took about six minutes to process. When it was done, the number of possible combinations had been reduced to four hundred and forty-nine. Yippee.

Now came the fun part.

He added the last set of variables. If anything was going to shit-can the possible results, these would do it.

He thought again of the Escher drawing *The Waterfall* as he reminded the computer that, since there was no break in the two contrasting patterns on the thumbprint, it was to proceed under the assumption that there would be no break in any contrasting patterns on the hand itself.

Then he told the computer that 1: the phalange at the

base of the index finger (the Mount of Jupiter, symbol-izing arrogance) would be more pronounced than any of the others, and 2: that the Mount of the Moon at the base of the hand (violence) and the Mount of Mars (lightheartedness, because this fucker was nothing if not an arrogant, smirking maniac) would also be pro-nounced.

Stan cracked his knuckles, bit his lower lip, held his breath, and pressed ENTER.

30

Arliss Hamilton later decided that it must have begun, as all things must, with seeds.

A man came into the store around nine A.M. carrying a large brown paper bag. For a while he contented himself with losing money in the pinball machine and annoying what few customers there were. Arliss stood behind the cash register and watched them all.

From 11:30 P.M. until 9:30 A.M. Arliss Hamilton was their watcher, their onlooker, their sentinel. With their tired and bloodshot eyes, chain-smoking filterless cigarettes, never looking at one another, the dead of spirit wander into this store for snacks, beer, cold cuts, and sometimes just to play the pinball machine. They never smiled, never stood very straight, and their sex was of little consequence. They shambled in from the darkness to this house of light, supplied themselves, and then vanished back into the night with the same familiarity one displayed when walking up the steps toward one's home. Arliss often felt sorry for them and wished there was something he could do to help.

"Would you like to buy some flower seeds?"

Arliss snapped out of his reverie and looked at the man standing near the register. Arliss expected him to stink of liquor but the man surprised him by smelling of talcum powder. His clothes were old but well-kept. His cheeks sagged and he could have used a shave, but Arliss knew almost at once that the guy had been at this all day and hadn't had the time.

"What are you selling them for?"

"I'm selling them for my daughter," he said (pronouncing it *dodder*). "She's a Girl Scout and they, well, they got this contest, see, and whoever sells the most seeds wins a scooter."

"A scooter?"

He looked worried by Arliss's question. "Look, I know this must look kinda weird, me bein' in here at this hour and trying to sell flower seeds, but she's been really sick lately and . . . well, she was doin' so good before and I just don't want to see her lose out again, y'know?"

Arliss did know. And believed him. It was the "again" that did it. Not a simple, *I don't want to see her lose out,* no; it was the "again" that told Arliss all he needed to know. Standing before him was a man who'd probably worked damned hard his entire life to provide for his family but never managed to give them anything they *wanted,* only the necessities—and perhaps sometimes even those had to be cut back because the paycheck was a little short. Arliss knew this by looking at the man's gaze. There is a certain sparkle that drifts across the eyes when desperation sets in, and Seed Man's eyes had it.

"How much?" asked Arliss, reaching for his wallet.

"Seventy-five cents a package. I know that might seem a little steep, but—"

"—it's for a good cause, I know." Arliss reached into his back pocket for his wallet, and that's when he felt someone else watching him—not Seed Man, he was still too busy trying not to look humiliated, so—

—Arliss glanced up and saw a little boy, holding what

looked like a curved section of broken glass, standing outside the front window of the store, looking right at him. He was nailed to the floor by the intensity of the boy's gaze. Arliss could almost physically feel the heat as it shot from the boy's gaze and passed through the window, catching the air currents and flying toward Arliss's face, circling around him, twisting around him, becoming tighter and tighter like a spring being wound up tight, and when it happened, when the spring uncoiled, it drilled right between Arliss's eyes, through his skull, and became liquid heat once again as it flowed into his brain. The sensation was sublime, causing Arliss to almost lose his balance. He leaned against the cash register and took a deep breath, closing his eyes for just a moment. When he opened them again, the little boy with his curved piece of glass was gone, but his resonance remained.

"Are you all right?" asked Seed Man.

"Huh? Oh, yes, yes. I'm fine. It's been a long shift." Arliss rubbed one of his eyes. "I guess I'm more tired than I thought. I'm good—thanks for asking. So, why don't you tell me about your daughter?" He genuinely wanted to hear.

Seed Man smiled, full of pride. "Her name's Pamela."

Pamela. What a pretty name. Gentle, lyrical, maybe a velvety laugh that sounded older than her years, perhaps she wore glasses, small, thin but not frail . . .

"She's ten, and she's been a Girl Scout since her mother died four years ago." His voice was soft and musical, not at all what you'd expect from someone of his rough appearance, and Arliss found himself thinking that if satin could speak, it would sound like a man pitching seeds for his dodder.

Seed Man spoke as if he were composing a poem to be written down for the ages yet to come; a turn of the page as he told of the fishing trips the family used to take when his wife was still alive, the way his mother used to put her hand against her bosom whenever she laughed, the certain look Pamela would get when she told a fib, another page, a new stanza to his poem of satin and seeds, the way his wife died of lung cancer when she'd never had a cigarette in her life, another verse, a new line composed, the hidden ridicule he saw behind the eyes of people when he tried to sell them the treasures from his bag, the sounds his dodder made when she was a baby . . . Arliss listened, enraptured, as Seed Man carefully chose his words, finishing the verse, completing the meter of his existence, one last line, and there: he folded the sweet, golden, sad, bitter, triumphant memories of his life into a perfect paper diamond and gave it to Arliss for safekeeping.

He looked at the clock on the wall. "I'm sorry. I didn't mean to go on for so long. How many would you like?"

"How many do you have left?"

"Fifty-eight."

"I'll take all of them."

Seed Man asked if he was serious, Arliss assured him that he was and handed Seed Man the money. Seed Man handed over the seeds, smiled, shook Arliss's hand, and thanked him several times on behalf of Pamela.

"She'll be so proud of me," he said.

She should be, thought Arliss. Of all the sights in this world, of all the valleys and temples and forests and pyramids and mountains, there is nothing so eternally powerful as the sight of a human being doing something out of love.

Arliss waved as Seed Man left—

—waited until the man had turned fully around—

—and made his hand into a fist, stuck out his index finger, lifted his thumb, took aim, and snapped his thumb down.

"Bang," he whispered. There. *You'll never know hurt again, never taste humiliation, never feel like a failure. I love you. Your dodder will be proud.*

And then the sound of words spoken in a voice not his own echoed in the depths of Arliss's skull: *Anima Christi, sanctifica me. Corpus Christi, salva me. Sanguis Christi, inebria me. Aqua lateris Christi, lava ma.*

He looked around at the lost who were wandering the small, cramped aisles of the market, saw the dark crescents under all of their eyes, thought about how tired and downhearted all of them were, and then remembered the .357 Magnum hidden under the counter. Drifting between those two thoughts was something that he knew connected them, made them one and the same, but he couldn't quite touch it and bring it into the light. Maybe on his way home . . .

31

The building that housed the headquarters of the Cedar Hill Police Department did indeed look like something from an old horror movie. A brown brick façade with an unused tower and tower room led more than one suspect to believe they were being dragged into a mad scientist's laboratory for experimentation, or (for those criminals who'd made it out of high school) the Tower of London where Richard III's black-hooded executioner stood beside the chopping block, ax at the ready. The heavy iron bars on most of the upper-floor windows did nothing to ease their anxiety, nor did the interior layout of the building with all of its mazelike corridors, scuffed wooden floors, doors with pebble-glass windows you just *knew* the cops were using to hide something behind. Add to this the smell of too much lemon wood polish, sweat, stale cigarette smoke, hot coffee left to sit too long in the pot, and a really unpleasant stench that everyone *said* came from the old plumbing, and by the time suspects made it to the interrogation rooms on the third floor, they'd be willing to confess to anything from petty theft to single-handedly creating the hole in the ozone layer—anything to get out of this creepy, smelling building and be taken to the adjacent jail building.

Ben could well understand why a lot of CHPD lifers wanted to retire early; if you spent nine to twelve hours a day trapped in this building or in one of the glorified walk-in closets that was supposed to pass for an office, it was a wonder more desk jockeys and officers hadn't gone a little wonky themselves by now: the place was enough to make even the most stable, healthy, phobia-free individual feel more than a little claustrophobic; add to that the plethora of security cameras, and you could add "paranoid" to that. It was not a calming environment. More often than not, Ben found that he felt cornered when inside. And he was definitely feeling cornered right now.

Goldstein looked up from the transcript of Ben's notes and said, "One more time?"

"There are fifteen brand-new headstones out at the old County Home Cemetery. I know that place by heart, I go walking out there all the time and I'm telling you, I *swear*, Captain, those things weren't there last week. The cemetery hasn't been used since the home burned down in '69."

"Nineteen sixty-nine was a bad year for fires around here," said Goldstein, handing Ben's digital voice recorder back to him. He then took off his glasses, massaged the bridge of his nose, and said: "Do any of the names on those headstones match the names of any of the victims?"

"No."

"So? There are six more headstones than we have bodies and—don't look at me like that, okay? I agree it seems like more than coincidence but the mayor and the chief are going to want something more solid—not to mention the city hall janitors. Damn cranky bunch."

"What's Stan have to say?"

"He's still running the prints on the coins and the Tec-9, but running the weapon itself is useless. No serial number, no skin fragments, no blood, saliva, nothing."

"What about the ME?"

"Before ten, I'm told." Goldstein rubbed his hands over his face, then propped his elbows on the edge of his desk. "Close the damn door, will you?"

Ben did so. "Where's Bill?"

"Still finishing up at the scene. He should be here shortly. I hope."

Ben took a seat near the side of Goldstein's desk. After a moment of prolonged silence, Goldstein lifted his face from his hands, looked at Ben, and said, "What?"

"Are you feeling all right, sir?"

"Why? Are you about to say something that's going to upset me?"

"I, uh—"

"Ignore that. What is it?"

"It's not so much the names on the headstones— though that was enough to unnerve me more than a little bit. It's the *number*."

"Did you run the names?"

"I fed them into the system before I came in here. With any luck, I ought to have something in about an hour."

"Assuming that they're the names of actual people and not just something else he's planted for us to waste time on."

"That occurred to me, sir—except that the names chiseled into the headstones *did* have wear on them. I mean, it looked as if they'd been there for a long time. May I ask, sir, if our deadline has been changed?"

"Not yet, but they're trying to find an excuse. You were saying something about the number of headstones?"

Ben took a deep breath, held it for a moment, and then exhaled. "If there had been only thirteen headstones, that would have matched the number of supposed bodies we're dealing with. But there are *fifteen*, and that . . . well . . . worries me."

Goldstein sat back in his chair. "You think he might've killed two more people that we don't about yet?"

Ben nodded. "Either that, or it's his way of telling us he's going to kill two more."

Goldstein chewed on his thumbnail for a moment—it seemed everyone who worked for the CHPD developed this habit after a while—and then pulled his hand away and fired up a cigarette. "You know, I can understand, Ben, I really can, how you could come to that conclusion. It does seem too coincidental that something like this would happen right now. So let's say that it's not some high-school prank or some frat pledges from Denison University trying to be funny and say that you're right, okay? Let's say that the killer *is* responsible for the sudden appearance of those headstones—and I can tell you right now that the Well-Pressed Suits won't buy that for a second—but here and now, between us, let's say it's true, that he's telling us that he plans on killing two more people. What can we do about it except wait for the bodies to turn up?"

"I *hate* this," said Ben.

"You see a smile on my face? It makes me sick that all we can do is have every officer and deputy from the sheriff's department driving around out there looking for anything suspicious. We're not looking for the proverbial needle in a haystack; we're looking for a goddamn ghost in a haunted house."

Goldstein's cell phone went off. He checked caller ID and then answered. "Stan, how nice of you to call. I . . . yes, I know, I know, but—please don't shout at me, just tell me what—" He bit his lower lip and closed his eyes. Even from where Ben was sitting he could hear Roth's voice; the man sounded both angry and excited.

Goldstein opened his eyes and exhaled, his upper lip twitching ever so slightly. "Finished with your little tirade? What? No, only Ben's here, Emerson's still on scene. No, we were reading *Wuthering Heights* to one another over a champagne breakfast—*what do you think?* Oh, *may I?* Yes, he'll come along, he was just saying how much he missed your whimsical wit and charming—" He held the cell phone away from his ear. "He hung up on me. Imagine that." He closed his cell phone, put it in the inside pocket of his dress jacket, and stood. "We have been cordially invited to join Charles Foster Kane at Xanadu. Try to contain your excitement. It seems—judging from his three-hundred-and-seventy-decibel side of the conversation—that something is amiss. We'll take separate cars in case one of us needs to leave in a hurry."

32

Maureen Cahill greeted them as soon as they entered the lab. "Did you guys remember to bring the garlic cloves and crucifixes?"

Goldstein smiled at her. "Oh no."

"Oh, yes," said Maureen. "Watch yourselves. He's in one of his *moods* again."

"Would this be the 'I'm-no-good-at-this-anymore' mood or the 'Damn-I'm-so-good-I-scare-myself' mood?"

"Somewhere in the middle." She gestured over her shoulder at Stan's closed door. "You'd best get in there. He's pretty anxious."

Goldstein put a hand on her shoulder as he walked past. "He doesn't deserve you, Maureen."

"Few mortals do."

"We have to do something about that self-esteem problem of yours."

Ben started to follow Goldstein but Maureen held him back. "Uh, Ben. Listen, I . . ." She seemed to wobble for a moment, then put a hand against her cheek, then her forehead.

"You okay?" asked Ben.

"Fine. It's been a long night. Stan got me out of bed at about a quarter of five."

Ben looked at his watch. "Christ. Have you at least eaten some breakfast?"

"I ran over to the Sparta. They make a good breakfast and the doughnuts were fresh. I'd've been back sooner but some guy who was standing in line with me over there insisted I hear this damn joke one of the waitresses told him." She seemed to turn inward for a moment, eyes staring out at nothing and everything. "Huh. I can't even remember it now. Only that it had Jesus in it and it was set on some beach." She shrugged. "I must be tired. I'm getting a headache and it sounds like there's all this static in my ears."

Been looked over at Stan's door and saw Goldstein standing there, his arms crossed in front of his chest, one foot impatiently tapping. "Uh, what did you need? I should be . . ." He shrugged in Goldstein's direction.

"Sorry, Ben. It's just I wanted to warn you about something he found." She glanced at the office door, then back to Ben. "It's about a couple of the matches. I was in there when he made the—"

At that moment the office door flew open and Stan wheeled himself halfway into the lab proper. "Is there some goddamn reason you two are milling about out here?"

"And a good morning to you, as well," said Goldstein.

"Spare me the snappy repartee, will you?" He rolled forward a little more, nearly running over Goldstein's foot in the process. "Excuse me, Littlejohn. Could you maybe confer with Maid Marian later? Thank you." He gripped the wheels and rolled backward into the office. Goldstein followed and Ben, giving a fast, apologetic grin to Maureen—*Tell me later*—was right in tow, closing the door behind him as soon as he was inside.

Stan was sitting with his back to them, furiously typing commands into the computer. Without turning around he said, "Sit down and be quiet for a second.

This is not insubordination nor is it disrespect, this is panic so you can infer the apology."

It took Ben and Goldstein a few seconds of searching amidst the piles of computer printouts and books and files and empty Styrofoam clamshells and cola cans and even a few articles of clothing that Stan hadn't yet gathered up for laundry, but eventually they managed to locate two folding chairs. They sat as close to the monitor as they could get and still allow Stan room to maneuver his wheelchair.

After another moment or two, Stan turned around and said, "I will start out with the merely odd part before moving on to the strange and then outright weird."

Goldstein huffed and looked at his watch. "Couldn't you just get to the punch line? We don't exactly have a lot of time."

Stan shook his head. "Correct me if I'm wrong, but aren't you guys sort of functioning under the microscope, as it were?"

"The Well-Pressed Suits are keeping a close eye on this one, yes."

"Then you'll want to be prepared for their questions. I find that having actual *answers* is helpful, so bear with me." He pointed at the left side of the monitor's screen, which displayed the suspect latent, then took them through the initial print problem step-by-step, just as he'd done with Maureen, making sure to emphasize the inconsistency of the whorl patterns and deltas, wrapping it up with his and Maureen's initial conclusion that the print was a forgery.

Goldstein looked at Stan and shook his head. "I don't want to parade my ignorance, but latents training was a long time ago. Refresh me: how can you forge a fingerprint?"

Before Stan could answer, Ben said, "Photocopy it."

Stan tilted his head to the side and almost smiled. "I may be close to being impressed. Go on."

"You photocopy the suspect's print from the file, then put print tape down on top of it while the copy's still hot and lift it off. Since powdered photocopy toner is used as fingerprint powder in a lot of situations, no one's going to question it. Then you simply take the tape with the fingerprint on it and attach it to whatever object you want to find the print on. Anyone asks why you taped it, you say it's because you wanted to protect the print."

"Very good, Ben. Very good, indeed."

"Wait a second," said Goldstein, "rewind a few inches. I may not remember much of the specifics but I do know that if you do that you risk being found out when the print is transferred to the lift card, then run against the file. I mean, in order to make a print you have to have a certain amount of identification points but they can't be exact."

"See," said Stan. "You remember more than you think. That's why they pay you the mediocre bucks. Right— you have to have 'X' amount of points of similarity, but in no way should every point exactly match up with the print on file. There are variables to think about—the angle of pressure when the print is taken from the suspect, the position of the finger, how smooth the finger rolls across the surface of the card . . .

"So you're with me on this so far, right?"

Ben nodded. "One thumbprint, two whorl patterns, no visual trace of inconsistency, possible forgery."

Stan moved back to the keyboard. "Or so I thought until I realized, Mensa material that I am, that it was lifted from an entire *handprint.*"

"C'mon," said Ben. "You know as well as I do you can forge an isolated section of a handprint if you've got the right tools."

"Well, *duh*. I think I might've picked that one up somewhere along the way."

"Sorry."

"As well you should be. I went on ahead and checked it against the accidentals file anyway. I didn't expect it to come up with any candidates but it gave me *ten*."

Ben and Goldstein exchanges surprised glances. Then the captain said, "How many points of identification matched up?"

"Watch closely," said Stan. "Nothing up my sleeve." He depressed another key. "Presto!"

Ten possible matching prints, shrunken to one-on-one size, appeared on the right side of the latent. "Interesting, isn't it?" Stan hit the next key. The first of the ten prints enlarged to the same size as the suspect latent. "We are now out of the odd part and into the strange." He depressed another key and the two prints quickly came together in the center of the screen, overlapping.

Goldstein's eyes widened. "Oh my . . ."

It was a perfect match.

"Do you have any idea of the odds against something like this happening on the very first comparison?" asked Stan.

Ben shook his head slowly, his gaze focused on the two prints. "There aren't enough zeros in the universe."

Stan laughed mirthlessly. "Then you're going to *love* this." He entered a series of commands, then sat back and watched their reaction as, one by one, each successive print was enlarged, then overlapped with the previous ones. The suspect latent remained off to the side.

Ben actually gasped. Stan couldn't blame him; he'd done it himself earlier.

All ten separate candidates matched one another exactly, right down to the last detail and reference point.

In his best Rod Serling imitation, Stan said, "You have just entered *The Twilight Zone*."

Goldstein leaned closer to the screen, chewing on his lower lip. "This can't be right. There has to have been a mistake somewhere. There was some kind of glitch and the computer just repeated the same print, that's all."

Stan raised his eyebrow and said, "Pull up the first candidate's card."

Goldstein scooted forward and tapped in the command.

The card appeared on the screen a few seconds later.

Goldstein stared at it in silence, then asked, in less than a whisper, "Where did this come from?"

Stan moved next to him and Ben stood behind the two of them. Stan said, "When DIM and AFIS were first installed I went right into the FBI's latents and downloaded every print they had on file. One of their ident technicians is a guy named Ryan Fosse. His humor's a bit on the ghoulish side but that's not uncommon with . . . persons of our sort.

"Anyhow, he told me about something the bureau's ident guys and gals had put together for us lucky few EXCEL Project participants who might be warped enough to be interested.

"They call it the 'Family Album.' You're looking at one of the pictures from it."

All three of them looked down at the image of the card and the name printed in the upper right-hand corner:

HUMBERTY, JAMES OLIVER

Once again, Stan laughed. "You might recall this is the guy in San Ysidro who had the serious Big Mac attack."

" 'I'm going hunting humans,' " Ben whispered to himself.

"What about the others?" asked Goldstein, swallowing once, very hard.

"Do you want them listed alphabetically or in order of body counts, highest to lowest?"

Goldstein rubbed his eyes and exhaled heavily. "Let's have it."

"All ten of these matching thumbprints came from the FBI's Family Album. In addition to Mr. Big Mac you've got Randolph Gene Simmons, who, between December 22 and 27 of 1987 murdered sixteen people and wounded four others in Russellville, Arkansas; then comes Marc Lepine who shot and killed fourteen women and wounded twelve others at the University of Montreal on December 6, 1989; also from 1989 there's Patrick Edward Purdy who killed five children and wounded twenty-eight others in a school yard in Stockton, California; next—"

"Stop it with the fucking scores, all right?" snapped Goldstein.

"Fine. On top of the first four, you've got Howard Unruh, James Rupert, Richard Speck, Theodore Bundy, Charles Whitman, everybody's favorite mailman Patrick Sherrill, and that king of clowns, John Wayne Gacy."

"And they all . . . I mean . . . did you . . ."

"Just so you'll know, we'll do it again," said Stan, who hit one last key.

All ten prints were enlarged, shuffled, and then layered again, one on top of the next, over the original suspect latent.

And they were still looking at the same print, point for point, with no deviations present.

"Oh, man," whispered Ben. "You're right, this is *weird.*"

Stan waved one of his hands. "Oh, no, this isn't the weird part."

"You're kidding," said Goldstein.

"Of course I am; I'm known for my whimsical humor." Stan leaned forward, grabbing Goldstein's wrists and getting right in the captain's face. "We're talking about some psycho fuckwad who slaughtered eight people and a *baby* in my hometown! You think I'm so antisocial I'd make goddamn *jokes* about something like this? I take my *parents* to the Moundbuilders Diner once a month. *We* could've been in there when it happened. Any of us could have."

"Calm down," said Ben, gently removing Stan's hands from Goldstein's wrists. "You know as well as I do that the captain didn't mean anything by it. If you'd been inside that diner, you'd understand."

Stan jerked back and took a deep breath, then wiped one of his eyes. "Sorry, Al. Sorry."

"It was a dumb thing to say. Forget about it. Can you just . . . get on with it?"

Stan reached under a pile of papers and pulled out a plastic, Tec-9-shaped squirt gun, offering it to Ben, who took it.

"Hold it like it's real and you're going to let fly."

Ben did so.

Stan grabbed a pencil and pointed at Ben's fingers. "Now, look at where the fingers are. The right index is on the trigger, the right fourth, third, and second fingers are wrapped around the grip, and the thenar zone—or lower thumb area—of the hand is pressed firmly against the grip. That's four solid prints and a partial thenar lift from the lower section of the weapon.

"The upper portion of the weapon—please don't move your fingers, okay?—the upper portion gives us the same thing, four solids and a thenar partial, only from the left hand. You can put it down now.

"Now, look at my hand. The pinkie side is called the ulnar and the thumb side is called the radial. Radial loops in a fingerprint flow toward the thumb, and ulnars flow toward the pinkie. The rules apply regardless of which hand you're talking about. Ulnar loops are more common than radials; radials tend to be found only on the index and middle fingers. Whorl patterns appear on the thumb, loops appear everywhere else. The direction of the flow tells me what hand the bastard was using and where he had it placed while firing the weapon.

"Still with me? Good. I lifted the ten prints from the Tec-9 you sent over from the diner and ran them through all of the files I have in the system. I'll get to the matches in a minute. The thing is—and this became evident early on—taken as a whole, the prints on the gun are a . . . a crazy-quilt phantasm.

"Don't say anything yet, Al, please? Thanks. There are only eight types of fingerprint patterns, all right? Plain arches, tented arches, right slope loops, left slope loops, plain whorls, central pocket loop whorls, double loop whorls, and accidentals. Take a look at these lift cards— I made them right before I called you.

"Those are both of my hands. As you can see, I have plain whorl patterns on both my thumbs, left slope loops on the fingers of my left hand, and right slope loops on my right. Average as average can be. There is a set number of combinations—but I'm getting off the point.

"Not only do *none* of the print patterns on the gun match—which is to say *all eight existing patterns* are present—but it would appear that your killer has thumbs where his third fingers should be, and that his right middle finger is on his left hand and his left middle finger is on his right. But that doesn't even matter because the two middle fingers have dissimilar patterns— the right is a tented arch, the left is a double loop. I don't even want to begin trying to come up with a scenario of how he could've done that.

"What it boils down to is this: all of the latent evidence I've examined thus far is impossible. You can't have contrasting patterns on the same finger, you can't have eight different print patterns on the same set of hands, you can't have ten different people with the same accidental pattern on their thumbs, and you sure as hell, short of a drunk-assed Dr. Frankenstein going a little loopy in surgery, can't have thumbs and middle fingers and loops and every other goddamn thing where they're not supposed to be.

"But what bugs the shit out of me is that all of the dis-similarities are *precisely* dissimilar. It's a mess, but it's a very *deliberate* mess, like the physics in an Escher painting." He looked back at the screen and shook his head once again.

"What about matches?" asked Ben.

Stan took a deep breath and recited the names in a rapid cadence: "The prints from the gun gave me Juan Corona, Albert Desalvo, Dennis Nilsen, Ed Gein, Christine Falling, Henry Lee Lucas, Joachim Kroll, and . . ." He cleared his throat and drummed his fingers against his leg.

"And who else?" asked Goldstein. "That's only eight."

When Stan spoke again his voice was thick and low, clogged with dread. He turned toward Ben and Goldstein. "Understand this: I like and respect both of you and would never purposefully do something that would hurt either of you, professionally or personally. I know that I am not the friendliest or the most professional of people and that my manners are at best slightly above those of a Neanderthal, but it's important that you know I like both of you and think of you as friends, even if I don't act like it most of the time."

"Jesus H. Christ will you *answer the question?*" shouted Goldstein.

Ben nodded at Stan and briefly touched his shoulder.

Stan looked at Goldstein and said, "Your father changed his name at Ellis Island, didn't he?"

Goldstein blanched. "He . . . uh . . . he was sponsored

by a couple named Goldstein who lived in Queens. The clerk got things mixed up that day. Dad was always saying how many people there were on the ships . . . anyway, the clerk got things mixed up and listed his name as Dozel Goldstein. He kept their last name because his own was hard for Americans to pronounce."

"Do you know what that last name was?"

Goldstein looked down at his hands. "Uh . . . no. As embarrassed as I am to admit it." He looked at Ben. "I don't expect either of you to understand but I wanted nothing from his past to connect me to fucking Germany." He turned his attention back to Stan. The two men stared at one another in silence for a moment, each understanding what the other did not voice. Then Goldstein finally said, "You're saying that one of those prints belonged to my father?"

"Fourth finger, left hand, top of the weapon."

Ben felt something in his gut twist into a knot of barbed wire when he realized it was this that Maureen had wanted to warn him about.

"The other print," said Stan, "belongs to Cheryl Denise Powell. I take it that was your wife's maiden name, Ben?"

"Yes," he replied, sinking down into his chair.

"Right index finger. On the trigger."

"God almighty . . ."

"I'm sorry, you guys. I really am. But their prints were in the system and they matched. Not quite as precisely as the others, but there were enough reference points for a positive make." He turned to Al and said, "Your father's prints were transferred from INS when he took the oath of citizenship, married your mother, and moved to Ohio." Then he looked at Ben. "Cheryl's prints were taken when she was eleven years old and toured the Columbus Police Station with her Girl Scout troop."

"I still have her uniform and merit badges," Ben said,

feeling something swell in his throat. He faced his captain. "So much for keeping this separate from my personal life."

"You see me jumping for joy?"

"No, sir. Sorry."

"Yeah. Me too." Goldstein looked at his watch, then at Stan. "You're gonna have to run this through the whole network now, aren't you?"

"I *have* to—it's one of the things we agreed to when the system was installed. The FBI has to be informed of anything like this as soon as all the results are available. Does this mean the feds get to come in and stomp all over you?"

"Yes."

Without blinking or shifting his gaze, Stan snapped his fingers and said, in a straight-faced monotone, "Oh, darn, and here I forgot to run cross-reference checks in our neighboring states. I'm still in Ohio's system. Gosh, this could take hours, maybe a whole 'nother day. Who knows, with a colorful character like myself at the keyboard?"

"Is that what you are?"

"Yeah. Twenty years in a wheelchair staring at prints and eating takeout makes you colorful."

"Put everything together and stuff it into an encrypted file. Does anyone besides Maureen and the three of us know about this yet?"

"No."

"Keep it that way for a little while. We've got to haul ass out of here and meet the mayor. Do me a favor? Make photocopies of the original latent and any six of the matches—excluding my father and Ben's wife. Then fax them over to the mayor's office. They should get there right about the time we do."

As soon as Ben and Goldstein were on their feet the door to Stan's office flew open and one of the Dispatch supervisors rushed in. "Sorry, sir, but a call just came in. Two officers down."

"Jesus. Who?"

"Number 19. Sanderson and Wagner."

Ben saw Goldstein's face go pale, but when he spoke his voice was tight and steady; grace under pressure.

"I want every available unit out there."

"But—"

"Now."

"Yessir, but the caller—"

"Now, goddammit!"

"The caller said they were dead."

33

Their throats had been clawed open, their eyes torn out, their eyelids stapled to their foreheads, silver coins jammed into the bloody eye sockets.

Sanderson's torso had somehow been pushed through the windshield and lay against the hood; Wagner was pulled from behind with such force that the seat had been wrenched off its track. A large hole had been ripped through the backseat from the trunk, enabling Ben to see the trunk was empty.

"Oh, Christ," he whispered. "The dog."

"What?" shouted Goldstein, trying to supervise the placing of roadblocks and barricades. It looked as if every cop in the city was there, all of them shocked, angry, and yelling at everyone or anything. To the best of Ben's knowledge it had been ten, maybe twelve years since a Cedar Hill police officer had been killed in the line of duty.

"The dog," he said again.

Goldstein shouted, "So where the hell is it?"

As the paramedics took the bodies away, Ben stopped a uniformed officer and asked if he or anyone in the neighborhood had seen a large black dog in the past thirty minutes; the officer shook his head.

Goldstein pulled Ben aside. "Is it possible the dog wasn't dead, only wounded? Maybe—"

"No, sir," said Ben. "That thing was *dead*. They put five rounds into it; three in the gut, two between its eyes. I saw the body. It was dead."

Goldstein peered into the back of the cruiser. "Looks like a fucking bomb went off in here."

An EMT shouted, "Captain! Over here!"

They ran over to the ambulance and climbed in back.

"What is it?" said Goldstein.

The EMT put on fresh latex gloves and gestured for them to do the same, then pulled back the sheet and pointed toward the mangled glob of meat and cartilage that had been Sanderson's throat. "Something's been jammed in there."

"Would you mind giving us a couple of minutes alone?" asked Ben. The EMT nodded her head, climbed out, and closed the doors.

Digging the tweezers from his pocket *(like you expect there to be fingerprints this time)*, Ben retrieved the object, carefully working the rolled note from inside the plastic bag.

"Well?" asked Goldstein.

Ben took a breath. "It says: 'I think the Hannibal question is a little beyond you, so try this one: Why does the dogwood have three red spots? You might ask Emily Modine that one, or even Mozart, if you can find his grave. The city of Vienna has been looking for it for almost two centuries.'"

Goldstein leaned forward and put his face in his hands. "And the other side?"

"The lyrics to John Lennon's 'Imagine.' And it's signed, 'Sincerely, Hoopsticks.'"

Goldstein exhaled and sat up straight. His composure was almost frightening. "Twenty years I've been a cop and in all that time the worst we've ever had to deal with were those .45-caliber killings a few years back. You hadn't made detective yet, Ben, but I figure you heard about it. Took us two weeks to track down those crankheads. A turf war. Boy, was the chief disappointed. He thought we had an honest-to-Pete serial killer on our hands, headlines, his picture on the front page." A small sneer appeared on his face, then just as quickly vanished. "Looks like we got one now." He rubbed his eyes. "Sanderson and his wife were gonna have a baby soon. Two months, maybe less. I don't suppose you'd care to volunteer to go tell the woman she's a widow? Don't bother answering, it wasn't a real question."

Ben closed his eyes and thought: . . . *we're gonna have a baby . . . a baby . . . we're gonna have a baby, Ben! God, I love you . . .*

"Okay," said Goldstein, taking the note from Ben after he'd slipped it back in the evidence bag. "This is the first concrete link we've got between the killings and the headstones at the cemetery. That'll give us some weight, so as far as we're concerned, the tapes still don't exist."

"We still have four bodies missing from the truck stop."

"I can add and subtract, thank you. I'm going back to the station to see if the ME's report is in yet. I'll send two units to search the cemetery grounds. You head out there and wait for them. Get your ass out there, as well. I'll send Emerson and the CSU team along as soon as they're finished at the diner. Walk them through the place. Try to remember the same route you took this morning. I want it treated as a crime scene—evidence, pictures, notes, plaster cast of anything that looks like a recent footprint, tire marks—you know the drill." He leaned forward, gesturing for Ben to do the same. "If you're asked about it later, you were out there on a temporary Code 5, got it?"

"A stakeout? I don't—"

"The WPS are going to want a list of everything we've been doing since the original killings took place. The chief and the mayor are always impressed with a Code 5. I'm not asking you to lie, Ben; I'm asking you to restructure the facts to create a more useful truth."

"Understood."

"Short of digging up the bodies, I want you to bring everything you possibly can back from that cemetery, got it? Find out if he's placed any more new headstones. I want this bastard's head for my personal piss-pot—but of course I never said that."

"Said what?"

"That's my boy."

Ben reached up and massaged his neck.

34

he's thinking about his dream again. i know. i'm the one who sent it to him. this promises to be interesting. but i knew that the first time i saw him.

a pity. his wife had such a lovely face. it's no wonder he misses her so much.

. . . .

yes, my torturer. i found another one.
and there's not a thing you can do about it.
is there?
not without finally showing mercy to me and my brother.
and you can't have that, can you?

. . . .

no. i don't imagine that would do at all.

35

Arliss had decided to stop at the Sparta for breakfast on his way home. The waitress smiled at him with tired eyes—always there were the tired eyes—and served him his meal. Her pale skin had too much makeup and told Arliss how much she wished she were beautiful, even just a little; even merely pretty. She told him a joke as she refilled his coffee, and it was a good joke, and Arliss laughed, and the waitress laughed, and something might have passed between them at that moment but Arliss couldn't tell. Too often laughter is mistaken for the sound of happiness.

As he left the waitress told him to have a nice day. Arliss wished her the same. Once outside he made a fist, stuck out his index finger and lifted his thumb, pointing at her through the window but she didn't see.

Bang.

There.

You'll never have any more nights longing for the warm body of a lover next to yours, touching you. You'll never again have to smile when you don't feel like it. I love you. Thanks for the joke. It was a good one. Maybe I'll share it on my way home.

And the dim and terrible voice in his head began to

whisper words he didn't understand, but knew were intended to guide him: *Passio Christi, comforta me. O bone Jesu, exaudi me. Intra tua absconde me. Ne permittas me separari a te.*

The bag of seeds tucked under his arm, Arliss began the long walk home. He needed to walk today. There were plans to make. He only hoped that Mom, Dad, and his sister wouldn't be too worried when he was late.

By the time he passed St. Francis on Granville Street, he'd already scattered a dozen bags of seeds. Outside the church, an old priest was crouching down, tending to a small garden in front of the statue of the Virgin Mary. Arliss stopped to admire his flowers.

"They're lovely," he said, because they were. The priest thanked Arliss for his kindness in noticing, Arliss told him there was no kindness involved, that beauty creates its own reward.

"That's a nice way to look at it," said the priest, returning to his work.

"Father?"

"Monsignor, actually."

"Might you be interested in some more seeds for your garden?"

He waved Arliss away. "I don't have the money to buy anything from you."

Arliss set down Seed Man's bag next to the monsignor. "I don't want to sell you anything. I just want to give these seeds to you for your garden."

"Well, then, I apologize for jumping to that conclusion, and I thank you kindly."

"I only ask that you listen to a story I have to tell."

The monsignor considered this for a moment, then gave a slow nod of his head. "I'll be able to make the place quite lovely with these," he said, looking through the different types of seeds inside the bag. "Please, then. Your story."

Arliss knelt beside him and began:

"On a Florida beach one afternoon, while everyone was sunning themselves or swimming or playing volleyball, a figure in a flowing white robe descended from the sky. He said that he was Jesus. The fun-in-the-sun crowd didn't believe him and asked him to prove it. 'Feed all of us with this bottle of mineral water and these two fish sticks!' said one girl. So Jesus blessed these items and soon everyone was munching happily away. But still the crowd needed more proof. 'I can't swim because my left leg is lame,' said a little boy. 'Can you heal me, please?' So Jesus touched the boy's leg and restored it to health. Still the crowd wanted more. 'Walk on the water!' someone shouted. So Jesus got into a rowboat and went out several hundred yards to where the water was deepest. Everyone watched breathlessly as he stood up in the boat and touched the surface of the water with his big toe. 'I do this so that your faith may be restored,' he said. 'I do this so that hunger and sorrow and loneliness and pain and despair will never again taint your spirits.' Then he stepped out of the boat and immediately sank.

"He swam back to shore and walked back onto the beach where everyone was laughing at him. Jesus looked at them for a few more moments, then began ascending back to Heaven. Before he disappeared from view, he looked down at the crowd and said: 'Give me a break. The last time I did that I didn't have holes in my feet.'"

The monsignor fixed Arliss with a cold stare. "I don't think that's very funny, young man."

"Neither do I, Father. I happen to think it's rather sad." Arliss rose to his feet. "Maybe you'll understand someday."

"Understand what?"

"That even the greatest failures are born out of love."

And with that, Arliss left the monsignor to his gardening.

36

The monsignor stared at Arliss's retreating figure for a minute, then turned his attention back to the overturned soil at the Virgin's feet, hoping he wouldn't have another dizzy spell like the one he'd experienced a moment ago when the young man had been telling that offensive joke. Odd, how that young man's intense eyes had made him feel slightly disoriented.

Once again, the monsignor found his thoughts going out to the families of the victims killed in that horrible shooting last night. He stopped his gardening, made the sign of the cross, and began to say a prayer for the souls of both the victims and those they had left behind.

A scream erupted from inside the church.

The monsignor snapped his head up, jumped to his feet, ran across the yard, up the cement steps, and through one set of the double oak doors that led inside.

37

Arliss had no idea how long he walked, the places he went, the people he smiled at, waved to, spoke with. All he could see was the sparkle in their eyes, the same sparkle, the one you learn to recognize when working nights. They all needed something so much, a sense of comfort, of belonging, of being loved and having that love returned in equal measure.

Arliss pointed at them—*Bang!*—took it all away, gave them peace.

Sometime later he passed a small retarded girl who was playing with a doll in her front yard. She seemed utterly content. There was no pain in her life for Arliss to take away and he immediately felt an affinity for her, a special love. He wanted to embrace her, to kiss her cheek, to tell her of all that he had learned. Only she would understand, being so much closer to God than everyone else.

From across the street Arliss waved at her, and she smiled.

"Dolly," she said, holding up her treasure. "Dolly dress."

"I love you, Dollydress," whispered Arliss. Then walked the rest of the way home.

His father was in the backyard, hobbling around on a

pair of metal arm crutches, trying to start the coals for a cookout. He liked cookouts, considered himself to be something of a backyard gourmet chef. Arliss stood by the broken fence and watched him; the way he stacked the charcoal, the way he measured the fluid, the way he tossed the match in *just so*. Things like this were his big projects now since the accident at the mill that had left him like this. Skilled hands going to waste, attached to a broken body that was never going to properly heal. He saw Arliss and smiled, so proud.

"Hope you're hungry, workin' man," he said. "I know it's a little chilly out, but I felt like grillin' today."

"No problem here," replied Arliss.

His sister was setting out paper plates on an old card table in the backyard and trying to arrange the lawn chairs so everyone would have enough elbow room. She'd recently lost out on a cheerleading position at school. Arliss could see that it still hurt.

Do you weep? he wondered. *Do you cry at night because you listen to all the latest music, read all the right magazines, and thumb through paperback books that tell you How You Can Be More Popular, but your weekends are still spent in front of the television with the rest of the family? Do you lie in bed wishing for a boy to call you, someone who's noticed all your efforts and wants to be your friend?*

She looked at Arliss and stuck out her tongue, then laughed. Arliss could always make her laugh, though he don't know how or why.

Inside the house, Arliss's mother was sitting in front of the television folding freshly cleaned clothes. All day long for the past twenty years she worked pressing clothes at Cedar Hill's only dry-cleaning shop, and here she was on her day off doing basically the same thing. She looked so tired, so worn and sad, but at least she had her favorite programs to look forward to.

Why, Mom? thought Arliss. *Do you dream? Do you? Do you imagine that someday you'll get lucky and hit the lottery? Is that why you always manage to scrape together enough to buy ten dollars' worth of tickets every week? And in this dream, is your family happy? Do we all smile and embrace you and tell you how the money doesn't matter because you've always been so good to us? Are these the things you dream about while pressing clothes and breathing steam? Does it help when your lower back is killing you? Does it comfort you when you go to the grocery store knowing that your family will again have to eat macaroni and cheese three times this week?*

He didn't know what he felt as he stood there watching her. He just hoped it wasn't pity. He leaned over and kissed her cheek. She seemed so interested in the television program.

"What're you watching?"

"Huh?" She looked at him, then at the television. "I don't know, just . . . some show." She looked at her hands, cracked her knuckles, and then sighed. "Did you remember to get some of that new kind of aspirin for your dad? You know, them capsule ones with the flag on the label? His hip's really been bothering him and those pills seem to be the only thing that help."

Arliss produced them from his pocket and she smiled.

"Oh, you're so thoughtful. Your dad was just saying the other night how proud he is of you. You didn't say no when we needed you. It was a wonderful thing you done for us, hon, puttin' off college to get a job and help us out with the bills."

"I love you, Mom."

"I love you, too, hon. Where have you been, anyway? We was gettin' worried."

"Just out walking. It's a nice day for it."

"I guess. I been folding clothes all morning. Isn't *that*

a pisser? One day off a week, and I spend it . . ." She
shook her head and laughed, but only a little. "I shouldn't
complain. I'm lucky to have a job."

How do you thank someone for caring for you? Arliss
asked the dim voice in his head. *I don't mean for loving
you, I mean for the little things—the laundry and food
and the toilet paper that's always there and the extra bit
of change when you're a little short. How can the words
"thank you" erase the ache of a lifetime's work that you
feel has come to nothing?*

He started up the stairs. At the top of the landing a
charcoal sketch of Christ hung on the wall. This picture
has been in Arliss's family for so long that no one could
remember where it came from, or who originally pur-
chased it. The eyes of this picture followed you everywhere, and until he was fifteen Arliss avoided going
anywhere near it.

Now he stood directly before it, hating the peaceful
expression on the Savior's face.

"Why?" he asked it.

Tell me.

*They've tried, they really have, we've all tried to get by
and keep alive a faith in something bigger, the idea that it
will all work out in the end, and beneath it all is the hope
that one day you'll hit the lottery, nothing spectacular, mind
you, just enough to help even things out. You wash the
clothes, you stack the charcoal, you sell seeds for your
dodder, and you try to believe. But every time you're lost
in a pleasant reverie or dream something happens that
snaps you back, and you find yourself sitting in your living room on furniture that needs to be replaced but you
can't afford it, and, hell, some of it's not even paid for yet,
just like the television and the house and everything else
around you, and you realize that your accomplishments
are fleeting but by God there has to be a reason . . .*

"I'm waiting," Arliss said.

The charcoal eyes stared at him. The picture offered no response.

No Dollydress scooter for the garden because love is a failure . . .

. . . to work all your life to provide for those you love, to do this thing, this seemingly inconsequential but ultimately selfless and remarkable thing, to do this and ask for nothing in return, to work like that without complaint or much hope of getting ahead with the next paycheck, to say your prayers at night and hope that someone somewhere is listening as you ask for courage and strength because your children gave up their education just so you could afford to live, and you want for them to have all the things you never could but now they can't even have less because the union turns its back on you when you're hurt and people go on suffering and feeling lonely and the only person who could understand is cooing over her dolly, so you sit there in front of an 18×20-inch box, hoping that something good is going to appear on the screen and make you laugh, make you think that maybe life isn't the dumper it seems, but it is and you know it because God, the Savior, GreatSavior, greatsavior who loves you and gave you gardens and dollydresses and weapons and televisions and unions, this greatsavior is also a sadist but doesn't even know it.

Arliss went to his father's room and unlocked the gun cabinet. His dad used to go hunting with his brother every year but dear brother didn't come around anymore. Dad always kept the guns cleaned and oiled in the hope that he'd get to go hunting again someday. Arliss emptied it of all weapons—shotguns, rifles, handguns, cartridges—and took everything to his room.

He laid out the rifles, just as the dim voice told him to.

Ab hoste maligno defende me.

He loaded the shotguns and handguns.

In hora mortis meae voca me.

He stacked up the cartridges along the wall.

Et jube venire ad te . . .

He then picked up one of the rifles and opened his bedroom window.

His mother had joined his sister and father in the backyard.   •

Arliss felt a tear brimming in his eye.

I wanted to take it all away and make everything better. I wanted to erase your sadness and loneliness. To make you forget about all the ways you've lost out in life. To give you something golden and true.

He took a deep breath as he focused his mother in the scope.

(—so proud of you—)

Forgive me, all of you.

Ut cum Sanctis tuis laudem te . . .

I wanted to save you.

(—didn't say no when we needed—)

Hold your breath, that's it, focus, steady, steady, c'mon . . .

I wanted so much for you.

In saecula saeculorum . . .

But I've got holes in my feet.

Amen.

The first shot was easy, just squeeze the trigger snap back and the recoil feels so hard like the Confirmation slap, the smoke spit out, threw the greatsavior's kiss, and Arliss saw something register on his mother's face and for a moment she looked just like—

—like—

—*like the time you lost twenty dollars from your check after you'd cashed it to go to the grocery store and I remember, Mom, how you cried because your feet had been hurting so much that week and that was money you'd had to stand for three hours to earn and now there you were having to put stuff back in the checkout line and three hours of your work and pain was for nothing because your family couldn't have some of the extra goodies like you'd wanted and even though I was little I cried just like you did, Mom, and your tears were seeds and I saved one for you, here—*

She caught it just below the base of her skull, Arliss's kiss, and fell forward over the table, wine spilling from her mouth, flowing wine, dark wine, come, all of you, and drink from this cup, this cup of my blood, which shall be shed for your sins, but then Arliss's sister was screaming, so—

—so—

—*so what if nobody asked you to the homecoming dance? You can go by yourself a lot of people do* I always go by myself I want to have a lot of friends even just one *but you never did, Sis, because you're plain, just like me, and the world doesn't embrace the plain to its bosom, we have to make due with the powdered milk of human kindness so I give you—*

—the smoke of a dozen black-red roses. She took them to her chest and clutched them there, the first roses she'd ever received from anyone, calling out, her mouth opening and closing but there was no sweet sound because suddenly Arliss's father, no fear in his voice, brave old broken man, was stumbling toward her as Arliss took a deep breath and sent—

—sent—

—*sent me to the store on my birthday because you knew how much I liked to roast marshmallows in the fireplace, so I went because I knew you were planning something special, and I got the marshmallows but you surprised me by meeting me when I was halfway home, and we walked together, and you had your arm around me, so proud of your boy, and I knew there was going to be a big, roaring fire waiting for us when we came*

through the door, but when we got home there was noth-
ing left of your fire but smoldering ashes and you looked
so ashamed because you'd tried to do something special
and failed again and you looked at me and said I wish—
      —I wish—

—and Arliss sent him that wish, sent it right to his
face, all over his face, through his face, and then there
was smoke and the heat from the guns and soon nothing but peace and silence and Arliss knew he'd been
forgiven because even in the bitter smoke of failure
there is still beautiful, fulfilling, triumphant love.

He fell back, sweating. He had done as the dim, terrible voice had told him.

He had saved them.

Arliss sat up, removed his shoes, and then pulled off
his socks.

The two holes were red and moist and he could easily see where the spikes had been driven through them.
He looked at his hands and saw that they too carried
the marks. He watched, smiling, as the holes began to
transform, becoming thicker, fuller, running their tongues
around their circumference, and he knew he was staring
at something truly miraculous, a miracle out of nowhere,
because the two holes had become lips, and the lips
were whispering to him, but their words were in a language he didn't understand, so he lifted the speaking
hands to cover his ears, maybe that was the secret to
understanding their message, and just to be safe he
pressed the soles of his feet together so their lips could
meet and soon, very soon, their unintelligible voices
merged into a single voice, dim and terrible, and it told
Arliss that he had done well, but there was one last
thing he had to do and he had to do it *now*.

Neighbors were screaming then, someone was pounding on the front door. The yard was filling up with people,
so Arliss grabbed the nearest rifle and began sending all

of them peace and roses and kisses as sirens came screaming in from the distance and the pounding downstairs gave way to an explosion and the sound of many footsteps running up the stairs toward his room—

—getting closer, they were getting closer, be here any second now, so he turned one last time toward the scene in the backyard, blew his family a kiss, chambered a round in his father's favorite handgun and turned it toward his face—

—screaming, yelling, getting closer—

—Arliss looked toward the sound, waited for them to enter; he had to time this exactly right—

—he took a deep breath—

—the door flew open—

—and Arliss decorated the wall behind him with the rose blossom that had always been inside of his head.

In saecula saeculorum.

Amen. . . .

38

From the bloody exit wound in the back of Arliss's head, a dark wing fluttered out, followed by another, and a moment later the black butterfly emerged and crawled out the open window.

39

Ben's radio squawked at him as soon as he climbed into his car. "D-19, D-19, you've got a 10-21, approximately 11:48 A.M. Urgent. Repeating, urgent."

Ben radioed Dispatch and got the number. Pulling out his cell phone, he cursed under his breath and punched in the number.

The person answered on the first ring. "Ben? This is Monsignor Maddingly at St. Francis de Sales on Granville Street." Ben had known Maddingly for most of his life—in fact, Maddingly had baptized him, married Ben and Cheryl, and presided over Cheryl's funeral. "Could you get over here right away? I know you've got your hands full right now but . . . please, Ben. Believe me, it's urgent. And don't use the siren. You don't want to draw attention to this just yet."

Ben hung up, then called Bill Emerson and asked him to get to St. Francis as soon as he could. He then rolled down the window of his car, and called to one of the officers on the scene. He told the officer to gather the rest of the uniforms assigned to stake out the County Home Cemetery, head on out, and wait there, he'd be along as soon as he could.

"I want a cruiser at each of the three entrances," he said. "Nobody goes in, nobody comes out, understand me?"

"Yes, sir."

Ben started his car, radioed in, then hit the gas and took off.

40

Stan Roth stared at the monitor. He'd been rerunning the Panic Hand Program since Ben and Goldstein had left in an effort to make sure he hadn't screwed things up. *No way* these results could be what they were.

"Son-of-a-bitch," he whispered, rolling his wheelchair closer. The screen went blank for a second, and then a code appeared in the upper right-hand corner: J-30. This meant that it was going to rebuild the handprint piece by piece, starting in the center of the palm. A one-on-one square appeared in the center of the screen, displaying a double loop whorl.

"You gotta be fucking kidding me," said Stan to himself, typing in a command to enlarge the one-on-one square. It was indeed a double loop whorl. Damn thing looked like an owl mask.

He checked the code again. This was supposed to be in the *center* of the hand? He called up the next square, I-29. It should have been the index finger with its pronounced Mount of Jupiter.

What he got was another owl mask.

He tried it three more times, requesting three different sections of the handprint, and was shown three more double-loop-whorl owl masks.

Fine.

"All right, then, smart-ass—" he pressed the PROCEED key "—put it all together for me and maybe I can figure out if and where you wandered off the highway."

Staring with the original J-30 center square, the program began reconstructing the hand square by square; one double loop whorl, then another, then another, the first three combining to form a shapeless cluster.

The next double loop whorl automatically rotated on its axis by thirty degrees, then was set in place next to the cluster. The next double loop rotated thirty-six degrees before being set in place over the previous one. This went on for several minutes, each trio of double loops appearing, being shrunken down to a one-on-one size, then set in place beside the previous cluster of three as the whole was magnified to show how all of the clusters were cumulatively constructing a large owl mask.

It wasn't until the "hand" was nearly finished that Stan realized what he was looking at, and even then he had to roll over to the bookshelf and find a specific reference book, and then riffle through the pages to make absolutely certain. He stared at the page in the book, and then his own hand, and then the image displayed on the screen, which was still rotating and layering double loop whorls on top of double loop whorls.

"*Fractals?*" he shouted at the screen. "You're showing me fucking *fractals?*"

The computer beeped. All finished.

Stan stared at the screen, feeling confused, numbed, and nearly defeated.

He wasn't even aware that Maureen had come in behind him. She stood behind him, looking over his shoulder.

"Glad to see you've been making the most of your time," she said.

Stan just shook his head.

"So this is what you've been doing?" said Maureen. "Using the computer to draw a picture of a big butterfly?"

"I don't know what the hell this is, Maureen. I've never seen anything like it."

She shrugged. "That's really too bad, Stan. No one was supposed to recognize the pattern for a few more hours." She bent down and kissed him, simultaneously pressing the business end of a pistol with a silencer attachment against his chest and squeezing the trigger.

The force of the blast blew the wheelchair back a foot or so. Stan was still alive, but just barely.

Maureen looked at him, her eyes filling with tears. "I loved you, too, you cantankerous old ass. I'm sorry. I tried. But I've got holes in my feet."

She pushed the gun into her mouth and squeezed the trigger.

She and Stan died at the same instant. Had he thought about it for a moment, Stan would have thought it kind of romantic.

For at least they died together.

41

Monsignor Maddingly was waiting in front of the church. Ben parked his car and threw open the door, nearly hitting Maddingly in the nuts.

"Jesus, Monsignor, watch it, will you?"

"Sorry, Ben, I was just—oh, screw it! Just come along, quickly, *please.*"

Ben joined him and they ran up the stairs to the center set of large double oak doors that led inside.

"Our cleaning lady found them," said Maddingly, opening the doors.

Even from where he stood—some thirty yards away— Ben could see the two bodies hanging by their necks from beams above the altar, bookends to the solid-gold crucifix that hovered in the center.

Ben and Maddingly approached slowly, the echo of their footsteps bouncing off the stained-glass windows depicting saints and prophets in solemn, multicolored meditation.

Both bodies were naked and had evacuated their bowels on the altar; the sickening, cumulative stench of piss, excrement, and incense made Ben's stomach turn. He stared up at the bodies and saw the deep, bloody scratch marks on their throats; frenzied marks, proof of panic, as if they'd been trying to—

"Oh God," he whispered. "They were still alive."

A soft shaft of sunlight resolved into a solid beam as it passed through the stained-glass eyes of the Virgin Mary and reflected off the silver coins that had been used to replace the eyes of both corpses.

A glob of piss-soaked excrement dropped from the leg of one body and spattered with a soft *ping!* against the rim of a gold chalice positioned in the center of the altar.

The chalice was filled to overflowing with human eyes and their still-attached stalks.

"Did you touch anything?" asked Ben.

"Of course not," replied Maddingly. Then: "No, wait—I *did* touch the phone in the sacristy and the left handle on the center door."

Covering his mouth and stepping to the altar, Ben saw four letters scribbled in shit on the white silk cloth that covered the marble:

DAMA

"Do you know what this means?" he asked Maddingly. "Is it part of something Latin?"

"Not that I can recall. But I'll check, I promise you."

Ben was impressed by the monsignor's outward calm. He stepped down and led Maddingly toward the sacristy. "You need to lock all the doors."

"All of the doors are already locked, except the ones we came through."

"Good. Where's the phone?"

Maddingly pointed it out, and Ben called Dispatch. Without going into details, he said that he needed Bill Emerson and the CSU team over here as soon as they were finished at the diner. After hanging up, he turned to Maddingly and said, "I hate to tell you this, but you're going to have to move all masses for at least the next couple of days."

"I figured as much. Just let me say a few more prayers over the bodies before you call this in."

Ben nodded, and for some reason felt compelled to ask: "Will you say a prayer for the soul of their killer?"

"Yes. But given my druthers I'd prefer to break his knees with a baseball bat."

"That makes two of us." Ben gripped Maddingly's hand. "Thanks for calling, Monsignor. We'll assign a surveillance unit for the next forty-eight hours, just in case he tries to get to you or the cleaning lady. I'll need to talk with her before anyone else arrives."

"She's been taken to the convent."

"What time did she discover the bodies?"

Maddingly looked at his watch. "No more than twenty minutes ago. She'd just come in to work."

"Where did she come in?"

Maddingly pointed to a side door, on the north side of the church, that led into the sacristy. "She has her own set of keys."

"Did she say anything about seeing someone?"

"No, she didn't see anyone, I asked. But I did." Maddingly described his encounter with the young man who'd given him the bag full of seeds a little while ago. Ben asked if Maddingly could remember what the young man looked like and much to his surprise the monsignor was able to give a rather detailed description. But something about Maddingly seemed to change when he repeated the joke the young man had told to him; it was as if the monsignor's mind were, for the moment, separating itself into two halves: the part that was telling the joke, the other half remembering—or *trying* to remember—something that might have crossed his thoughts when he was listening to the joke for the first time.

As Maddingly finished recounting the joke, he put a hand to his head and wobbled slightly. Ben slipped an arm around the monsignor's shoulders. "Are you all right?"

"I, uh . . . sorry. Sorry, Ben, a little wrung out, I guess."

Ben led him over to a brown leather recliner that sat in front of the sliding-door closet that contained the cassocks and surplices worn by the celebrants for Mass. After getting Maddingly situated, Ben went into the restroom and ran some tap water into one of the disposable cups sitting on the counter. He handed it to Maddingly, who emptied it in a single gulp.

"Thanks," said Maddingly, handing the cup back to Ben. "I don't know what came over me. The same thing happened right after that young man told me that joke. I felt . . . felt . . ."

"Nauseous?" said Ben.

"Oh, no, no . . . not at all. More . . . dizzy and disoriented than anything else. I . . ." He closed his eyes for a moment, then exhaled and shook his head.

Ben asked: "What is it?"

"Nothing. It has nothing to do with—"

"—stop right there," said Ben. "With all due respect, Monsignor, right now you're a witness, and I have to treat you as such—and that includes *not* letting you decide what does and doesn't factor into this. I don't want you to hold back anything, regardless of how inconsequential or even stupid it might seem to you. I need to know it all, including anything that might have crossed your mind during the encounter. You'd be surprised how often a stray, seemingly unrelated thought will trigger the memory of some forgotten detail."

Maddingly looked up at him and suddenly Ben saw in the old man's eyes the same confusion, disgust, and sadness that had been there on the morning of Cheryl's funeral.

Don't think about that now, Ben told himself. *Just . . . just don't.*

"Listen, Ben, I don't know if . . . if . . ."

"If what? C'mon, Monsignor, *please.*"

"Look, I haven't exactly been the most popular person in this parish for a few weeks. Do you remember that priest in Zanesville who was accused of molesting those three little boys?"

Ben nodded. "Yes. The boys later confessed they were lying and the charges were dropped."

"But that's not the point, Ben. The point is that I have been friends with Father Reynolds since he served at this parish over ten years ago. I *knew* he was incapable of having done what he was accused of, and while I don't deny that the Catholic Church does have its share of . . . of priests like that, I also know Jim Reynolds isn't one of them. The bishop, the parish council, and a good majority of our congregation made it abundantly clear to me that I was not to testify on his behalf at the hearing if I were asked to."

"I remember," Ben said. "You'd volunteered to be a character witness for him."

"Yes. And even though those boys confessed to lying before Jim even *had* a hearing, the fact that I'd volunteered to be a character witness for him painted a target on my forehead, as far as some of the more powerful parishioners here are concerned. I am not naive, Ben. I know damn well there are people here who're just waiting for me to screw up so they can petition for my transfer. I am sixty-seven years old and have been at this parish for over thirty years. When I retire in a year or two I'd rather it be my own choice and not because people think I've become mentally incompetent. I don't mind the bullshit that goes along with this position, and Heaven knows I've locked horns with the parish council before, but it would . . . it would kill me to lose this parish in that way."

"How bad can it be?"

"Bad enough that I don't want any written or recorded record of what I have to say."

Ben held out his hands. "Do you see a notebook or my recorder?"

"I need your word that what I'm about to tell you will stay in this room."

"I can't promise that, Monsignor, not if it's something that could help us catch this guy—but I *will* promise you that I won't make any notes or record your voice. If it comes down to it, if something you have to tell me is important to this investigation, then I'll credit it to an anonymous tip."

Maddingly nodded his head. "Thank you."

"What happened after he told you the joke?"

Maddingly sat forward, resting his elbows on his knees. "As I said, I felt unbelievably disoriented for several moments—detached from my surroundings, as if I were no longer completely inside my body. I thought I was going to pass out. But when I came back to myself—and mind you, this took maybe five, ten seconds—I blinked and looked at the young man and . . .

"The only thing I can liken it to was something I saw on television a few years ago. I was watching a PBS special on how animators worked back in the old days. One of the fellows they talked to was a very old gentleman who'd worked at Disney on both *Fantasia* and *Snow White and the Seven Dwarves.* He talked about these things called 'cellophanes'—'cells,' as he called them. He showed how part of the background for a scene would be hand-drawn on one clear cell sheet, then another cell with a different part of the background would be layered on top of it, then another and another until you had perhaps a dozen cells, each with something different drawn on it, and all of them, combined, made up the picture on the screen.

"*That's* what everything looked like to me for a few moments after I came back to myself, Ben. It looked as if some unseen hand was peeling back the cells one sheet at a time to give me a clear look at what truly lay underneath the surface of the everyday world.

"I consider myself to be a man of strong faith, but there is still a pragmatist in me, a skeptic. I personally don't put much stock in so-called 'visions' and I can't *not* help but question the truthfulness of someone who claims they've had one—look at how many times Elvis Presley has been sighted since he died, or the amount of people who claim to have seen the face of Christ in the surface of a potato. I am also, despite my advanced years, in good physical health and not prone to fits of dementia . . . but I can't think of any other term except 'vision' to describe what I saw at that moment. The 'cells' had been peeled back, and what lay underneath was not very pretty. Or kind. Or compassionate. Or even *human,* for that matter. I won't be so melodramatic as to call it 'evil,' but I can tell you that I have felt that kind of . . . of *darkness* only one other time in my life."

Ben stared at Maddingly for a moment, and then cleared his throat. "Monsignor, I don't mean to sound—"

Maddingly held up his hand, silencing Ben. "I can tell from the expression on your face that you need me to be more specific, correct? Fine.

"When I first began attending seminary there were these two old women who lived in a trailer park just a mile or so away—the Knox sisters, Emily and Flora. Part of our early training was to accompany one of the priests to visit them each week and assist in administering Holy Communion. Emily and Flora had a car but neither of them was particularly fond of driving, so they didn't get into town to attend church on a regular basis, except on holy days. They were passionate in their religious beliefs, Ben—it *defined* them. There were times I fancied I could actually *feel* the heat of their evangelical fervor wafting on the breeze whenever I approached the trailer.

"Flora Knox, who was only fifty, had recently agreed to watch her daughter's infant son while her daughter served a ninety-day jail sentence for . . . I forget what it was she had done, but it doesn't matter. This was not a healthy baby. In the few weeks he'd been in the sister's care he'd suffered a recurrent ear infection, warning signs of asthma, and two bouts of colic. In all fairness to them, Flora and Emily did all they could for him and cared for the baby as best they could. I never doubted for a moment that they loved that baby and wanted nothing but the best for him.

"No one knew why it happened, but suddenly the sisters stopped interacting with the outside world. They bought new locks for their doors and windows, always kept the windows closed and the curtains drawn, and whenever someone would come to the door, they refused to answer, just told the person to go away. The sheriff came by the seminary one day and asked Father Spense if he would accompany him to the sisters' trailer. The sheriff figured that Flora and Emily might give in if both a priest and law-enforcement officer demanded to see them.

"Father Spense asked me to come along. 'The only way to learn proper crisis intervention,' he said to me, 'is to experience it firsthand.' So I went along.

"As we climbed out of the sheriff's car and began walking toward the trailer . . . I knew that all three of them were dead. That heat, that evangelical fervor I'd always felt in the air surrounding the trailer, it was gone, replaced by something . . . I don't know how to describe it, I only know that it terrified me. What surrounded that pathetic silver cigar they called home was more *tragic* than it was evil, but it was as equally destructive—does that make sense? And everything was so silent. I swear I heard not only my blood pulsing through my veins but that of the sheriff and Father Spense, as well. Rarely in my life have I dreaded anything as much as I did entering that trailer—but at the same time, I'd never felt so *alive,* so in tune with all that surrounded me. It was incredibly intimate, almost sensual. I could feel worms burrowing underneath the dirt at my feet. I could hear each individual leaf of every tree sigh as the wind flowed through it. I looked at the sheriff and Father Spense and knew that they were feeling the same way. I think I could have captured the twilight in my hands and drunk it down as if it were well water. For a moment everything was so in sync with that essence of tragedy it would not have surprised me if the whole world were bowing its head and weeping.

"The sheriff had to force the door open, but we managed to get inside.

"The stench was unbelievable. Emily and Flora had evidently convinced themselves that the baby was suffering from demonic possession and not colic or asthma or an ear infection, and that it was screaming so much because of the pain the demon was inflicting on it. They'd tried baptizing the child in boiling water to rid it of the evil spirit. The baby had been scalded to death. It was still floating in the large pot on top of the stove. What skin hadn't sluiced off its tiny body had blistered like bacon left on the griddle for too long.

"Then both Flora and Emily—this was my guess at the time—must have decided that the demon had left the baby at the moment of the child's death and entered both of them. Both of them had swallowed drain cleaner to cast the demon from their bodies. Their insides had bubbled up through their mouths and noses—or at least, that's what it looked like to me. Their bodies were unnaturally swollen. I remember thinking that they looked like a pair of gorged leeches.

"None of us became sick, despite the stench. Mostly what we did for a minute or two was stand there and cry. It was horrible, sickening, pathetic and tragic and sad—a sadness so vast, deep, and merciless it seemed . . . infinite.

"*That's* what I felt when I looked in that young man's eyes and saw the 'cells' peeled back, that sadness. Beyond the brief glimpses of ugliness and terror and violence and depravity and countless abominations that I saw and sensed, there was an infinite sadness a million times or more stronger than what I'd felt in the Knox sisters' trailer that day.

"That's what happened. And then the young man said something to me about failure and love, and then he walked away. The bag of seeds is right where he left them, at the feet of the Virgin Mary statue outside.

"Now, Ben Littlejohn, would you mind telling me how knowing that is going to assist in your investigation?"

Ben shook his head. "I'm sorry, Monsignor. It's my job to ask these questions."

"I understand." He reached out and gave Ben's hand a hard, affectionate squeeze. "Is there anything more I can tell you? Something that might actually *help* you?"

"Yes."

"Name it."

Once again Ben cleared his throat, and then rubbed his neck. "Can you tell me the fable of the dogwood?"

Maddingly stared at him for a moment. "For the investigation? Seriously?"

"Seriously."

Maddingly shrugged, and then said: "There are actually two versions of the fable. The one I tell to the children goes like this: When Jesus was crucified some of His blood dripped onto the petals of a white flower growing at the base of His cross. The flower was so saddened by His suffering that it kept His blood on its petals to remind the world that He tried to save it from suffering. That's why when the dogwood blooms it has a red spot on each of its three petals, to symbolize where the nails went through Christ's hands and feet.

"The other version isn't nearly as sentimental, which probably accounts for it being lesser known."

"Thanks. I'm going to—"

—the growling stopped him.

Low, guttural, and wheezing; from outside the sacristy, near the altar.

Then, the sound of a familiar voice echoing from inside the church proper: "Ben? Ben, you need to get your ass out here. *Now.*" Bill Emerson.

Ben pulled out his .45 and stepped back into the church from the sacristy.

The dog from the truck stop was sitting on top of the altar, staring up at the hanging bodies. Hearing Ben chamber a round from the clip, it snapped its head down and glared at him, dark eyes clouding over into bright silver. Ben could see all five of the large, seeping bullet holes from where it had been shot, and knew that it *had* been dead when it ripped through the back of the trunk and attacked Sanderson and Wagner, and he knew that it was *still* dead—

—*so how?*

It bared its teeth and tensed its legs to pounce as Ben readied to shoot—

—but then it stretched low, threw back its head, and released the longest, loudest, most preternaturally mournful cry Ben had ever heard; it was the cumulative wail of a million broken-hearted men shrieking their anguish into an uncaring night coupled with the screams of a million babies doused in gasoline and set aflame; a rabid, ragged cacophony of fury and despair that shook the overhead beams with such force that the golden crucifix snapped loose and crashed down onto the altar. The keening grew in volume and potency until the stained-glass windows began to rupture in spiderweb patterns, casting off sections of Mary, John the Baptist, St. Francis, and even Jesus Christ.

Maddingly, who'd followed Ben out of the sacristy, pressed his hands against his ears.

Bill Emerson was down on one knee, taking careful aim at the dog's head. "Just give me the word, partner."

Ben felt as if his bones were rattling loose as he also leveled the gun and took aim at the dog—

—that ceased howling, gobbled up a mouthful of eyes from the chalice, and leapt into the aisle, disappearing within the rows of pews. Bill Emerson fired off three rounds and then threw himself between a row of pews as the dog ran past, then fired two more rounds that went directly into the dog's body, but the damned thing kept running.

Ben turned around to make sure Maddingly was all right.

The pipe organ in the loft over the main entrance suddenly began playing "Don't Get Around Much Anymore."

"What the—?" said Ben. He, Bill Emerson, and Maddingly looked up in time to see a shadow move across the loft so quickly that if either of them had blinked they would have missed it.

Maddingly shouted over the deafening music: "There are twenty-five hymns programmed into the organ's memory—and that isn't one of them."

The music suddenly lowered in volume—

—the now-unseen dog howled again—

—and just as soon as Bill Emerson stepped into the aisle machine-gun fire erupted from the loft, splitting one of the beams over the altar; it cracked in half and the two bodies came slamming down.

Bill Emerson also went down.

Ben plowed three shots into the loft but the machine-gun fire didn't stop; as the bodies struck the marble base of the altar a barrage of bullets bounced them around like crazy puppets jitterbugging to the music.

Maddingly, pressed against the door of the sacristy, made the sign of the cross.

"Get back in the sacristy!" shouted Ben, just as the strafing veered to the side and began shattering the solemn statues.

He ran forward, jumping the small carpeted steps that led from the aisle up to the altar, and skidded on his knees to the unconscious heap of his partner. Checking for a pulse, Ben was relieved to find that Bill was still alive but he'd taken two shots—one to the shoulder, the other lower. Near the base of the spine.

Dear God, let it have missed; please let it have missed.

"Call 911!" he screamed. "We need an ambulance! *Now!*"

Hopefully, Maddingly heard him over the racket.

Ben took a deep breath, said another prayer *(Just let me get to the entryway)*, bolted past Bill Emerson, and ran toward the organ loft, pumping round after round toward the flash of gunfire from above.

The machine-gun fire stopped abruptly and a dark shape appeared near the loft's rail.

"Does the flapping of a butterfly's wings in Brazil set off tornadoes in Texas?" it shouted—

—then, with the last few rounds in its clip, blew out the large stained-glass window beside the pipe organ and flung itself outside.

Ben slammed through the unlocked double oak doors and burst into the bright sunlight.

Before he was halfway to the sidewalk he saw the two crucified bodies in the yard of the convent, each nailed to their cross with railroad spikes—one spike through each hand, another through both feet. Both were naked except for the small section of torn and blood-stained cloth tied around their waists.

Ben swung left, then right; the broken glass of the organ-loft window lay scattered about but there was no sign of whoever had jumped through it.

Still holding the .45 in front of him, he walked slowly toward the crucified bodies, oblivious to the screams of passersby and the screech of tires as shocked drivers slammed on their brakes, some colliding with others; the howl of twisted metal, the belch of shattering windshield glass, cries of panic and disgust and horror.

Ben felt the tears on his face but made no move to wipe them away.

Nailed above the head of each body was a piece of wood into which letters had been burned.

The one on the left read *EL.*

The one on the right, *HAC.*

He stared up into the dead glinting silver-coin eyes and felt the world surrender to madness. He felt helpless. Useless. It happened so fast, too damn fast and there wasn't a thing he could do about it so what the hell good was he anymore—

—and so Ben Littlejohn simply stood there, screaming inside.

42

and now, my torturer, he is somewhat aware of what he is dealing with.

. . . .

i wasn't sure that he would do.
but that was just you trying to confuse me, wasn't it?

. . . .

he'll do nicely.
he'll do nicely, indeed.

43

As Ben and Goldstein approached the mayor's office, the secretary looked up from his desk, buzzed open the office door, and shook his head in pity.

They entered.

The Honorable Rachel S. Moore was sitting behind her desk, one hand supporting her bowed head, the other holding a telephone receiver to her ear.

"Yes, sir, I understand. Tomorrow." She hung up and gestured for Ben and Goldstein to sit down. "That was the governor. He's decided that the entire Cedar Hill Police Department couldn't find its ass with both hands, a floodlight, and a fifty-man search party, so he's calling the feds at noon tomorrow—and the *only* reason he agreed to wait that long is because I begged him. I hate to beg, so I'm in a lousy mood, which means you'd better have something for me."

Ben and Goldstein alternated their recitation of the events since the massacre at the diner. When they finished, Mayor Moore shook her head and asked Goldstein for a cigarette. "I don't give a shit if this *is* a smoke-free building." She produced an ashtray from her desk and the three of them lit up.

She looked at Ben and said, "How long were you in the church?"

"Not more than seven or eight minutes. I have no idea where the crosses and bodies were hidden or how he could've gotten them up so quickly without being seen. When he jumped through the window I couldn't have been more than five seconds behind him—but he was gone and the other crosses were up outside. I've been trying to figure it out and it's just not possible. Granville Street is the most traveled in the city."

"No chance the bodies could have already been there and you—"

"Absolutely not."

"I didn't think so. I don't have to tell you how pissed the governor is, what with this being an election year. He doesn't want to call in the feds any more than the rest of us but this has to be taken care of fast or he'll look bad. I guess he took pity on my begging—did I mention that I hate to beg?—and he agreed to make all facilities and personnel at his disposal available to us, including state troopers and National Guard units." She leaned forward and gave both men a hard, unblinking stare.

"One of the people crucified outside the convent was Esther Simms. That grand old woman practically raised me after my mother died." She rubbed her eyes and tried to smile. "I hope that if you get the chance to shoot this psycho you'll have the decency to fire an extra round into him for me."

"With all due respect, Your Honor," said Ben, "my partner and best friend is in surgery right now with a bullet near the base of his spine. He might not be able to move ever again. I understand your feelings. But *one* extra round is not acceptable at this point."

Mayor Moore stared at him for a moment, then nodded her head. "I didn't hear that, of course."

Ben and Goldstein remained silent.

"What about the lab report and the ME's office? Anything there?"

Ben cleared his throat. "We got a detailed report from the lab before we came over here. The coins in the eye sockets of all the victims . . . the minting dates coincide with the birth year of whoever they were attached to."

"Jesus," said Moore. "How in hell could the killer know that?"

Goldstein said, "We wondered if the minting dates might also coincide with the dates of death on the new headstones in the old County Home Cemetery, but they didn't."

"We've got three units stationed out there, along with two from the sheriff's department," added Ben. "They made a thorough search of the grounds but didn't find anything. Those headstones are heavy. He has to store them somewhere nearby."

Moore said, "You do have positive ID on all the victims from the diner, right?"

Ben exchanged a worried look with Goldstein, then said, "Sort of."

"What's that mean?"

"All bodies matched their identification and were positively identified by either friends or relatives, but Stan Roth ran the fingerprints from the bodies and . . ." He exhaled and cracked his knuckles.

"If you want my attention," said the mayor, "you've got it, but my patience is getting a bit strained."

"According to the fingerprints the first half-dozen victims were Richard Speck, Theodore Bundy, Edward Gein, Charles Whitman, Herbert Mullen, and Juan Corona. Those're the only names I can recall without looking in the files, but every set of fingerprints identifies one of the victims as either a dead mass murderer or a dead serial killer. The same goes for the prints left on the weapon and the door of the diner. In some cases, the same killer shows up several times; in other cases, only once. The killer had to have gotten into the system somehow, though Stan didn't say so. He was supposed to fax some material to you."

Rachel Moore lit another cigarette. "I haven't gotten anything from him yet, but that's no surprise—he's always worked on his own bizarre schedule. Anything else?"

"Just that the coins are whole silver and not sandwiched."

"Come again?"

Ben took a quarter from his pocket and showed it to her as he explained. "The U.S. Mint manufactures what are called 'sandwiched' coins for mass circulation. They stopped making whole silver coins before WWII. The majority of coins today are made of nickel and copper." He pointed to the copper strip around the circumference of the quarter. "The coins attached to the victims, despite all of them being dated *after* WWII, were whole silver."

"Any ideas on that?"

"None."

The phone bleeped. Rachel Moore pushed the intercom button. "What is it, Steve?"

"The station manager from WLCB radio is on the line for Captain Goldstein. He says it's an emergency."

She punched the line and handed the receiver to the captain.

Goldstein listened for a moment, then said, "And this was how long ago? Can you run the tape for us? Yes, *now.*" He looked at Moore. "We need the speaker. The killer phoned them about ten minutes ago. The DJ recorded the call."

A crackle of static came over the speaker, followed by a hiss, then the sound of Jack Donovan, Cedar Hill's favorite morning DJ: "WLCB request line. This is Donovan. What would you—"

"This is the person who visited the Moundbuilders Diner this morning, then left an offering at the St. Francis de Sales Church."

"That was all on the news," said the mayor.

The killer: "I have a question for the police: Does the flapping of a butterfly's wings in Brazil set off tornadoes in Texas?"

"*That* wasn't," whispered Ben. "He said the same thing to me at the church."

The killer continued, his words edged with a profound weariness, even sadness: "There are one hundred and fifty-seven bodies buried in the old County Home Cemetery. I have placed headstones on fifteen of their graves for you, one in exchange for each person I have killed thus far. There are also seventy-eight additional unmarked graves on the property where the Hangman's Tavern is located—these being the bodies of blacks who were hanged by the Ku Klux Klan. I am willing to give you some time before I kill anyone else so Captain Goldstein and Detective Littlejohn can piece things together—but if anyone tries to take them off the case I will not hesitate to kill the remaining two hundred and thirty-five people that are needed for . . . balance.

"By the way, I would like Captain Goldstein and Detective Littlejohn to know that Bill Emerson will not die, nor will he be paralyzed from his wounds. Emerson is needed for other things, other events, other investigations, some of which have not yet occurred, but I mustn't get ahead of myself.

"I believe that Detective Littlejohn took physics for a little while when he went to college, so he might understand about the flapping of a butterfly's wings in Brazil; a theory of chaos math, fractals and such, with just a touch of Markov's chain of disintegration. It'll come back to him soon enough.

"As for the letters found in the church and on the

crosses, I've decided to let you chew on that for a while, just to see if you're as bright as I think you are, Benjamin.

"I'm sorry about the people I've killed. And I'm sorry about the people I'm going to *have* to kill. I've spent an eternity being sorry, but for some, 'sorry' just doesn't cut it. Try apologizing to a baby being eaten away by cancer, or to an old woman whose family dumps her in a nursing home to die; try saying 'I'm sorry' to a country filled with starving people or a homeless man who freezes to death on a park bench. You may offer your sympathies to the lonely and broken-hearted people who shamble through the ruined places of this world but, in the end, you walk away. Apologize, then walk away, and feel no responsibility whatsoever.

"That is part of the seed from which the black butterfly was born. And that is why you have to deal with me.

"You cannot protect yourselves.

"Ever.

"Only I can do that."

Click.

Rachel Moore looked first at Ben, then Goldstein, asking respectively: "What the hell does he mean about butterfly wings?"

"Physics was a long time ago," said Ben. "I flunked out of the course after one semester."

Goldstein raised his hands, palms out. "Don't ask me about anything Jewish. I fell away from the faith a long time ago."

She considered all this for a moment. "All right. I'll need a copy of that tape for the governor. Is anyone checking the records at the new County Home? If there's some way we can identify the rest of those bodies—"

"—already doing it," said Ben. "Sheriff Jackson is co-ordinating the searches at the Home, the courthouse,

the county land office, and we've got volunteers checking the burial register of every parish. A record has to
exist somewhere."

"Providing someone thought to make copies and
transfer them before the old Home burned down," said
Goldstein.

"Yeah," said Ben, absentmindedly massaging his throat.

44

you feel it, don't you, benjamin? the memory of your dream?

before you take your wife's place at the all-night market, you're running through a dead field with tears in your eyes. your arms ache because you're carrying something heavy. your chest is crackling with anger, sorrow, confusion, and guilt. you want to be rid of it all.

then you see the tree, and it becomes the first of the teenagers who killed your wife—who killed you—and you wake up choking . . .

. . . and i wonder how you'd react if i said i know what your son's face looks like?

45

Ben and Goldstein were heading back to their cars when Ben's cell phone went off again.

"Hello?"

"Ben?" It was Eunice Emerson. She sounded steady. The woman was a rock. Ben suspected that was one of the reasons Bill had married her.

"How's Bill?"

"He's still in surgery, but one of the interns told me that it's looking good. The bullet in his shoulder was easy, but they're taking their time with the other one. It could be hours. It's in a bad spot, but it *didn't* hit his spine. Isn't that wonderful?"

Ben felt a tear slip from his eyes, then regained his composure. "Best damn news I've heard all day."

"He's going to live."

"That's . . . that's great news, Eunice. Do you want me to come over to the hospital and wait with you?"

"Figured you'd make that offer. No, Ben, you've got your hands full right now, I know. But there is one thing you can do for me."

"Name it, Eunice."

"Find the son-of-a-bitch who shot my husband and make him sorry he was ever born."

"If it's the last thing I do. You got it."

"He really loves you, Ben. So do I."

"I love you too, both of you."

"Tell me that some day we'll all have a good laugh over this. I know we won't, but I need to hear it for now."

"Some day we're all going to have a good laugh over this."

"You're a terrible liar, but thank you."

"I know I am, and you're welcome."

"I'll call you as soon as he's out of surgery."

"You'd better."

Ben had no sooner disconnected the call than his cell rang again. He looked at Goldstein, shrugged, and answered.

"Eunice?"

"Sorry, Ben, no." It was the Reverend. "But how's Bill doing?"

"He's still in surgery, but it looks like he'll make it. What can I do for you, Reverend?"

"Can you get over to the shelter? Something was just delivered that you need to see right away."

"What, exactly?"

"Not over the phone. Please—I know how insane things are right now, but you *have* to see this."

Ben closed his eyes, sighed in frustration, then exhaled. "Give me twenty minutes."

"Thank you."

Ben disconnected the call and relayed the information to Captain Goldstein.

"He wouldn't tell you what it was?"

"No, sir," said Ben. "But he sounded anxious."

"The Reverend doesn't get 'anxious.' That's one steely guy, so it *must* be important. All right, you head over to the shelter and see what's going on there. I'll go back to the station and see if Stan's finished yet. We'll meet at the radio station in—" He checked his watch. "—forty-five minutes."

"Yes, sir."

Goldstein took hold of Ben's arm. "I only heard part of the first call, but I assume that was Eunice?"

"Yes, sir. The killer told us the truth. Bill's going to make it."

Goldstein shook his head. "How the *fuck* could the killer know that?"

"His aim is fairly precise, Captain. He didn't hit one face in the diner."

"So you think he purposefully shot Bill?"

"Yes, sir."

"Why Bill and not you, as well?"

Ben thought about it for a moment. "He knows who we are, and my guess is that, for some reason, he doesn't want Bill to be a part of the investigation. Don't ask me why I think that, I'm not sure I could explain it."

Goldstein stared at Ben for a few moments, began to say something, thought better of it, and then slammed his fist down on the hood of his car. *"Goddammit!"* He turned back to face Ben. "You know, under any other circumstances, I'd question the path of logic that led you to that conclusion, but you know what? I think you're right. He's playing us."

"Maybe the Reverend's got something that will help us get a step ahead, sir."

"Is that your way of telling me we need to get a move on?"

"In so many words."

Goldstein opened his car door. "I'll see you at the radio station in forty-two minutes."

"Yes, sir."

Ben climbed into his own car, and wondered—only momentarily—how the Reverend had gotten his cell phone number.

46

are we now moving toward the end-game, my torturer?

. . . .

i see. have I not done as you've commanded?

. . . .

so a little while longer, yes?

. . . .

i did not want to harm the other detective. he is a decent man, not unlike someone we both once knew and . . .

. . . .

very well. i'll not bring that up.
not yet, anyway.

. . . .

what more can you possibly do to me?
may i have an answer, my torturer?
may i may i may i may i may i may i may i may i may i . . . ?

47

Regardless of how many times Ben saw the interior of the Open Shelter, he could never get over the chandelier hanging from the middle of the ceiling; it was easily the most disparate thing in the city, in his opinion.

The Reverend greeted him at the door. "Sorry for all the commotion," he said.

The place was filled not only with the homeless, but with dozens of sheriff's office deputies—as well as Sheriff Ted Jackson himself.

"Ted's using this place as a sort of command center," said the Reverend, taking Ben's elbow and leading him through the crowds of people, officers, and tables. Ted Jackson looked up, saw that Ben was here, and broke away from a table surrounded by deputies and volunteers who were going through thick stacks of what looked to be old maps and county records.

"Any luck?" asked the Reverend.

"I can tell you where the water goes when you flush the toilets in here, but as far as the names for the bodies at the County Home—not so much." He turned toward Ben. "Good to see you, Ben."

"Thanks for all the help you're giving us, Ted."

Jackson waved away the thanks. "No need to thank

me. On top of all my deputies, we've got about two dozen volunteers from the VA working on this, as well. I swear to God, Ben, we must have every physical record from the courthouse basement in here."

"What about electronic records?"

"I've got three people on that. Hopefully one of them will come up with something."

"Your lips to God's ear," said Ben.

The Reverend gave an odd little smile at that, but it didn't really register with Ben. Jackson went back to the volunteer table. Ben and the Reverend made their way through the kitchen area where Grant McCullers, owner of the Hangman's Tavern, was preparing box meals for everyone. Grant nodded at them, and then came over.

"I can't believe that crazy son-of-a-bitch knows the exact number of bodies buried on the Hangman's property," he said to Ben. "I've owned that place for years and even *I* have no idea how many bodies are buried there, or even *where.*"

"Which is why Ted's got deputies out there with shovels right now," added the Reverend. "Personally, I think it's a waste of time. Even if they find some of the bodies, there's not going to be any identification on them."

"And you have no idea if there are any written records of the names?" asked Ben.

"We're talking the *Klan* here," said Grant. "They didn't give a shit about names, only about hanging folks."

The Reverend nodded. "Good point."

Grant shook Ben's hand. "I'm sorry for all of this."

"Makes two of us."

Grant went back to preparing the meals for the volunteers. Ben knew from the Reverend that Grant often brought food to the shelter, and that he, Ted Jackson, and the Reverend were close friends.

"My domicile, such as it is," said the Reverend, opening a door that led into a small but uncluttered room. A

television set with both a VCR and DVD player hooked
into it sat on a rolling stand. The Reverend pulled up a
chair close to the TV and gestured for Ben to take a seat.

"About half an hour ago," said the Reverend, "a videotape was left in the donations box out front. Sometimes
people will dump old movies in there for the TV in the
main area—people can relax a little when they're
watching movies, so I—never mind.

"It was unmarked, but I get a lot of donated movies
that are like that. I brought it back here and checked it
out to make sure it would play and that's when, well . . ."
He picked up the remote control and started the tape.

It was footage that someone had filmed outside the
Moundbuilders Diner this morning after the crowd had
started to form. The picture was surprisingly clear and
sharp; Ben got a good look at every face in the crowd,
and even caught a glimpse of himself and Captain
Goldstein through the windows. It was when the camera turned back at the crowd that he saw them.

The Reverend paused the tape; the image froze, still
surprisingly clear.

"Ben, correct me if I'm wrong, but isn't that—?"

". . . Cheryl," he replied, his voice barely more than a
whisper. There was no doubt at all in Ben's mind that he
was looking at the ghost of his dead wife, but what
made it even worse, what made it hurt right down to the
marrow of his bones, what twisted his stomach into a
knot, was the face of the little boy, perhaps two years
old, whom Cheryl was holding: there was no mistaking
Ben's own features in the child's face.

Ben sat there, shaking his head back and forth, back
and forth, trying to convince himself that it was just
some woman who *looked* like Cheryl, holding some little boy who *looked* like he could be . . .

"This can't be," said Ben.

The Reverend put a hand on Ben's shoulder. "That's

what I thought, and then this happens." He pushed PLAY once more, and as the camera lingered on Cheryl and the little boy, the child held up a picture.

It was a smaller but quite visible copy of the same photograph Ben had on his nightstand: he and Cheryl on their wedding day.

Ben reached for his wallet in his back pocket, removed it, and took from it a copy of the same photograph.

There was no doubt about it.

It was the same photo.

The Reverend squeezed Ben's shoulder. "It *is* her, isn't it?"

"Yes."

"And that little boy she's holding, the one who looks so much like you, he's—"

"Yes."

"I thought as much."

"Please pause the tape."

"No. You need to see the rest of it."

The camera moved in for a close-up of Cheryl and the little boy, both of whom waved and mouthed the words "Hi, Daddy" before the image went momentarily black. A beat, and then another image appeared, this one of Cheryl, sitting at the kitchen table in her and Ben's house, feeding baby food to their son, who sat in his high chair and actually managed to get as much food in him as on him. Cheryl wiped off the baby's chin, set down the baby food, and turned toward the camera.

"Hi, honey. Happy anniversary."

Ben felt himself getting dizzy: it was her voice. It was her voice. It was her voice. It was *her.*

"I know you spoke with Monsignor Maddingly earlier," she said. "Is he still the character I remember? *Of course* he is, forget that I asked. The story he told you about the dogwood, that's only one of them—the sentimental one, I think he called it.

"There are some who believe that the cross used to crucify Jesus was made of dogwood. As the fable goes, during the time of Jesus, the dogwood was larger and stronger than it is today. After his crucifixion, Jesus supposedly changed the plant to its current form, shortening it and twisting its branches to make sure it would never again be used in the construction of crosses, and he transformed its inflorescence into the form of the crucifixion itself. The four white petals are cross-shaped, each bearing a rusty indentation like one of the nails; the red stamens of the flower represent Jesus's crown of thorns; and the clustered red fruit represents his blood. I like the other version better, don't you?" She turned back to the baby and played nosey-nose with him for a moment, the baby squealing with delight, making her laugh. "I have to get back to Ian—that would have been our son's name, Ben, Ian. But before I leave you again there's something that Hoopsticks wanted me to pass along to you—and by the way," she whispered, as if about to share some delicious secret, "that's not his real name, but he kind of likes 'Hoopsticks' because of the local legend. You'd be surprised at what his real name is." Her gaze shifted, and for a moment Ben thought she was looking at the Reverend, but then she smiled and looked back at him and that thought fled his mind.

"*Anyway* . . . he wants me to tell you that the letters you found in the church and on the crosses spell 'Haceldama.' It means 'The Field of Blood.' You can ask the Reverend to explain it to you.

"I don't want to make you feel any worse than you already do, honey, but this might be the last time you ever see me. Or it might not. The choice is yours."

No sooner had she said that than Ian began bouncing in his high chair, arms extended, shouting, "Daddy! Daddy! *Daddy!*" And the tape went blank.

The Reverend stopped the VCR. "Do you want to see it again?"

Ben covered his mouth with both of his hands, trying to hold back the terrible sound trying to emerge from inside his chest, lungs, and throat. Shaking his head, he turned away from the Reverend and wiped his eyes and face.

The Reverend came around, knelt down, and took hold of Ben's wrists. "Ben, you have to listen to me, all right?"

"How in God's name is this possible?"

The Reverend stared at him for a moment. "Look at me—*look at me, all right?* Thank you. Before I tell you anything more, I need to ask you something; do you believe that the person you just saw was Cheryl?"

"Yes."

"If I were to tell you that something supernatural is at work here, would you believe me? Think about all that you've seen today, think about all the impossibilities you've been witness to. Would you believe me?"

Ben could only nod his head.

"Good," said the Reverend. " 'Haceldama,' the Field of Blood, is the name that was given to the pauper's field where the body of Judas Iscariot was buried after his suicide. For thousands of years its exact location has remained a mystery. Even now, no one knows where it is. Now . . . look over at the far wall."

Ben, still in a state of near shock, did as he was instructed. The surface of the wall rippled and began bowing outward, as if something were pushing against a sheet of plastic; he could make out the shape of a face, then a shoulder, an arm, a torso and legs, the whole shape forming into something that looked like a piece of bas-relief art, but then the shape was through the wall, corporeal, breathing . . . and disfigured.

The figure's face was like something out of a horror movie. There was very little soft tissue on the upper portions of its face, and what flesh there was had become hardened to the point where it more resembled scales on a lizard's back; in places this scalelike flesh was semitranslucent, allowing Ben to see the red and blue veins that spiderwebbed the areas where most people had cheeks. The figure had no nose, only two tear-shaped caves through which he breathed, both of which seemed to leak constantly. His left eye was a good quarter-inch lower on his face than his right, and he had no ears to speak of, just bits of dangling flesh on either side of his head. Though his jaws were intact, he possessed almost no chin; the flesh under his lower lip had only the smallest of rounded bone fragment beneath it, the rest simply blended into his neck like melted candle wax, creating a thick, disturbing wattle that pulsed with every leaking from his nose caves.

The worst part, though, was the overall shape of his face and head; his skull seemed to have been wrenched apart with a crowbar, then pieced back together by someone with no knowledge whatsoever of human anatomy; there were lumps where none should have been, craters where there should have been lumps, and one section, beneath his too-low left eye, where the cracked and yellowed bone was actually exposed to the elements; Ben caught a glimpse of something metal and realized there was a rusty pin holding those two small sections of the figure's faceplate together.

"As usual," said the figure to the Reverend, "another person has been struck dumb by the awesomeness of my beauty."

"What the hell happened to you?" asked Ben.

The disfigured man looked at the Reverend. "*Why* is that always the first question anyone asks me?" He looked back at Ben. "I tried to French-kiss an airplane propeller as a college prank—what the fuck does it matter?"

"Can it, Rael," said the Reverend.

"What? I'm not entitled to a little fun, a little sarcasm, I can't spread my sunshine all around?"

The Reverend glared at him.

"Fine," said Rael, taking an object from his pocket. "I got better things to do, anyway." He tossed the object to the Reverend, then looked once again at Ben. "No review of my dramatic entrance? No questions or comments? I'm . . . I'm crushed. Sincerely."

The Reverend shook his head. "I keep forgetting how sometimes a little bit of you goes a long way."

Rael glared right back at him. "Yeah, well, since you've been around almost as long as I have, you've gotten a little picky about who you choose to befriend."

"This isn't the time for this discussion, Rael."

Rael snapped his fingers. "That's right, you've got a direct line to the Big Guy, so you're in charge." Making a mock-theatrical bow, he then said: "Your wish is my command, oh master."

"Stop being an obnoxious ass for once, will you?"

Rael stood back up. There was some genuine hurt in his eyes. "Come on! I don't mean anything by it. Not since that business with Londrigan."

At the mention of that name, Ben sat up, his attention suddenly intensely focused. "Londrigan? Do you mean *Robert* Londrigan?"

Rael spread his hands before him. "Unless you and Bill Emerson know another one."

"How do you know about Londrigan?"

"I know about him," said Rael, "because he and I are I guess what you'd call roommates."

"He's alive?" said Ben.

"And well, and kicking. He sends his regards to you and Bill Emerson, by the way."

For a few moments, Ben could only stare at Rael. Robert Londrigan had been a popular local newscaster whose wife and child had died during childbirth and their bodies stolen from the morgue. After giving Bill Emerson a description of a man who, Ben now realized, looked a lot like Rael, Londrigan's behavior had gotten more and more erratic until he'd vanished altogether. Some of the more fantastic aspects of the case had left both Ben and Bill Emerson confused and more than a little frightened . . . so now, neither of them ever spoke of it.

"You're not gonna ask me *where* he is, are you?" said Rael. "It'd be a waste of breath, because where he is, and where I come from, you wouldn't find yourself welcomed. So just give me a little smile and look upon me as the deliverer of the deus ex machina."

"You give yourself too much credit, Rael," said the Reverend.

Rael smiled at him. " 'Let he who is without sin . . .' and all that happy horseshit."

"What are you?" asked Ben.

Rael did not answer; instead, he looked to the Reverend, who sighed, gave a nod, and then said to Ben: "Remember what you told me, that you accept and believe that there is something supernatural at work here."

"For fuck's sake, Reverend, I just watched this guy *come out of a goddamned wall! Of course I believe it!*"

"Excitable boy, isn't he?" said Rael.

Ignoring him, the Reverend said: "Rael is something of an angel. To be more specific, he is the offspring of a Fallen Angel and a human woman. He and I . . . well, let's just say we go back a ways."

"Always the King of the Understatement," said Rael; then, turning his attention back to Ben, said, "You have to understand that there are two types of time, buddy; in one, you go along with your everyday life, get old, get sick, punch a time card, retire, go fishing, and eventually die. In the second type of time, you are ageless, you cannot be touched by the passing of years, disease, age, any of it." He gestured to the Reverend. "Because Mr. Help-Your-Fellow-Pile-of-Carbon here has done a lot of favors for me and my kind in the past, I agreed to give him a little help—which is to say, we're giving *you* some help, providing you do exactly as he says. Me, I gotta go. Got a soufflé in the oven and those things are motherfuckers to time properly." He looked at the Reverend, tipped a nonexistent hat, said, "Always a thrill, Boss," and then simply disappeared; there one moment, gone the next.

The Reverend looked at Ben. "He's actually not the asshole he tries to make himself out to be."

"If you say so." Then: "What did he give to you?"

The Reverend handed Ben the object: an old-fashioned pocket watch with a spring-loaded brass cover. Ben automatically began to press on the mechanism atop the watch to open it.

"No!" said the Reverend, grabbing the hand in which Ben held the watch. "Don't open it yet."

"Then . . . then what? When do I—?"

"You'll know the moment when it comes, trust me."

Ben stared at the watch. "What is this supposed to do?"

The Reverend looked down at his feet. "I wish I could tell you, but I . . . I can't. And I'm sorry."

Ben slipped the watch into his pants pocket.

"It would be . . . inconvenient were you to lose that, Ben."

"Another understatement, I take it?"

The Reverend shrugged. "It's a slight character flaw."

The two men smiled at one another.

"Can I have that tape?" said Ben.

"Absolutely. And don't worry—I won't tell anyone what's on it, not unless you give your okay."

Ben took the videotape from the Reverend and then shook the man's hand. "Can I ask you something?"

"Anything."

"I have no memory of either telling you about Cheryl or giving you my cell phone number. How did you know?"

"Maybe you told me and then forgot about it. Or maybe someone close to you said something—Bill Emerson stops by here a lot. He's a loquacious sort, your partner."

Ben nodded. "He's still in surgery."

"I heard about what happened at St. Francis. Do you need to talk about it?"

Ben looked at his watch. "Yes, but right now I haven't got the time."

"I understand."

"If the killer contacts you again—"

"—I'll call your cell right away, don't worry."

And with that, still stunned, confused, and mournful, Ben Littlejohn made his way out of the shelter and back out to his car, half-stumbling along the way.

48

While Goldstein was inside getting the tape from the WLCB station manager, Ben sat in his car outside the radio station and tried not to surrender to depression or hopelessness.

He reached into his pocket and removed the picture that had been taken on their wedding day, the same one that sat on his nightstand, the same one the child had held up in the videotape.

God, she'd been so beautiful. And he was so god-damned confused right now. None of this made any sense, but yet he could sense, on the periphery of all the horror he'd witnessed in the past fourteen or so hours, the promise of something in the shadows that was waiting for him to find it; the final piece of the puzzle that would make all the tumblers fall into place.

His vision blurred for a second and he realized he was crying.

"God, honey," he whispered so low it was almost a prayer. "I miss you so much. Still."

Christ! He had to stop this.

Call in and see if there's any word on Bill's condition.

He put the picture away, then reached toward the radio—

—as the killer's voice sliced through the static.

"She was quite lovely, Ben. You're right to miss her so much."

"What the—"

"After you wake up from your dream, what happens?"

He snatched up the microphone. "How did you get on this frequency?"

"The rope burn that's around your neck for just a second. Remember? You have to be familiar with the term 'stigmata.'"

"What do you *want?*"

"*Oro, fiat illud, quod tam sitio; ut te revelata cernens facie. Visu sim beatus tuae gloriae. Amen.*"

A great pressure coiled around Ben's neck. He fell forward, gasping, his lungs screaming for air as the pressure intensified, crushing his larynx—

His world spiraled downward into darkness where—

—a man named Herbert Mullin killed thirteen people as a sacrifice to the gods, claiming the deaths would prevent earthquakes in California; during police questioning he hinted that the deaths had been "preventing other things" as well—

—into darkness where—

—Juan Corona took a machete and slaughtered sixteen migrant workers on his farm and claimed that the murders were "an act of holy preservation"—

—where—

—William "Theo" Durant strangled and mutilated four women of his parish in 1895, then dragged their bodies to the tower of Emanuel Baptist Church and hanged them by their necks, claiming their corpses would serve as "a reminder of God's anger against humanity for turning away from its fellow men."

Ben became Mullin and Corona and Durant, as well as Bundy and Gein and Whitman and others like them in the past, the present, and the future. He raped and mutilated, he flayed and cannibalized, he stared at victims from the scope of a rifle and bathed in their blood and clothed himself in their dead flesh—

—and every savage act was filled with release and redemption, for even though part of him knew the acts were unspeakably depraved, a deeper, stronger part sensed that the butchery was somehow preventing a final act of even greater violence and destruction.

Dum vista est, spes est: Where there is life, there is hope.

A motto for the smorgasbord of slaughter.

He clutched the steering wheel so tightly his knuckles began turning white. Staring ahead with the intensity of a man being led into the gas chamber, Ben remembered the voice of the killer over the radio, remembered looking at Cheryl's picture, remembered the pain that twisted through him before he'd black out, remembered the sound of her voice, her impossible voice on the tape, and the baby, their son, Ian, calling out *Daddy! Daddy! Daddy!*—

—but he didn't remember coming to, or driving away.

He didn't even know where he was going.

He was dressed differently—

—his hands looked so old—

—and his head felt so heavy—

—and this wasn't his car—

—so what in the . . . ?

49

He pulled into the parking lot of a public cafeteria. There were six cars, plus three semi tractor-trailers, one of them hauling gasoline. He reached into his shoulder holster and removed a Colt Commander 9mm with a nine-round magazine and special silencer attachment. He jacked open the chamber and inserted a tenth round, then shoved it back into his shoulder holster and put an extra clip in his pocket.

Pulling four sticks of dynamite from under the front seat and stuffing them into the lining of his coat, he wondered: *What the hell am I doing?*

Buying time, came the answer. He looked in the rearview mirror. He didn't recognize his face.

Inside, the overhead lights were far too bright, giving the place a cavernous feel, accentuated by the pinging echo of silverware clattering through a dishwasher.

Three large men were sitting in a room at the far end marked TRUCKERS ONLY.

He took a seat at the counter. The waitress was a big old friendly gal named Margie who smiled through slightly discolored teeth and never stopped talking to the cook—a short, nervous-looking young man wearing a silver skull earring.

Two other waitresses were sitting at a far table. Probably on break.

A well-dressed man came out of the restroom and sat at a booth near Ben.

A small office window near the trucker's room revealed a stooped bookkeeper within.

He turned and spoke (with the killer's voice) to the well-dressed man. "I've been thinking about Edward N. Lorenz, the mathematician-turned-meteorologist who opened up the field of chaos math. He applied certain convection equations to the short-term prediction of weather and watched them degenerate into insanity. He wrote: 'Does the flapping of a butterfly's wings in Brazil set off tornadoes in Texas?' Yes—because that seemingly harmless movement creates a small yet potent change in atmospheric pressure, which interacts with other minute changes, and these combine with still more unpredictable variables that come down through the exo-, iono-, and stratosphere to mingle with the cumulative 'butterfly effects' in the troposphere, and before you know it—WHAM!—you've got thirty people dead in a Kansas trailer park while hundreds more stand weeping among the ruins of their homes. And this can happen in *seconds*. Think about that. A monarch flutters its wings, and in less than a minute chaos can come crashing down on your world and reduce it to smithereens."

"I don't know what you're talking about," said the man, "but I'm minding my own business, so why don't you—"

With a *snick!* from the Colt his face peeled back and slapped against the window, hanging in place for a moment before slithering down.

Margie came next, a shriek barely having time to escape her throat before the round punched through her chest, lifted her off her feet, and sent her walloping backward into a row of metal shelves that groaned and buckled as their contents plunged to the floor with her in a bloody shatter-glass shower.

Cook Silver Skull hurtled sideways as the bullet demolished a quarter of his head, landing on top of the grill and convulsing as his blood sizzled and his flesh scorched and his body spasmed before he shit his pants and rolled onto the floor oozing and smoking.

Eight seconds had elapsed.

The two waitresses screamed and vaulted toward the doors but two quick *snick!*s decorated the tables with squirming bits of their skulls and gray matter.

At fifteen seconds and counting the truckers were on their feet, one of them pulling an eight-inch bowie knife and rushing full-force, screaming, "YOU PSYCHO-FUCK SON-OF-A—" A round *snick!*ed through his throat but he kept coming, arms pinwheeling as he spewed blood and tried to ram the knife home as he collided with Ben and they fell, the knife skittering under a chair.

Ben pumped another round into the trucker, this one at a vicious angle, flipping up through the trucker's stomach and blowing out just above the tailbone, dragging a gummy white loop of lower intestine with it.

Twenty-nine seconds.

The other two truckers had armed themselves with knives snatched from place settings.

Snick!—one lost his balls and collapsed, screaming at the top of his lungs and clutching the soggy-meat hole between his legs.

The other one dove behind the counter, skidded in a puddle of Margie, and smashed through the kitchen door. Ben pulped his knees with two shots. The trucker hit the side of his face against a stove knob on the way down, tearing a thick gash from cheek to temple.

Ben grabbed him by the hair, dragged him to his feet, ejected and replaced the empty clip, put a fresh round through the trucker's chest and shoved him against the deep-fat fryer, ramming his face into the bubbling oil. The trucker managed to get his face out of the oil for a moment, the skin sloughing off like wax melting down a candle before Ben plowed two more shots through his back and he slumped forward, head submerging into the scalding pit as dozens of blackened french fries writhed around his skull.

Catapulting himself out the kitchen door with such force he wrenched the hinges out of the frame, Ben lunged toward the small office and blasted the window into a puking supernova of fracture-burst fragments. Someone inside tried to choke back a moan as Ben kicked away the remaining shards of glass and climbed inside.

An old woman with palsied, liver-spotted hands was lying face-down on an adding machine behind a small metal desk, a phone receiver clutched against her chest.

Heart attack.

Ben held the receiver to his ear and heard ". . . aine County Sheriff's Department, is this an emergency? Hello?"

Jerking the phone cord out of the wall, he spun around and clamped the old woman's head between his hands, snapping it sideways and shattering her neck.

Back in the restaurant the last trucker was still screaming and clutching at the raw, gushing chasm where his nuts used to be but Ben walked past him and toward the entrance; one of the waitresses was still alive.

He grabbed the bowie knife, flipped the girl onto her back, and rammed the knife into her forehead. To the hilt.

He crossed the gore-slicked floor and straddled the last trucker's waist, pressing the gun into his cheek.

Fifty-eight seconds.

Chaos rules.

"Getting back to the 'butterfly effect,' " Ben said. "Human behavior is a lot like that—determined by preexisting yet uncontrollable events which, when considered in the context of inviolable laws of momentum, completely account for all subsequent events. So what causes behavior to suddenly veer toward the self-destructive? The butterfly effect."

"P-p-please m-mister," choked the bleeding man beneath him. ". . . it . . . ohjesusgod . . . it hurts so . . . so m-much . . . please d-don't . . . kill me . . ." He closed his eyes and began to whimper, then weep, fear and hysteria burrowing inward to a place beyond fear.

". . . don't wanna . . . die . . . I got k-kids who . . . ohgod . . ."

Ben continued speaking in the killer's voice. "Imagine the butterfly is the embodiment of everything that causes us to ignore or add to the suffering of others, and the flapping of its wings is the force of our apathy spilling outward. In less than a second it combines with the myriad emotions we expel—anger, lust, happiness, despair, whatever—until they become a single entity. Multiply that by however many times a day a person turns away from the suffering of others, then multiply that by the number of people in the world, then multiply *that* by the seconds in a week, a month, a year or a decade, and pretty soon you've got one hell of a charge building up. After the point of maximum tension is reached the combined forces rupture outward and target whoever or whatever is closest at the time. Gives a whole new meaning to 'shit happens.' "

"*OHGODPLEASEMISTER—*"

Snick!

Blowing out its pilot light, he shoved two sticks of dynamite under the gas stove and lit their extended fuses.

Outside, he shoved a stick halfway into the tank of the gasoline truck, another under the semi next to it.

Two minutes later, when he was almost six miles down the road, the cafeteria went up in a titanic mushroom-cloud blast that roared two hundred feet into the air and sent shockwaves rippling over one-third of the county. Debris rose so high it took almost ninety seconds to come back down.

Staring in the rearview mirror, Ben saw the cloud assume a very appropriate shape.

A blink and a breath, then he said: "Two thousand days more."

And was answered by an echo:

that was nebraska. september of 1977. look it up if you want. just a snapshot from the scrapbook of my memory. hope you appreciated it.

With a sick feeling in the pit of his stomach, Ben realized that he had not only appreciated it, but *enjoyed* it, as well. God forgive him, he'd enjoyed it.

50

He awoke to pain, bright light, and the sound of many people running by.

He was on a bed behind a plastic green curtain.

A hospital emergency room.

Monsignor Maddingly: "Are you all right? Al said you had some kind of seizure."

Ben swallowed once—it hurt; twice—a little less; three times—still uncomfortable but he could live with it. "How long was I—"

"A little over two hours."

"Where's the captain?"

"Called away on some kind of emergency. Said he'd try to get back."

Ben sat up and pressed his hand against his head to stop the dizziness. "W-what're . . . what are you doing here?'

"I was administering extreme unction to a patient when you were brought in. Al told me about the call to the radio station and it triggered a synapse in this old brain. Let me ask you something—did all of the bodies have coins in place of their eyes? Silver coins?"

". . . yeah . . . ?"

"Fifteen bodies?"

"Yes."

Maddingly nodded his head.

"What?" said Ben.

"You were baptized in the Catholic Church. Think about it: fifteen bodies, two coins each—"

"—thirty pieces of silver." Ben touched his still-tender neck.

"Judas Iscariot," said Maddingly.

"Then, the Reverend was right . . . the Field of Blood—"

"Haceldama. The potter's field in Israel where Judas was buried in an unmarked pauper's grave. To this day no one knows the exact location of that field. Thousands of bodies buried there, and nothing to mark the spot."

The curtain was yanked back and Goldstein stepped through, looking as if he hadn't slept in a week. "The dead have arisen."

Ben asked, "Where did you go? What happened?"

"All fifteen bodies disappeared from the morgue. Right in the middle of the autopsies, there was a blackout, some kind of small boiler explosion, the building was evacuated, and by the time the ME's team went back inside the bodies were gone. The building was empty less than fifteen minutes."

"What did you do?"

"Christ!—sorry, Monsignor—what *could* I do? I had Moore phone the governor and request some help. Every available cop is on the street and this guy is playing ring-around-the-rosy with us. There is no doubt in my mind now that he's capable of killing as many people as he claims. And that scares the hell out of me. So the National Guard comes in and Cedar Hill goes under curfew." He ran a hand through his hair and looked out at the doctors and nurses and the suffering patients with wounded souls.

"Al?" said Maddingly. "What is it?"

"Just tired, I guess. Thinking about . . . things."

"Like what?"

Goldstein watched a woman holding a towel against her bleeding face roll by on a gurney, then sighed. "I used to listen to my father tell stories about the camps. He saw his parents die at Gunskirchen Lager. I got so sick of him going over and over the details, as if the only reason he was allowed to survive was so he could become this living memorial tape loop. The only time he ever really acknowledged my existence was when he needed an audience for his perpetual eulogy. One day I screamed, 'I'm sorry I wasn't there. I'm sorry you had to see it. I'm sorry I haven't suffered and died like they did so you'd love me, too.' He never spoke about it again, but the ghosts stayed with him. That's why I fell away from the faith and left home: I couldn't stomach the sight of what his faith had done to him. He wasn't my father, he was a repository for phantoms. Every time I saw those ghosts in his gaze I felt diminished. So I walked away. I didn't even go back for his funeral.

"The thing is," he said, turning to face Maddingly and Ben, "sometimes I look in a mirror and catch a glimpse of his ghost in my own eyes, and I wonder if we're not all just walking graveyards, our memories serving as coffins for all those we've seen die, and the people they saw die, and the people they saw die. I just"—his voice cracked—"can't . . . *look* at it anymore. It feels like this guy . . . this *thing*, has beaten us. And if he has . . . if he has . . ."

A nurse stepped in and said she had a call for Ben at the desk and the caller had said it was an emergency.

Ben stumbled his way to the desk and lifted the receiver.

"How was Nebraska?" said the killer. "Figure anything out yet? I hope so—"

"—wait a second, I—"

"—because I weary of this. It's come-and-get-me time, Benjamin. Meet me at the cemetery in fifteen minutes. Come alone."

"There're cops and sheriff's deputies stationed there, you know."

"They've all been called away on an emergency."

"What do you—"

Just as the line went dead a patrolman rushed to the desk, trying not to shout as he said, "A call just came in from downtown, sir. We got a sniper."

51

so, my tortuurer, here we are again. will you divinely intervene, or will this end the same way as all the times before?

like benjamin and his captain, i, too, have been thinking about things.

the caterpillar that crawled into my mouth as i hung there. how it slipped down my throat and made its cocoon inside me.

caiaphas had his "servant" cut down my body and bury it along with the coins of my so-called betrayal. then, as the season changed, the traditor papilio emerged from me.

how terribly clever of you to stigmatize it.

your quote son's unquote blood marked the dogwood with holiness.

my death marked the black butterfly with disgrace.

and the rest of it . . .

you really outdid yourself.

have you ever asked yourself if they really deserve this?

i didn't think so.

time is short. dum vista est, spes est.

52

The storm clouds were already gathering by the time Ben arrived at old County Home Cemetery. Low rumbles of thunder were accentuated by vivid flashes of silent lightning that dazzled his eyes and seemed to dance across a nearby pond, turning it into a sheet of fire before everything pitched into darkness. A blink and a breath, then his gaze recovered from the preceding flash, enabling him to see the tendrils of mist rising from the graves, twisting and coiling, forming semihuman shapes.

The .45 gripped tightly in his left hand, he climbed out of the car and climbed the small hill that led to the cemetery proper. Goldstein hadn't been crazy about Ben coming out here alone but the situation downtown was serious; eight people had already been wounded—but none, thank God, had yet been killed.

"Why didn't it ever occur to us that there might be two of them?" he'd asked as Ben started the car.

"Damned if I know."

"Twenty minutes," said Goldstein. "If I don't hear from you by then, sniper or no sniper I'll come to get your ass and bring three units with me."

"You'll hear from me."

Goldstein had grabbed Ben's arm then, and said, "You be careful. Don't fuck with him. I hate heroes, got it? They're mostly all dead."

Ben had nodded then driven away as Goldstein and Monsignor Maddingly (who'd insisted he go to the scene, perhaps he could talk the sniper down) climbed into a squad car.

Ben checked his watch.

He had nineteen minutes.

At the far end of the grounds, near a foot trail that had once led all the way around the place, a lone mercury vapor lamp came on, its murky light coming downward to illuminate a thin figure hunched over a shattered headstone.

Ben jacked a round into the chamber and moved slowly forward. His breath was staggered and heavy and he couldn't shake the feeling that he and this figure weren't alone.

Another burst of lightning spiderwebbed across the sky and Ben had to bite his lip to keep from crying out.

Suspended from various trees surrounding the cemetery, some hanging by their necks, others by their ankles, still others impaled on the ends of jagged branches, the bodies stolen from the morgue dangled, pale, naked, gutted angels. Their opened, empty chest cavities looked like the gaping maws of giant insects. Flesh flaps swayed in the rising wind; faces no longer capable of further expression were frozen into grisly smirks; and arms devoid of conscious impulses swung witlessly back and forth as if beckoning him forward.

Ben took a deep breath and strode onward.

The figure rose to its feet.

Ben froze mid-stride and almost choked. ". . . *ohGod* . . ."

"Hello, my love," said Cheryl.

One thousand days of cumulative grief, loneliness,

anger, and confusion instantaneously welled up in Ben's chest, shaking him within and without. He lowered the gun and tried to move but couldn't, part of his mind screaming that this wasn't happening, it couldn't be true, and as he worked his mouth and jaw to form words that refused to be articulated, his wife moved toward him, her smile filled with spring, her arms parted for his embrace, and Ben Littlejohn suddenly didn't give a damn about the killer, all that mattered was Cheryl, who was here, who was real, who was his life and reason and oh God she was so close, he could smell the scent of her skin, tender and sensual as the horror of the last fifteen hours faded, the taste of one thousand days of bitter longing withered, and the chaos that had so long been the core of his existence turned in on itself and hinted at order.

He lurched toward her, tripped over a section of headstone, and dropped to one knee, then, through a veil of near-blinding tears, wrapped his arms around her waist and buried his face in the center of her torso as the sobs exploded.

". . . ohjesus baby I've missed you so much so much ohgod I love you I missed you I need you so much . . ."

"Shhh, there, there," she said, stroking the back of his head. "It's almost over now."

". . . love you so much . . ."

He began to stand, blinking the tears from his eyes——she was gone.

And there, at his feet, at the corner of the headstone, was the black butterfly he'd seen this morning.

The killer's voice echoed: "When Hannibal arrived at the gates of Rome he saw the black butterfly resting there, and knew his victory would be futile. What good is it, after all, conquering a city that would fall to flames anyway?"

Taking in a deep breath filled with steel, rage, and snot, Ben snapped up the gun and clenched his teeth.

"Where are you?" he whispered.

"Turn around," said the killer.

He was much smaller than Ben had imagined but it was easy to see, even through the shabby clothes he wore, that his body was tight and powerful; layers of sinewy muscles rippled whenever he moved.

His eyes, so clear and startlingly blue, nailed Ben to the spot; they were the most haunted he'd ever seen, brimming with ghosts. So many, many ghosts.

"Hello, Ben."

"What did you do with Cheryl? Goddammit, where's my wife?"

"Nearby. Don't worry, you'll see her again. Maybe. Depends on how much you cooperate."

Ben raised the gun, pointing directly between the killer's eyes.

"Shoot if you want, but it won't do any good. I've tried it so many times it's almost funny."

"Who are you?"

"I'd have thought that was obvious by now." He smiled then, a wistful, tired expression that turned his windburned face into a mask of lattice-work lines. "So, are you going to use that thing, or what? Nice gun, by the way."

Ben glanced quickly and saw the .45 shimmer in his hand, then turn into the Colt 9mm Parabellum he'd held in the Nebraska dream.

It was a testament to his professional composure that he did not throw it down.

The killer shook his head and walked past Ben, kneeling down by the headstone and extending his hand. The butterfly moved toward it on dozens of tiny insect legs until it nestled securely in the center of the killer's palm.

"If you want Cheryl and Ian back, Ben, you won't pull that trigger."

"Who's your partner?"

"My what?"

"Your partner. Who's the sniper?"

"Oh, right. His name's Randy Perry. He's a mechanic from Heath who's been getting treated for depression. He'll manage to shoot seven more people before the SWAT team takes him down. They'll check into his background and find enough evidence to link him to the truck-stop killings. Case closed. Another chapter for the Time Life serial killer books."

"How do you know that?"

The killer stood, cradling the butterfly in his hands. "Have you ever said or done anything that you later regretted, Ben? Of course you have, who hasn't? You wish you could take it back but you can't. A loss of control in a moment of confusion or weakness or anger and suddenly you've contributed to the damage in the world. It's out there, it's done, and you can't change it.

"When you were attending Catholic school, did anyone ever ask your religion teachers that classic smartass question: 'Can God create a rock so big that even He can't lift it?' Well, He can.

"On the day Christ died God's rage was so overwhelming that He lost His mind for a moment, and in that moment he created a day when the world would end. He spit out that day and sent it flying into the multiverse where it still waits. And He can't take back that day, He's tried. So there you have that 'rock' so big even God can't lift it.

"Did you know that Hell is technically not a separate place from Heaven? It's located on the north side of the Third Heaven. It's funny, because—well, *to me* it's funny, because when I entered this branch of the multiverse this time, which is to say when I arrived in Cedar Hill, I did so in the place that used to be called 'Old Towne East.' Hell is basically Heaven's Coffin County.

"After my suicide, from my corner of Hell, I screamed at God not to punish the world for the wrong I had committed. 'The sin is mine!' I cried. 'Let the suffering be mine, also. Torture me, not them.'

"So He sent me back. It took a long time but eventually I realized the nature of my punishment. Do you remember thinking 'two thousand days more' after the killings in Nebraska? That's how much time those deaths bought. By killing those nine people I put two thousand days between humankind and the end of the world."

Ben, repelled yet fascinated, asked, "Was there a cemetery near that place?"

"Half a mile away in a farmer's field were nine hoboes who'd been beaten to death by railroad men in 1931 and buried without being identified. There was nothing to mark their grave. No one knew they were there. Still don't, as a matter of fact."

"So for each person who dies and is buried without a name or anything to mark their grave—"

"—I have to kill a person whose death *will* be noticed, whose grave *will* bear their name, whose friends *will* weep and whose family *will* remember them. It helps to restore the balance of pain and thus postpones the . . . end of everything."

The storm clouds dropped lower, churning and thundering and flashing jagged lightning as Judas Iscariot parted his arms toward the cemetery. "There are hundreds of thousands of places like Haceldama, like *this* sad little cemetery, all over the world, with new ones being dug every hour. It didn't take long to understand there was no possible way I could maintain the balance of pain on my own.

"So I begat Bundy and Whitman and Corona and Gein; Cowan and Gacy and Berkowitz and Haarman; Gilles de Rais and Starkweather and Rojas and Dahmer and Speck and countless others, some of whom won't even be born for another fifty years. Their tallies add to the time the world has left."

"*How do you know?*" shouted Ben. "What proof do you have?"

Judas tensed his jaw, his eyes narrowing as his voice became a deep, grieving, deadly whisper. "Do you see this?" He held out his hand to show the black butterfly. "A species of lepidoptera so rare it has been classified as extinct for over a hundred years. Its Latin name is *traditor papilio*—'betrayer butterfly.' Also called the 'Judas Moth' because of its white strip, symbolizing the rope burn around my neck after I used the cattle halter to end my wretched life. There are only thirty of them in existence, one for each piece of silver I accepted. They can only be found on unmarked graves—they were born in one, so they are drawn to the same. They move by crawling. They never flap their wings—oh, they might give out a little flutter every now and then, but they never take flight. They are indestructible but capable of unbounded destruction."

"The 'butterfly effect'?" asked Ben.

"Taken to a hideous extreme. The day will eventually come when all thirty of them will go back to the place of their birth. Once gathered upon my grave they will simultaneously flap their wings, and next will be Nothing. Unimaginable Nothing. Vengeance, as the saying goes, will be the Lord's."

The gun held limply at his side, Ben whispered, "Why me?"

Judas shook his head. "Can't answer that one. I don't do the choosing. The butterflies do. I simply . . . beget."

"Why the theatrics, then?"

"I have found, over the centuries, that chaos helps to speed up the . . . I guess you'd call it the recruiting process. And, as terrible as it sounds, it amuses me to watch how people react. If that sounds cold-blooded I won't apologize. After ten thousand years I'll take my enjoyment when and however I can get it. You simply cannot think of them as people, merely a means to an end."

Ben stared at the spot where his wife had stood just a few minutes ago, trying to deny all of it. After a moment he raised his head and asked: "Why are you white?"

Judas grinned. "Because this body is not the one I was born into. My spirit can move into and out of any body at will. This particular body is that of one of Cedar Hill's dead settlers. I find it rather comfortable, as does your friend the Reverend."

"The Reverend is like you?"

Judas shrugged. "Depending on which text you believe—the Bible, the Conical Texts, Thomas Aquinas's *Summa Theologica*, about a dozen or so others—the man you know as the Reverend is actually my step-brother. But I like to call him brother because it pisses him off and causes this little vein in the middle of his forehead to pop up. That amuses me."

"Who is he, really?"

"It is not my place to answer that, Ben. And you don't really need to know. Suffice to say that he was the man responsible for both cutting down and burying my body, as well as helping pry Christ's body from the cross. His hands had open wounds on that day, so the blood of both the Betrayer and the Betrayed mingled with his own. His punishment is due to a sin of omission. But you'll understand better, one day. Maybe.

"You know, you have more of a conscience than most possible recruits," said Judas. "But, being a policeman, you will also have more opportunity and freedom." He stood next to Ben, his long gray hair blowing backward, and placed a hand on his shoulder. "So I have a proposal for you: continue this work along with me, continue helping to maintain the balance of pain, and I'll let you use this." He held up the pocket watch the Reverend had given to Ben at the open shelter.

Ben checked his pocket and discovered it was empty.

"Yes, I count 'pickpocket' among my many acquired talents," said Judas, pressing down on the watch's latch and opening the cover before handing it back to Ben. "Note the time."

Ben looked and saw that the watch's hands were set at exactly 10:45.

"The same time I entered the Moundbuilders Diner last night," said Judas. "If you agree to join me, then all you have to do is press the small button atop that watch and it will run backward for one minute, going back to 10:44 P.M., *before* I entered the diner.

"Are you getting this, Benjamin? Start that watch, and once the second hand has gone around once in reverse . . . *none* of this will have happened, and only you, I, and the Reverend will carry the memory. Think about it. All of those innocent people, back among the living, going about their sad little lives as if nothing had happened, because nothing *will have* happened."

Ben looked at the watch. "Why did the Reverend and . . . and Rael give this to me?"

Judas smiled. "Rael is in debt to the Reverend for several reasons, so he cannot refuse a request. The Reverend—and how I wish I could tell you his real name, just to see the look on your face—the Reverend and I are a sort of . . . tag team, to use a wrestling term."

"He knew that you were going to make this offer to me?"

"*Knew?* My dear Ben, it was his idea."

Ben shook his head and began stepping backward. All around him the semihuman clouds of mist were becoming more solid, more corporeal, the nameless dead rising from their forgotten graves. Even the bodies hanging from the trees seemed to be twitching back to life.

"I don't believe you," he said to Judas.

"I didn't expect you would, so let me sweeten the deal. I will promise you this: for every death at your hands you will be given one hour with your wife and your son, Ian—as he would have been had he lived."

The first spattering of rain began to fall on their heads. The sky was fracturing.

"Come on, Ben," said Judas, looking toward the sky. "There is no more time for you. You can't help Al or Maddingly or anyone else now. What's done is done. This is why you were born.

"Your wife and son, Ben. Erasing everything that has happened since 10:45 last night. And the continued stillness of butterfly wings."

53

And now we are nearly at the end of our story, dear friends, one that no one in Cedar Hill except me remembers. Ben Littlejohn *did* start that watch and erase all that had happened since the night before. He accepted Judas's offer. The promise of being with his wife and son was more than he could resist.

As for me, I chose to remain in Cedar Hill as its guardian, its sentinel. There is nothing that happens here of which I am not aware; no event, no dying blade of grass, no ill thought, no pang of hunger, no moment of despair, no spoken word I do not hear, no memory that does not cross my mind as well as that of whomever calls it up from the shadows.

And here I shall remain, in this borrowed body, until such time as I am called to leave.

Were I to tell you who I really am, you would shake your head in disbelief. So allow me to tell you instead an old story that might help you figure it out for yourself.

A merchant in Baghdad sent his servant on an errand to the bazaar and the man came back white with fear and trembling. "Master," he said, "while I was in the marketplace, I walked into a stranger. When I looked him in the face, I found that it was Death. He made a threatening gesture at me and walked away. Now I am afraid. Please give me a horse so that I can ride at once to Samarra and put as great a distance as possible between Death and me."

The merchant—in his anxiety for the servant—gave him his swiftest steed. The servant was on it and away in a trice.

Later in the day the merchant himself went down to the bazaar and saw Death loitering there in the crowd. So he went up to him and said, "You made a threatening gesture at my poor servant this morning. What did it mean?"

"That was no threatening gesture, sir," said Death. "It was a start of surprise at seeing him here in Baghdad; for you see I have an appointment with him tonight . . . in Samarra."

I once had such an appointment, but my friends—such loyal friends—did not want for me to keep it. They stole me away by force and found another man to take my place.

But this isn't about me. And I can sense from the look on your faces that you may have figured it out by now.

Come, then; we need to follow Ben Littlejohn for a brief moment, and then I and this story will take our leave.

Three days after Cedar Hill was restored to how it had been before the man in the parka had entered the Moundbuilders Diner, Phil Dardis of Cedar Rapids, Iowa, along with his wife and their three kids, pulled out of their clean suburban driveway, and drove toward their big family reunion picnic twenty-two miles away.

Fifteen minutes later, right smack the hell in the middle of a country road lined on both sides with dense trees, they came upon a young, good-looking priest whose car had died on him. Despite his wife's protests, Phil, a good Catholic all his life, pulled over to give the priest some help.

"Is there something I can do for you, Father?"

"I'm afraid my fan belt snapped. Could you do me the kindness of driving me to the nearest phone?"

"Of course. There should be one at the park. That's where we're heading."

"Lovely family."

"Thank you. Here, let me help you with that. Don't wanna leave your bag out here where someone could grab it. Lucky for you we came along. Not many folks drive this road, too out-of-the-way. Whoa—this bag's pretty heavy, Father."

"Church decorations. I'll take it if you can't—"

"Shit! Oops, sorry. Darn thing came open and—what the hell?"

"I'll take that."

"Jesus, wait a second! You ain't no—hold it! *JESUS GODDAMN CHRIST LUCY GET OUT OF—!*"

It was a few hours later before Ben saw them standing by the side of the road. He pulled over and flung open the door. Cheryl climbed in first, then Ian. They had to fumble around the guns and rifles and other weapons, but that was okay, they were finally reunited. There was a lot of crying and kissing and hugging and rejoicing.

Cheryl told Ben that if he wanted to make love they'd have to find a place soon, they only had five hours and oh by the way the Dardis family bought another ninety-eight days and where did you get that big black dog in the backseat Ian just loves it.

Ben nodded his head and said the dog's name was Caiaphas and it was a gift from a friend. Then he stared out at the road and thought five hours with his family wasn't enough.

Forty minutes down the road they picked up a couple of hitchhikers before getting on the interstate—New Agers with crystals around their necks and one of those ersatz–Native American backpack things to carry their baby in.

Ben smiled later as he tossed their heads into a rest area Dumpster.

It was all worth it; and it was good.

Here, with his family; to have the time.

"Look," said Cheryl, pointing at a patch of flowers. "What a beautiful butterfly."

AND NOW, A BONUS:

Two Cedar Hill stories, featuring Grant McCullers and Sheriff Ted Jackson

I'LL PLAY THE BLUES FOR YOU

"I went to the crossroad, fell down on my knee,
Went to the crossroad, fell down on my knee,
Asked the Lord above to have mercy, save poor Bob
  if you please."
                                        —Robert Johnson

"The thing you got to understand is that people have
died *for this music."*
          —John Lee Hooker, BBC radio interview, 1973

1

Paying the Cost to Be the Boss

The legend says that if an aspiring bluesman waits by the side of a deserted country crossroads in the dark of a moonless night, then Satan himself will come and tune his guitar, sealing a pact for the bluesman's soul, guaranteeing him a lifetime of easy money, women, and fame. They believe there walks on the earth a very special few of them deal-makers, who must have waited by the crossroads and gotten their guitars fine-tuned.

Like all legends, son, things get a little mixed-up in the telling down through the years.

It's gonna be time soon for you take over; there's things you need to know about that responsibility.

Sit yourself down and listen to me.

There was a deal struck at the crossroads, but old Scratch—and don't let anyone tell you different—he had almost nothing to do with it . . .

2

Boogie Chillun'

I knew this was going to be the night when the old juke-box in the corner came on all by itself. The damn thing's nearly fifty years old, hasn't been used in almost as long, and so sets behind some crates, covered by tarp. We've got a computerized jukebox next to the dance floor that the customers prefer.

How'd I know it was the sign?

That old jukebox has never been plugged in; not for as long as I've run this place, anyway. Dad showed it to me the night he decided to retire.

I stood behind the bar, massaging my bad hand and staring at the eerie light that tried to push through the tarp as the miraculous opening croaks of John Lee Hooker's "One Bourbon, One Scotch, One Beer" managed to pull a king-snake crawl from underneath, twisting its funky tail in a snap-rattle dance and spitting in your eye if you didn't like it.

I looked at the clock.

Eleven P.M.

One hour and counting.

It's funny, the way Purpose works: You spend most of your life preparing for something, yet you still get a mondo case of the willies when it's upon you.

I took a quick shot of Jim Beam to steady my nerves and kill the pain in my arthritic hand (which is more of a claw at this point in my life), then flipped up the serving panel and came out from behind the bar to set about the preparations.

The first things I retrieved were the netting and the skulls.

My name is Grant McCullers, and my place is called Hangman's Tavern. It's located halfway between Cedar Hill and Buckeye Lake, but if you look for a sign to guide you there you'll never find it.

Watch for the crossroad two miles after you get off the highway. Can't miss it. And if the weather's bad and you can't see very far, then keep an eye peeled for the eight-foot "T" post on the left, the one with the noose dangling from it. The Klan used to bring blacks out here and hang them, then go on down the road for a few drinks. That's how our family business got its name. My great-grandfather was Klan and built this tavern. The male descendants who followed him decided not to pursue membership in that particular boys' club. Not that it helps erase the shame of our family's history.

The skulls—six of them altogether—belonged to blacks whose bodies had been cut down from the post and buried in the field that stretches for two miles behind tavern property. My grandfather found the bodies and, knowing what had to be done, took the skulls and left the remains to lie in peace.

I tried very hard not to look at the things as I gathered them up and put them one by one into the net sack; the idea of staring into those ancient, empty eye sockets gave me the shakes: Who knew what kind of phantoms waited in that bone-grave darkness.

I tied the top of the sack together with chicken wire, then slung it over my shoulder—the rattling from inside almost made my knees buckle—and made my way out the side door.

The night was cool and crisp and clean; darkness made into a jeweled blanket by the glittering stars above, each one winking down at me as if knowing I needed all the moral support I could get. I smiled at them, astonished as always at the thought that, the farther away a star was from the Earth, the closer it was to the moment the universe began; the closer it was to the Secret of where the Music came from, and what exactly it was the Songsters wanted.

I never dwelled on that for too long. It not only frightened me . . . it depressed me, as well.

I trudged down the road until I reached the hanging post, then tied the net of skulls to the noose and—as I'd been taught—spun them around hard, until the rope knotted at the top and began twisting itself back into position.

The skulls shifted and clattered.

So did my spine.

A sharp breeze came out of the south, holding the faintest traces of ozone.

Big storm a-comin'.

The clouds moved in almost at once, obscuring a section of sky perhaps five miles in circumference: the property boundaries of the tavern.

A small break in the center of the clouds allowed a single, intense moonbeam to cast its glow down into the center of the crossroad, a spotlight on an empty stage.

I closed my eyes, gripped the small mojo-bag in my pocket, and held my breath.

The faint, breathy sound of a train whistle drifted toward me, underscored by the melodious *clackitty-clack* of iron wheels against the track *(grab dat sack 'cause you ain't comin' back, jack)* and when I opened my eyes I saw Smokestack standing in the moon's spotlight.

Dressed in a raggedy coat and sporting an even raggedier fedora on his head, he was looking not at me but up at the light. He pulled the harmonica away from his mouth and whipped the hat off his head as if preparing to take a bow. His smile was lightning against the deep ebony of his skin. He tossed his hat in the air, let fly with a whoop and a holler, then caught the fedora, slapped it to his skull, and placed the harmonica back to his lips, one hand firmly grasping the harp, the other whirling in the air as he waved hello to the spirits that were out and about this night.

Kick-a-tap-tap, shuffle-tap-kick was the song his feet sang as he danced in the moon's follow-spot. For the next two hours, no one—human being, spirit, or otherwise—could pass this way without his permission.

Kick-a-tap-tap, shuffle-tap-kick—

—and his harp sang: *Oh, de Rock Island Line, it's a mighty good road, oh de Rock Island Line, it's the road to ride, oh de Rock Island Line is a mighty good road, if you want to ride it gotta ride like it you find get your ticket at the station fo' de Rock Island Line!*

"I may be right and I may be wrong," I sang.

"Know you gonna miss me when I'm gone," he replied in song, his baritone spiritual voice melting the chill of the dark.

Then his harp again: *Oh, de Rock Island Line is a mighty good road . . .*

I turned and started back toward the tavern.

Kick-a-tap-tap, shuffle-tap-kick.

I had marked this spot well; Smokestack had given me his blessing, as had those spirits whose ghostly voices joined in his chorus.

3

Good God Have Mercy

Some say it started with the War in Heaven. You know how that went down—Lucifer didn't win and got himself banished, but there were some of the angels who fought with him who went to God and said they was sorry, but God didn't want to hear it. He said they had to be punished and sent them away while He thought about their punishment. But the Good Lord, He got all caught up in creating mankind. The Fallen Angels, they didn't much care for all the attention God was givin' to mankind, so they stole the Book of Forbidden Knowledge from the Good Lord's library, and they came down here to Earth and they scattered, each of them taking a piece of the Forbidden Knowledge with 'em.

Some of 'em got down here and acquired a taste for human things—food, drink . . . women. And they laid a little angelic tube-steak on the chosen human women, and the children who were born from those couplings . . . they were Gifted in ways no regular human ever could be.

There are certain things that Man was never meant to know, understand. Poetry, Art, Sciences and such . . . and Music. That was maybe the worst of them all, Music, because it was supposed to belong only to the angels;

didn't matter which Master they served, Music was supposed to be theirs and theirs alone. But the Fallen Angels, they didn't have a place in either Heaven or Hell on account of what they done, especially after stealing the Book and getting their celestial rocks off and all. So Music was the first thing they gave to mankind, and damned if mankind didn't quite know what to do with it.

It took a long time before the Fallen Angels figured this out, and by then, well . . . Music was everywhere. There were some—damn few, truth be told—who knew how to use it, who were born with the Gift of Understanding on account of having an angel as one of their parents— Bach and Mozart and some of them fellahs—but most folks, they could only try to reach for what the music held before them.

So a few of these Gifted Ones—the Songsters—they came up with a plan.

One cold midnight.

At the crossroads.

They drew lots, and some of 'em snuck into Heaven, and the others . . . well, I guess you can figure out where they went.

And those bands of Gifted thieves, they managed to get what they went after.

4

(They Call It) Stormy Monday

I wasn't the least bit surprised to find the backup musicians already on stage and setting up their instruments when I returned. I nodded at one of them—the drummer whose face I recognized from a *Rolling Stone* story last year that came out two weeks after he died—and made a beeline for the bar.

The area within the bar itself is safe because it's blessed. The marble used for the top came from an altar my granddaddy bought from an old church that was being demolished, and forms an almost perfect sixteen-foot square around the serving area. The only vulnerable spot is the flip-up wooden serving board; once I was back behind the bar I immediately hung another mojo bag from the corner of the glass rack directly above it. It wasn't the most potent form of majick I could use to protect myself, but it would do for right now.

Thunder rumbled from outside, and the flashes of lightning became ever more intense.

The backup musicians finished setting up, then wandered over to the bar.

I set each of them up with a shot of whiskey and a beer, taking care not to look any of them directly in the eyes—even though I knew their gazes were fixed on me. Not that that bothers me. Having the use of only one hand has made me something of a local legend, so I'm used to patrons staring. It's an accomplishment of sorts, I guess: Even with only one hand, I can flip a glass, pour a shot, and open a bottle faster, smoother, and neater than bartenders who've got the use of all ten fingers.

You'll see things in their eyes, boy, that you'll spend the rest of your life trying to forget, my dad had told me. *Just sling the booze like you're supposed to and don't get too friendly and you'll be okay.*

I wondered if Dad would approve of the way I was handling myself. He'd died two years ago. I still missed him so much that I'd start crying like a baby if I thought on it for too long.

But there wasn't time for that tonight.

The lightning fried the sky again as the next clap of thunder threatened to blow the roof off the place.

The old jukebox finished playing its Hooker records and started in on its B.B. King collection.

Another flash of light, this one more focused and steady than the lightning but no less intense, drilled through the front window, hot on the heels of a roar that sounded like it came from the guts of an ancient dinosaur awakening. Godzilla arriving at the tavern, lawdy, lawdy, lawd.

"Ankou's Chariot," murmured one of the backup musicians.

I squinted my eyes and saw that the "chariot" was a screaming-chromed hog, its engines smoking and sparking as its midnight rider brought it to a screeching halt.

The backup musicians finished their drinks in a hurry and got back to the stage.

The light died, the roar choked into silence, and a

few moments later the front doors were kicked open with such force they banged against the walls and loosed some plaster from the ceiling.

Ankou stood there holding his ax of choice—a banged-up Fender Strat—by the neck, its body balanced on his shoulder.

His height was a good seven feet even, at least. He wore a black duster that looked more like Dracula's cape from my viewpoint, and his long white hair hung down over his shoulders. Adding to the effect was the wide-brimmed hat on his head, part of which was bent down to hide his eyes.

He stormed toward the bar. The doors slammed closed behind him even though he made no move to touch them. He took a seat at the bar, gently laid the Strat across the wooden serving board, and snapped his fingers.

I pulled the pack of cigarettes from my pocket and shook one out for him. He took it, put it in his mouth, then flicked index finger to thumbnail and brought forth a small flame from his thumb. Once the smoke was lighted, he blew the flame out.

His flesh was not charred in the least.

Then he reached up and pushed back his hat.

Even though Dad had warned me over the years about what to expect, the sight of his face still made my parts wither.

His skin had the gray pallor of a corpse, pulled so tightly over his skull that for a moment he appeared to be only a skeleton. Two tear-shaped holes squatted in the center of his face where a nose should have been, and he stared at me through two empty, tomb-dark eye sockets.

"I was a lot prettier when the day started," he said. His voice was the echo of rat's claws scratching against the cement of a crypt pit.

I reached up and pulled a whiskey tumbler from the overhead rack but my hand was shaking so badly that I dropped it.

It never hit the floor.

The second it fell from my hand Ankou opened his mouth and from it shot a long, thin, forked toad's tongue that whipcurled around the glass and sucked it back toward the bar.

"Hit me," he hissed.

I filled the tumbler with Jack Daniel's Black. Ankou slammed it back and demanded another.

"Gettin' a little greedy in yer old age, ain't'cha?" came a voice from somewhere beyond the bar.

I whirled around in time to catch a glimpse of a small, fiery circle throbbing to life, then dying away.

The sickly-sweet stink of cigar smoke wafted toward me.

"Just look at 'im, will ya? You done went and damn near gave 'im a case of the screaming meemies, Ankou."

"My heart bleeds, J.J."

The man in the darkness chortled, then slowly walked forward into the light.

Understand something: I am not a racist, but the only way to describe this man was to say that he was *astoundingly* black. I had never seen a black man of that impenetrable hue: It was a blackness of such intensity that it reflected no light at all, achieving a virtual obliteration of facial features and taking on a mysterious undertone that had the blue-gray of ashes. He flashed me a blissful grin, revealing deathly purple gums, the yellowish stumps of several teeth, and oddly colorless lips.

"Doesn't look to me like you're up for the fight tonight, J.J.," said Ankou.

"Hear that?" J.J. asked me. "He's concerned for my

well-bein'." He took a seat at the opposite end of the bar. "I'm touched, Bone-Bag; really, I am."

"Don't call me that."

"Then don't call me 'J.J.' like we're life-long buddies, asshole."

"Is that any way for the son of an angel to talk, Juke-Joint?"

"Angel this," he said, turning both thumbs down toward his crotch.

After a moment of the tensest silence I have ever endured, JukeJoint looked at me and said, "You gonna peer or you gonna pour? I just came across time, space, and Highway 61 to get my sorry butt here, and I'm a bit thirsty."

I reached up for another glass and immediately recoiled in revulsion.

I have this recurring nightmare where my right hand—my good hand—swells up like some dead bloated thing and begins to rupture, its tendons turned to cotton. I sit there in the nightmare and bend down my head and start pulling the cotton out with my teeth until all that's left at the end of my wrist is a limp, useless, bony starfishlike *thing*, and usually wake up in tears because now I have no hands left.

The cotton tendons of my right hand were bursting forth now, and as I recoiled in horror a shriek escaped my mouth and Ankou laughed.

"How you sleeping these days, pal?"

"*Knock it off!*" snarled JukeJoint.

I blinked several times, took a deep breath, and looked at my hand.

Intact, no cotton tendons bursting.

I swallowed very hard, trying to stop the single tear from slipping out my eye, but it did no good.

"It's all right, boy," said JukeJoint. "Now, how's about my drink?"

I gave him a whiskey and a beer.

I hoped that neither of them sensed how much I was trembling inside.

Finally Bone-Bag Ankou looked at me with his grave-gaze and said, "You got the strings for us?"

"Right here," I said, ashamed of the little-boy terror in my voice as I pulled the ancient wooden box from under the bar and inserted the key in its lock.

5

I'm On My Last Go-Round

What these thieves did, each of 'em stole a hair: One from God's beard, the other from one of the Devil's cloven hooves. And when they got back here to this world, they twisted them two hairs together to make a string, a very special guitar string, forged in Evil, Holiness, and Steel.

Then they cut that string in half so each side'd have equal power for the fight.

They say that those strings can produce sounds the likes of which no axman, regardless of how skilled he is, can ever hope to reach.

I always used to dream about hearing them sounds, but you and me both know I ain't gonna be around much longer. Spent my whole life waiting to hear that kind of music. You know, ever since your mother passed on, it's been one of the few things that's kept me going, hoping to hear that sound. That—and knowing what a good son you been to me.

If you get picked, son, if you're still running the place on the night of the showdown, and if you are honored to hear them sounds, listen real good for me, will you? Remember that music, and maybe I can snatch me a little listen, wherever it is I'll be.

6

People Get Ready

I wish I could tell you that the two guitar strings looked to be spun from gold or crackled with lightning or felt ethereal to the touch, but the truth is they just looked like any pair of E-strings you could buy at any music store. Each was rolled very carefully and sealed inside an airtight plastic bag. I handed one to Bone-Bag and one to JukeJoint and stood there in respectful silence as each of them added it to their guitars.

Where Bone-Bag had the Strat, JukeJoint, surprisingly, had a new-looking Les Paul with a brilliant sunburst finish. I'd expected something a little more, I don't know, *worn* for his ax of choice. Something whose age was as unfathomable as his.

As they finished stringing, I took a brandy snifter and set in on the bar, then pulled out my switch and freed the blade.

The two of them looked at the knife and laughed.

"You call *that* a knife?" said JukeJoint.

Bone-Bag shook his head. "I pick my teeth with things bigger'n that."

Both of them proceeded to reach into their coat pockets and produce knives that were only quarter-inches short of qualifying as machetes.

They looked at each other, nodded their agreement, climbed down from their stools and met in the middle of the bar where the snifter waited, then each one very quickly twisted their blades to make a small cut on the other's thumb.

They bled into the snifter until it was half full, then each put their bleeding thumb into their mouth, sucked once, and healed the wound.

I wasted no time: I took the snifter and poured their mixed blood in a straight line across the floor in front of the serving panel. I was now completely safe from any unfriendly spirits or harmful majick that might try to find a way behind the bar.

"All right, boy," said JukeJoint. "You pour the liquor, you got the power, you say yeah or nay: We do a warm-up set or what?"

I looked at my watch: 11:40 P.M. "Five minutes to tune, five minutes to warm up."

Bone-Bag gestured toward my left hand. "Arthritis's a bitch, isn't it?"

"Crippled up that hand before I was twelve."

"Looks like a damned claw."

"Thank you. And that night cream's doing wonders for your complexion."

"Hoo-wee!" shouted JukeJoint, slapping his hand to the bar. "He got you with that one, Ankou."

"Lucky shot."

Something in his voice told me that if he won tonight, I was going to be in deep sewage.

They each laid straps to their axes, then slipped them on over their shoulders.

JukeJoint cocked his head at me. "Gonna wait 'til the Midnight Hour, eh?"

"I thought it would be a nice touch."

"One thing I always despised about your race," hissed Ankou, "is that you people always have to make everything so *dramatic*. Like afflicting something with ritual will somehow make it important. Well, get this: None of it means shit to us. Only the music, only *this*"—he held up his guitar—"means a damn—and then only because of what it can produce, not because of the thing itself."

"I knew he'd be in one of his moods," whispered JukeJoint. "By the way, *you* can call me J.J."

Ankou glowered. "Don't encourage him."

J.J. grinned. "You never were any fun."

"Go to Hell."

"We're trying to move back into the *other* neighborhood, asshole. At least get the zip code right."

I checked my watch again. Almost 11:50. "Better get yourselves on the stage."

"Not just yet," said J.J. "Since you pour the liquor and provide the stage, you get one question and we *gotta* answer it. You wanna ask it now or after it's over?"

I thought about the implied threat in Ankou's voice earlier and figured this might be the only chance I get. "Look, I know *what* you are, and I know what it is you're here to do . . . but what I don't understand is why."

Ankou snorted a derisive laugh. "That's not a question."

"He's right," said J.J. "Like on that one game show, you gotta ask it as a *question.*"

"Why do you have to do this?"

J.J. looked over at Ankou. "You wanna take that one?"

"Not without another shot in me."

I filled his glass and watched him slam it back.

"You know that old saying about monkeys and typewriters?" he asked.

"No."

"Somebody once said that if you put enough monkeys in a room with enough typewriters, eventually one of them would write *Hamlet.* It's the same way with Music, you little pissant. Despite how primitive your race is, something got screwed up. You weren't *supposed* to inherit the gift of Music, but our daddies, they done went and gave it to you, anyway. Dipshits." He shrugged his massive shoulders. "For the longest time no one really worried about it—I mean, what the hell was the chance any of *you* were going to even come close to reaching into the heart of song? Only *we* could do that—and then only with lifetimes of practice behind us.

"But something went wrong. Too many monkeys got their filthy hands on too many typewriters and . . . your race started to tap into the Secret of Music. Not often, and sometimes not very well, but some of you showed promise. And so it was decided that maybe, just maybe your race might actually be Worthy of Music. One day you might get it right, and so long as that potential existed, it couldn't very well be taken back from you.

"So every so often, when Music starts to change—like when, say, rock 'n' roll was getting started, or all that electronic progressive garbage infected the '70s—we have to come to dumps like this and fight it out on our axes. We gotta box heads. We gotta play our way through cramp-inducing variations on every goddamn form of Music your race has managed to cough up by accident and see if it all hangs together." He cracked his knuckles. "Personally, I'd just as soon make all of you deaf and be done with it, but nobody's left it up to me."

"But which one of you is fighting for us to keep it and which one—?"

"*One* question, boy," said J.J. "One to a customer."

I nodded, suddenly very frightened.

It was quite possible that before the next hour was over, Music would be taken away from humankind.

"Is everyone in?" whispered Ankou in a pretty good Jim Morrison imitation. "The ceremony is about to begin."

And the jukebox went dead.

7

Goin' Down Slow

One more thing, son, then I need to rest my eyes for a while.

Ritual is important when the time comes. I know it sounds kinda silly, but you got to remember that even in them cases when Music has no connection to the ritual act, folks'll still tell you that they get something outta Music of all kinds. Know why that is? 'Cause Music is the emotional substitute for the ritual—and why the hell not? Christian angels're supposed to be consummate musicians, and performing Music's believed to be a suitable occupation for timeless life in Heaven. Hope to hell I get to tickle the ivories up there, over there—wherever.

The words of the Scripture are sung as well as spoken; temple, church, and synagogue musicians, choirs and cantors, songs and hymns, rhythms and Hindu whatchamacallits—ragas—ain't all of those things considered an important part of their religion?

Music represents the struggle of reaching the . . . the wholly other, which most musicians can never express. But for it to be true, to be alive and have some meaning, it's gotta come not just from the heart but from the belly and guts and every living part. That's why I envy you, and cry for you, too, truth be told: Weren't for your hand being all crippled up like it is, you coulda been one of the real ones. Me? Sit me down in front a piano and I can play the notes, sure, play 'em just as sweet as you please, but that . . . that extra thing, the thing that exists between the notes and beyond the song itself . . . I'll never know what it feels like to reach it.

Just remember, son, that even though you'll never reach it, either, you could have.

And that ought to comfort you. Maybe not much, but some.

We gotta do this because we can't have Music taken back, understand? Can you imagine a world without Music? Even the sound of the morning birds? Gives me the willies just thinking about it.

Okay . . . I done told you everything I know about it. Now you go on about your business and let me . . . let me rest my eyes for a little bit, okay?

8

The Midnight Special

I thought they'd get up there and loose hellfire on the world.

Not even close.

At least, not at first.

Ankou stood on one side of the stage, J.J. on the other. One of them—to this day I can't tell you which—began playing Bach's "Sheep May Safely Graze," fingers so light and gentle against the strings, a whisper, a ray of warm sunlight on your face after the storm clouds had passed; the other began playing "Joy of Man's Desiring," a sigh of thanks because you'd lived to see another morning and hadn't really expected to, the sound of dreams laughing quietly because they know something you don't, something great; and despite these two pieces of music being written by the same composer several years apart, Ankou and J.J. played them in perfect opposing harmony, as if the pieces had always meant to be joined together, "Sheep" filling in the empty spaces left after "Joy" 's refrain, and I couldn't help but wonder if Bach had planned it that way all along, the two pieces simply components of a much larger musical puzzle, because the two skilled guitarists on the stage before me merged the two separate themes to-

gether to create a third and—believe it or not—even
more moving theme.

I looked down at my crippled hand and felt a sting of
something like regret, but a quick shot of Jim Beam put
that back in storage.

Their warm-up evidently over, J.J. moved to the side
of the stage while Ankou crossed to his amplifier and
used his knife to split the speaker cones right down the
middle.

The backup band was looking ready for battle.

Nodding to J.J., Ankou struck strings with pick, his
Strat gave out with a little shriek, but it didn't end there
because he bent those strings and played with his volume knobs and in a breath took that little shriek and
turned it into feedback that he pulled down into his
whammy bar and rebuilt right before my ears, taking
the atonal and filtering it through the pickups and
strings and his surprisingly deft fingers and before you
knew it those tones and feedback were singing a portion of Bach's "Fugue in G," building higher on the final
note, higher, louder, wider, until at last Ankou hit and
sustained a note that must have pulled from the guts of
all the Fallen Angels, and he threw back his head and
let fly with a laugh that was equal parts glory and grotes-
querie, then stomped his foot four times, real slow but
not too slow, and on the fourth stomp the backup band
kicked in all at once, bass and piano and drums and
guitars—

—and the sound was that of a flaming 747 screaming
down from the sky as they broke into a traditional blues
riff, the classic twelve-bar harmonic progression of one-
four-five, and God it was something to hear, the band so
into it, so tight, so together, thrashing out the four bars
of tonic, then two of subdominant, two more of tonic,
two of dominant, and the final two of tonic, laying the
groundwork that Ankou built upon, and I wish I could

tell you that there was something evil in Ankou's playing but there wasn't, it was *pure,* man, as pure as you can get and still expect to be breathing once it's over, and as the band kept it together underneath, Ankou's finger dragged and ripped over the strings, bringing forth the ghostly voices of every slave who worked in every field and coal pit—*Born a day when the sun didn't shine*—bending the strings until they shrieked in agony and desperation—*Picked up my shovel and I went to the mine*—spitting out notes like bullets from a machine gun, hammering it out at double-time, then quadruple-time but never sacrificing a sense of order—*Loaded sixteen tons o' number nine coal*—his touch isolating overtones by playing one string with his pick while simultaneously brushing another with his fingernail—*And the straw boss he said well bless my soul*—and now he was Up There someplace, someplace where the Music lived, his ax releasing the vocalized screams of a Pentecostal church choir trying to overpower the sliding-trail notes of a hillbilly steel guitar—

—and then it was J.J.'s turn, and he took over in the middle of a note as if he'd been the one playing it; only where Ankou ended in fire and brimstone, J.J. started in gentle waters: mercurial, warm, yet defiant and biting: subtle and tender, to be sure, yet just as often brutal and cool. He knew the value of playing few notes with frightening precision, standing there as proof of what a man could become when he resisted easy answers, and just when you thought he couldn't make his ax sound any more loving, there was a sudden eruption at his fingertips, naked, razor-blade howls of anger and power—*Take this ol' hammer, take it to the captain*—and Ankou answered him, just as cocky and mad—*Take this ol' hammer, take it to the captain*—then it was the two of them together, opposing harmonies in perfect sync—*Tell him I'm-a-goin', I'm-a-goin' HOME!*—

—and that's when they reached even higher, sounds swirling around me like mythical winged creatures dancing on the unforgiving metallic truth of their guitars, and the bass, it was a-thumping, and the cymbals, they were a-crashing, and the piano keys, they were a-crying as the pianist's fingers made glissandos over the ivories, and I was *there*, I was with them, hanging on to every note and nuance, letting fly with ol' spirituals, the work songs and field hollers and arhoolies . . . I swear I could still hear the griots of all the old tribes in there, as if the bodies of the slaves buried in the field had risen up, risen up high, ohLord, singing loud and true and fine, the bent-pitch blue notes of the guitars giving these ghosts back their collective voice—

—and just as quickly as I was with them, I was suddenly apart, because somewhere in there, between Ankou sliding out of his second solo and J.J. starting in on his third, I saw my dad during the last weeks of his life: Broken and sick, spending too much time in his near-empty room that writhed with loneliness and defeat and sadness and drift, and I wished he'd lived to see this, to hear this, to be here and experience this sound for himself, but he hadn't, he'd died in his sleep after missing one shot too many of his insulin, and I missed him more at that moment than I ever had before, and I wept, Jesus! I wept like a baby and didn't give a damn who or what saw me, just stood there crying in the middle of a Music that no human ear had ever heard before and probably would never hear again—

—my hand. My stinking hand. God, how I wanted to be able to play like they were, and I knew that was never going to happen because boys with crippled hands, ohLord, they don't get to Reach for the sound, they don't get to step into the wholly other, no, they stand behind bars and sling the booze and listen to the Songsters from all walks of life, even those who don't cross time and space and Highway 61 to get here, they stand and sling and listen and long for some way to achieve even a little piece of that dream—

—but isn't that what it's all about? I asked myself suddenly, my dad's voice strong in my head. Isn't that what Music is supposed to do, give you dreams, give you songs to sing when you're feeling down, songs that'll make the hurt go away and, if not go away, at least loosen its grip on your spirit?

Damn straight, I thought.

And I *put* myself back into the battle with them. I listened, I listened good for my dad and hoped he was able to snatch himself a little listen, wherever or whenever he was.

Hellfire and Angelic song loosed on the world then. I couldn't tell which of them was playing what because their hands and fingers were moving so smoothly, so fast and furiously, for several moments I couldn't even *see* their fingers.

I swear to God, until the day I die I'll swear on a stack of Bibles, I tell you, that right at the end, just as everything was winding up and grinding down and the guitars looked like they wanted nothing more than to limp off stage and whimper in a dark corner—right at the end, I *swear* that flames leapt from the strings.

And then it was over.

Silence.

Not even fuzz-tone feedback from the smoking amps.

Ankou and J.J. put down their guitars, shook hands, and invited the band up to the bar for a drink.

I was still crying when they all took their seats, crying so hard, so openly and unashamedly, that I couldn't get my good hand to steady the bottles, so I just sat the booze on the bar and told them all to pour to their hearts' content.

And you bet that's just what they did.

I couldn't blame them.

Creating that kind of Music had to be thirsty, thirsty work.

I have no idea how long I stayed that way, bawling my head off behind the bar, but eventually I became aware that they'd stopped talking among themselves and when I was able to wipe my eyes and look, everyone was gone except for J.J.

"Feel better now, do you?"

"I don't know." I blew my nose and managed to pour myself a shot. "Which one of you won?"

J.J. laughed. "Neither one of us did. Which means that y'all get to keep the Music for a while longer."

"But I don't understand—"

He held up his hand, silencing me. "The whole point behind our doing this, son, is that there *ain't supposed* to be a winner. As long as your race keeps the Music evolving, you get to keep it. You didn't hear the mistakes we started makin' toward the end—hell, maybe you couldn't even *tell* they was mistakes, but we made 'em, you bet'cha. And you know why? Because it's starting to look like you folks are getting the hang of it. You're getting closer and closer to getting it right. Ought to make you feel good."

"It should . . . but it doesn't."

"That hand of yours?"

". . . yeah . . ."

"You ever hear the story about Paganini? Wanted to be a concert pianist, had his heart set on it, but his fingers was just too damned long to master the keys. So he took up the violin and became a virtuoso."

"Meaning?"

"Meaning that you done spent so much time crying over what that crippled-up hand of yours *can't* do that you never once gave a thought to what it *can* do." He got up from the bar, handed the two E-strings back, and said, "Take a little stroll with me."

We went down to the crossroad where Smokestack was still playing.

"Remember Paul Butterfield?" asked J.J.

"Yes, I do. I wept the day he died."

"Did you know he had arthritis in one of his hands?"

"You're kidding?"

"Yeah, I'm a real cut-up. No, I wouldn't lie." He snapped his fingers, and Smokestack stopped playing, tossed his harmonica to J.J., then disappeared. Just like that.

J.J. handed the harp to me. "You'd be surprised what a claw-hand like yours can do when it comes to holdin' on to one of these, to movin' it back and forth while your other hand does the easy part." He shoved the harmonica in my pocket. "You're a good kid, and I'll be sure to let your daddy know you're doin' right by him and the Music."

Before I could say anything, he picked up his battered guitar case and walked into the shadows, wrapping them around him like a blanket and vanishing back into time, space, and the shortcut to Highway 61.

I looked up to the stars and heard the music of the night birds, of passing cars and the dying storm.

And suddenly I didn't feel so dreamless.

9

Further On Up The Road

Stop in sometime.

My place is called Hangman's Tavern. I'll tell you the story behind it over a drink.

I don't know that I'll ever marry, ever have a son to pass the legacy on to, but there's a gal who waits tables for me on the weekends who makes no secrets that her eye's on me. I give her a lot of looks, too.

So, maybe . . .

So you stop in here some night. Listen to the band, or to the old jukebox (I got rid of the newer one, finally). Stick around afterward, and when the place closes we'll sit down at the bar and I'll tell you the story of a great battle that was fought here once, years ago, a battle for the soul of Music.

Maybe you'll believe it, and maybe you won't.

But it makes for a good whiskey-drinking story.

And after the story, if you feel like it, I'll take out my harp and tell you how it came to be mine, and if you've a notion, I'll try to Reach what the Music has to offer and make you hear the sounds that Angels have fought and died for.

Men, as well.

And maybe you'll leave feeling a little less dreamless.

Stop in some night. Have a drink. Listen to a few stories. Listen to a few tunes.

And then . . . throw a pebble in the ocean . . . if you've a notion . . .

. . . I'll play the blues for you.

*In Memory of Paul Butterfield, Roy Buchanan,
and Rory Gallagher*

UNION DUES

"It is one of the great tragedies of this age that as soon as man invented a machine he began to starve."
—Oscar Wilde, *The Soul of Man Under Socialism*

(here is my son
does he have the makings of a factory man?
does he have the mark of a worker?
will he do me proud?)

1

A man works his whole life away, and what does it mean?

Please don't ask me that question, Dad.

On the line your hands grow aching and calloused, your body grows sore and crooked, and your spirit fades like sparks between the gears. The roar of machinery chisels its way into your brain and spreads until it's the only thing that's real. The work goes on, you die a little more with each whistle, and the next paycheck is tucked inside the rusty metal lunch pail that really ought to be replaced but you can't afford to right now.

A man works his whole life away. For twenty-three years he reports to work on time, punches the clock, takes his place on the line, and allows his body to become one-half of a tool. He works without complaint and never calls in sick no matter how bad he feels, and for this he gets to come home once a week and present his family with a paycheck for one hundred and eight-seven dollars and sixteen cents. Dirt money. Chump change. Money gone before it's got. Then one day he notices the way his kid looks at him, he sees the disappointment, and he wants to scream but settles for a few cold beers instead.

And what does it mean? It means a man becomes embarrassed by what he is, humiliated by his lack of education, ashamed that he can only give his family the things they need and not the things they want.

So a man grows angry—

—because even in his dreams—

(. . . doors open and the OldWorker is cast away . . .)

—the work goes on—

—and the machines wait for him to return and make them whole again—

Don't say these things, Dad.

I can't help it, boy.

Sometimes it gets to be too much.

2

Sheriff Ted Jackson held a handkerchief over his nose and mouth as he surveyed the wreckage of the riot.

(. . . as the production line begins again . . .)

A cloud of tear gas was dissipating at neck level in the parking lot of the factory, reflecting lights from the two dozen police cars encircling the area. Newspaper reporters and television news crews were assembling outside the barricades along with people from the neighborhood and relatives of the workers involved. Silhouetted against the rapidly setting cold November sun, the crowd looked like one massive duster of cells; a shadow on a lung x-ray—sorry, bud, this looks bad.

Men lay scattered, some on their sides, others on their backs, still more squatting and coughing and vomiting, all wiping blood from their faces and hands.

A half foot of old crusty snow had covered the ground since the first week of the month, followed by days and nights of dry cold, so that the snow had merely aged and turned the color of damp ash, mottled by candy wrappers, empty cigarette packs, losing lottery tickets, beer cans, and now bodies. The layer of snow whispering from the sky was a fresh coat of paint; a whitewash that hid the ugliness and despair of the tainted world underneath.

A pain-filled voice called out from somewhere.

Fire blew out the windshield of an overturned semi; it jerked sideways, slammed into a guardrail, and puked glass.

The crowd pushed forward, knocking over several of the barriers. Officers in full riot gear held everyone back.

The snow grew dense as more sirens approached.

The searchlight from a police helicopter swept the area.

A woman in the crowd began weeping loudly.

You couldn't have asked for an uglier mess.

Jackson pulled the handkerchief away and took an icy breath; the wind was trying to move the gas away but the snow held it against the ground. He turned up the collar of his jacket and pulled a twenty-gauge pump-action shotgun from the cruiser's rack.

"Sheriff?"

Dan Robinson, one of his deputies, offered him a gas mask.

"Little late for that."

"I know, but the fire department brought along extras and I thought—"

"Piss on that." Jackson stared through the snow at the crowd of shadows. The strobing visibar lights perpetually changed the shape of the pack; red-*blink*—a smoke crowd; blue-*blink*—a snow-ash crowd; white-*blink*—a shadow crowd.

"You okay, Sheriff?"

"Let's go see if they cleared everyone away from the east side."

The two men trudged through the heaps of snow, working their way around the broken glass, twisted metal, blood, grease, and bodies. Paramedics scurried in all directions; gurneys were collapsed, loaded, then lifted into place and rolled toward waiting ambulances. Volunteers from the local Red Cross were administering aid to those with less serious wounds.

"Any idea how this started, sir?"

"The scabs came out for food. Strikers cut off all deliveries three days ago."

"Terrible thing."

"You got that right."

They rounded the corner and took several deep breaths to clear their lungs.

(. . . the shift whistle blows like a birth scream, and the factory worker springs forth, with shoulders and arms made powerful for the working of apron handwheels . . .)

Jackson remembered the afternoon he'd had to come down and assist with bringing in the scabs—the strikers behind barricades on one side of the parking lot while the scabs rode in on flatbed trucks like livestock to an auction. Until that afternoon he'd never believed that rage was something that could live outside the physical confines of a man's own heart, but as those scabs climbed down and began walking toward the main production floor entrance he'd felt the presence of cumulative anger becoming something more fierce, something hulking and twisted and hideous. To this day he couldn't say how or why, but he could swear that the atmosphere between the strikers and scabs had rippled and even torn in places. It still gave him the willies.

He blinked against the falling snow and felt his heart skip a beat.

Twenty yards away, near a smoldering overturned flatbed at the edge of the east parking lot, a man lay on the ground, his limbs twisted at impossible angles. A long, thick smear of hot machine oil pooled behind him, hissing in the snow.

Maneuvering through the snowdrifts Jackson raced over, slid to a halt, chambered a shell, and dropped to one knee, gesturing for Robinson to do the same.

Jackson looked down at the body and felt something lodge in his throat. "Damn. Herb Kaylor."

"You know him?"

Jackson tried to swallow but couldn't. The image of the man's face blurred; he wiped his eyes and realized that he was crying. "Yeah. Him and me served together in Vietnam. I just played cards with him and his wife a couple nights ago. *Goddammit!*" He clenched his teeth. "He wasn't supposed to be workin' the picket line today. Christ! Poor Herb. . . ."

He turned away, shook himself, and looked back at the man whose company he'd known and treasured, and cursed himself for never letting Herb Kaylor know just how much his friendship had meant.

Kaylor's neck was broken so badly that his head was turned almost fully around. Jackson reached out to close his friend's dead eyes—

—his fingers brushed the skin—

—*I barely touched him*—

—and the eyes fell through the sockets into the skull. There was no blood.

"Jesus!" shouted Robinson.

"I hardly—!" Jackson never completed the sentence.

With a series of soft, dry sounds, Herb Kaylor's skull collapsed inward; the flesh crumbled and flaked away as his face sank back, split in half, and dissolved.

Robinson was so shaken by the sight that he lost his balance and pushed a hand through Kaylor's hollowed chest. He tried to pull himself from the shell of desiccated skin and brittle bone but only managed to sink his arm in up to the elbow. Jackson pulled him out; Robinson's arm was covered in large clumps of decayed, withered flesh. Bits and pieces of Herb Kaylor blew away like so much soot.

Jackson stared into the empty chest cavity.

Robinson backed away, dry-retching.

A strong gust of wind whistled by, leveling to a chronic breeze.

(. . . the factory man turns his gaze toward the plant's ceiling . . .)

Unable to look at Herb's body any longer, Jackson rose to his feet and turned toward the sliding iron doors that served as the entrance to the basement production cells.

He could feel the power of the machines inside; at first it was little more than a low, constant thrum beneath his feet, but as he began to walk toward the doors the vibrations became stronger, louder, snaking up out of the asphalt and coiling around his legs, soaking through his skin and latching onto his bones like the lower feed-fingers of a metal press, shuddering, clanking, hissing and screeching into his system, fusing with his bloodstream as carbon fused with silicon and lead with bismuth, riding the flow up to his brain and spreading across his mind: it became a deep, rolling hum in his ears, then an enveloping pressure, and, at last, a whisper.

Welcome, my son—

—a powerful gust of wind shrieked around him, kicking against his legs—

—*welcome to the Machine.*

It came from the opening between the doors, and as Jackson moved toward them something long and metallic slipped out, flexed, then vanished back into the darkness of the plant before he could get to it. Jackson blinked against the snow and shook his head. Every so often he'd see something like that in his dreams, a prosthetic hand, its metal fingers closing around his throat . . . and the thing he'd glimpsed had been like the hand in his dreams, only much, much larger.

Jesus, I gotta start sleeping better, can't start seein' shit like that while I'm awake or—

"Christ Almighty!" shouted Robinson.

Jackson whirled around and instinctively leveled the shotgun but the wind was so strong he lost his grip and the weapon flew out of his hands, slamming against a far wall and discharging into a four-foot snowdrift.

He stared at the body of Herb Kaylor.

No way, no goddamn way he can still be alive—

—moving, no mistaking that, Herb was moving; one arm, then another, then both legs—

—Jackson reached out and grabbed the iron handrail leading down the stairs; it was the only way he could keep his balance against the wind—

—that seemed to be concentrated on what was left of Herb's body, lifting it from the ground like a marionette at the end of tangled strings, its limbs twisted akimbo, shaking and flailing in violent seizurelike spasms, flaking apart and scattering into the wind, churning into dust and dirtying the funneling snow; even the clothes were shredded and cast away.

It was over in less than a minute.

Jackson slowly climbed the steps and rejoined Robinson. They stood in silence, staring at the spot where Kaylor's body had been—

—the steps into the basement—

(*It sure as hell* looked *like a hand* of *some sort.*)

—but the pressure returned to his ears, three times as painful—

—*what are these marks, Daddy? They're just like the ones on your back only mine don't bleed—*

—he shook his head and pressed his hands against his ears as he spiraled back to that morning so many years ago, during a strike not unlike this one; his own father, so desperate because the strike fund had gone dry and he'd been denied both welfare and unemployment benefits, had decided to cross the picket line. He remembered the way his mother had cried and held Dad's hand and begged him not to go, saying that she could get a job somewhere, maybe doing people's laundry or something—

—and the look on her face later, when the police came to tell her about the Accident, that Dad had somehow ("We're not sure how it happened, ma'am, no one wants to talk about it.") been crushed by his press, and Jackson remembered, then, the last thing Dad had said to him before leaving that morning, something about being welcome to come and see his machine—

—Jackson took a deep breath and stood straight, clearing his head of the pain and pressure.

"What the hell happened, Sheriff?" asked Robinson, handing back Jackson's shotgun.

"I never saw anything like it," whispered Jackson. "How do you suppose a man could get crushed in a press like that and no one saw it happen?"

"What are you talking about, Sheriff?"

Jackson blinked, cleared his throat and faced his deputy. "I mean . . . Jesus . . . how could a body just . . . *dry up* like that? You had your arm in there, Dan. The man had no internal organs. When his head collapsed there was no brain inside the skull." He fished around inside his pockets, found his cigarettes, then lit one for himself and one for Robinson.

They smoked in silence for a moment.

Around the corner, the sounds of the crowd grew angrier, louder. The chopper made another sweep of the area. Sirens shrieked as ambulances sped from the scene with their broken and bleeding cargoes.

Jackson crushed out his cigarette, turned to Robinson, and said, "Listen to me. I don't want you *ever* to tell anyone what happened out here, understand me? Not the other guys, your girlfriend, your parents, *nobody*. This stays between us, all right?"

"You got my word, Sheriff."

A gunshot cracked through the dusk and the crowd erupted into panic. Jackson and Robinson grabbed their weapons and ran to lend what assistance they could.

(. . . the iron support beams in the factory's ceiling ripple and coil around one another, becoming sinewy muscle tissue that surges down and combines with the cranks . . .

. . . which become lungs . . .

. . . that attach themselves to the press foundation . . .

. . . which evolves into a spinal column . . .

. . . that supports the control panel as it shudders . . .

. . . and spreads . . .

. . . and becomes the gray matter of a brain signaling everything to converge . . .

. . . pulsing steelbeat pounding faster and faster . . .

. . . moist pink muscle tissue, tendons, bones, sparks, tubes, metal shavings, flesh, iron, organs, and alloys coalescing . . .

. . . and the being that is the Machine stands before the factory man, its shimmering electric gaze drilling into them as it reaches down and lifts them to its bosom, feeding, draining them of all essence until they are little more than a clockwork doll whose every component has been removed . . .

. . . doors open and the OldWorker is cast away . . . a hiss . . . a clank . . .

   . . . the next shift arrives . . .
   . . . as the production line begins again . . .)
   The east parking lot was empty now. No one was there to hear the sounds from behind the iron doors.
   Squeaking, screeching, loud clanking, heavy equipment dragging across a cement floor.
   Something long, metallic, and triple-jointed pushed through the doors, folding around the edge. Another glint as more metal thrust out and folded back.
   Throwing sparks, the mechanical hand raked down, gripped the handle, and pulled the doors closed.
   The structure of the factory trembled.
   The breeze picked up, swirling snow down the steps and up against the doors with a low whistle; a groan in the back of a tired man's throat.
   A man works his whole life away, and what does it mean?
   The wind stilled.
   It means he has the makings of a factory man.
   Shadows bled over the walls.
   He has the mark of a worker.
   A shredded section of Herb Kaylor's shirt drifted to the ground, floating back and forth with the ease of a feather. It hit the dirty snow and was covered by a rolling drift of chill, dead white.

3

Hearing the noise is nothing at times. No, the worst part is that, after a while, you start to wear it. All over your face, in your eyes, on your clothes.

Stop it, Dad, just knock it the hell off!

It's a mark, this sound, that people can see and recognize. You might be at the grocery store or just walking outside to get the mail and people will look at you and see what you are, what you can only be, and that's a factory worker, a laborer all your life, and they know this by looking at you because you wear the noise.

I never asked you to give up any of your hopes or dreams to go work there, you gave those up on your own!

A man works his whole life away and he grows angry because he can't make anyone understand how it feels to scrub your hands so hard after a day's work that the palms start to bleed.

Goddammit, Dad, shut up! I know it's crummy but it's not my fault!

I remember my daddy's hands, the machine stink on them. The day he had my dog put down he tried to apologize to me, told me about how sick old Ralph was, but I was too hurt to listen. He just stood there and touched my cheek. I opened my eyes and looked at his hand and saw it was stained with machine grease. It was the hand that fed me but it was also the hand that killed my dog. He did it. Because he had to. Had to and hated it. He knew he'd never have to tell me he was sorry because his hand against my face, trying to wipe away my tears, said it all. His cruel dog-killing hand with its grease and machine stink so lightly against my face.

Take a good look at *my* hands, boy. A man's flesh was never meant to be like this, the lines so dark from oil stains they might as well be cracks in plaster. Sometimes I hate the idea of touching your mother with these hands, having her feel the callouses and cuts, the roughness on her cheek. She deserves tenderness, boy, the soft, easy touch of a lover, and she ain't never gonna feel it from these hands.

But she loves you, we all do, you should know that.

I know you do, boy. And I wish it helped more than it does, but sometimes it don't and that just makes me sick right down to the ground.

4

Jackson climbed the front steps of Herb Kaylor's house and knocked on the door. Darlene answered, nodded, and invited him inside.

The house smelled like coffee, uneaten dinner, and grief.

"I made meat loaf tonight," whispered Herb Kaylor's widow. "It was always his favorite. Don't know what I'm gonna do with it now . . ." She bit her lower lip and closed her eyes, locking her body rigid against Jackson's embrace. Pulling away, she ran a hand through her thinning gray hair and coughed. "I have to . . . apologize for how the place looks. I, uh . . . I—"

"Place looks fine," whispered Jackson as she led him toward the kitchen.

"Nice of you to say so." Her eyes were puffy and red-rimmed, making the lines on her face harsher.

Her son, Will, was making coffee; the teenager exchanged terse greetings with the sheriff and took his coffee into another room.

"Would you like a cup?" asked Darlene. "I grind the beans myself. Herb says . . . *said* that it made all the difference in the world from the store-bought kind."

"Yes, thank you."

As she handed him the cup and saucer her hand be-gan to shake and she almost spilled the coffee in his lap. She apologized, tried to smile, then sat at the table and wept quietly. After a moment she held out her hand and Jackson took it.

"Darlene," he said softly, "I hate to ask you about this but I gotta know. Why was Herb working the picket to-day? He wasn't supposed to be there again until Friday."

"I swear to you I don't know. I asked him this morning right before he left. He just kind of laughed—you know how he always does when he don't want to bother you with a problem? Then he kissed me and said he was sorry he'd got Will into this and he was gonna try to fix things."

"What'd he mean?"

"He got Will on at the plant. Was even gonna train him." She shook her head and sipped at her coffee. "You know Herb's father did the same for him? Got him a job workin' the same shift in the same cell. I guess a lot of workers get in that way. Didn't your father work there, too?"

Jackson looked away and whispered, "Yeah."

"Place is like a fuckin' family heirloom," Will said standing up in the doorway.

Jackson turned to look at him as Darlene said, "What did I tell you about using that kind of language in the house? Your daddy—"

"—was stupid! Admit it. It was stupid of him to go down there today."

Darlene stared at him with barely contained fury worsened by weariness and grief. "I won't have you bad-mouthing you father, Will. He ain't"—her voice cracked—"here to defend himself. He worked hard for his family and deserved a hell of a lot more respect and thanks than he ever got."

"*Thanks?*" shouted Will. "For what? For reminding me that he put his obligations over his own happiness, or for getting me on at the plant so I could become another goddamn factory stooge like him? Which wonderful gift should I have thanked him for?"

"You sure couldn't find a decent job on your own. Somebody had to do something."

"Listen," said Jackson, "maybe I should come back—"

"When was I supposed to look for another job? Between running errands for you and helping with the housework and cleaning up after Dad when he got drunk—"

"I think you'd better go to your room."

"No," said Will, storming into the kitchen and slamming down his coffee cup. "I'm eighteen years old and not once have I ever been allowed to disagree with anything you or Dad wanted. You weren't the one who had to sit down here and listen to him ramble on at three in the morning after he got tanked. To hear him tell it, working the plant was just short of Hell, yet he was more than happy to hand my ass over—"

"He was only trying to help you get some money so you could finally get your own place, get on your own two feet. He was a very giving, great man."

"A *great* man? How the hell can you say that? You're wearing clothes that are ten years old and sitting at a table we bought for nine dollars at Goodwill! Maybe Dad had some great notions, but *he* wasn't great. He was a bitter, used-up little bit of a man who could only go to sleep after work if he downed enough booze, and I'll be damned if I'm gonna end up like—"

Darlene shot up from her chair and slapped Will across the face with such force he fell against the counter. When he regained his balance and turned back to face her, a thin trickle of blood oozed slowly from the corner of his mouth. His eyes widened in fear, shock, and countless levels of confusion and pain.

"You listen to me," said Darlene. "I was married to your

father for almost twenty-five years, and in that time I saw him do things you aren't half man enough to do. I've seen him run into the middle of worse riots than the one today and pull old men out of trouble. I've seen him give his last dime to friends who didn't have enough for groceries and then borrow money from your uncle to pay our own bills. I've seen him be more gentle than you can ever imagine and I've been there when he's felt low because he thought you were embarrassed by him. Maybe he was just a factory worker, but he was a damn decent man who gave me love and a good home. You never saw it, maybe you didn't want to, but your father was a great man who did great things. Maybe they weren't huge things, things that get written about in the paper, but that shouldn't matter. It's not his fault that you never saw any of his greatness, that you only saw him when he was tired and used-up. And maybe he did drink but, goddammit, for almost twenty-five years he never once thought about just giving up. I loved that . . . *factory stooge* more than any man in my life—and I could've had plenty. He was the best of them all."

"Mom, please, I—"

"—You never did nothing except make him feel like a failure because he couldn't buy you all the things your friends have. I wasn't down here listening to him ramble at three in the morning? You weren't there on those nights before we had kids, listening to him whisper how scared he was he wouldn't be able to give us a decent life. You weren't there to hold him and kiss him and feel so much tenderness between your bodies that it was like you were one person. And twenty-five years of that, of loving a man like your father, that gives you something no one can ruin or take away, and I won't listen to you talk against him! He was my husband and your father and he's dead and it hurts so much I want to scream."

•

Will's eyes filled with tears. "Oh god, Mom, I miss him. I'm so . . . sorry I said those things. I was just so angry." His chest began to hitch with the abrupt force of his sorrow. "I know that I . . . I hurt his feelings, that I made him feel like everything he did was for nothing. Can't I be mad that I'll never get the chance to make it up to him? Can't I?" He leaned into his mother's arms and wept. "He always said that you gotta . . . gotta look out for your obligations before you can start thinking about your own happiness. I know that now. And I'll . . . I'll try to . . . oh, Christ, Mom. I want the chance to make it all up to him . . ." Darlene held him and stroked the back of his head, whispering, "It's all right, go on . . . go on . . . he knows now, he always did, you have to believe that . . ."

Ted Jackson turned away from them and swallowed his coffee in three large gulps, winced as it hit his stomach, and was overpowered by the loss that soaked the room. He'd never felt more isolated or useless in his life.

Someone knocked loudly on the front door. Darlene turned toward Jackson. "Would you . . . would you mind answering the door, Ted? I don't think I'm . . . up to it just now."

Jackson said of course and went into the front room, quickly wiped his eyes and blew his nose, then turned on the porchlight and opened the door.

5

Even if you manage to scrub off all the dirt and grease and metal shavings, you've still got the smell on you. Cheap aftershave, machine oil, sweat, the stink of hot metal. No matter how many showers you take, the smell stays on you. It's a stench that factory workers carry to their graves, a stink that's on them all the days of their lives, squatting by them at the end like some loyal hound dog that sits by its master's grave until it starves to death, reminding you that all you leave behind is a mortgage, a pile of unpaid bills, children who are ashamed of you, and a spouse who will grow old and bitter and miserable and empty and will never be able to rid the house of that smell.

Stop it.

That smell is your heritage, boy, don't deny it. You were born to be part of the line, part of the Machine, and it will mark you just like it marked me.

I won't listen to this.

Breathe it in deep.

SHUT THE FUCK UP!

That's a good boy.

6

Seven men stood on the porch, each with some sort of bandage covering a wound. Though Jackson recognized all of them as strikers, he only knew a few by name.

A barrel-chested man in old jeans and a grimy sweatshirt stepped forward and offered a firm handshake. "Evenin', Sheriff. We come to . . . to pay our respects to the family. Herb was one of the good guys and we're sorry as hell that he died because of this."

"Darlene's not feeling up to a bunch of company," said Jackson. "I shouldn't even be here myself but—"

"Nonsense," said Darlene from behind him. "Herb would never turn away a fellow union man, and neither will I."

Jackson stepped back as the men entered and stood in a semicircle, each looking sad, awkward, lost, and angry.

The barrel-chested man (Darlene called him "Rusty") offered the group's sympathy—each man muttering agreement and nodding his head—and said that if there was anything they could do she was to give the word and they'd be right on it.

Darlene thanked them and offered them some coffee.

The men seemed to relax a little as each found a place to sit.

Then Will came into the room.

Once, when Jackson had still been a deputy, he'd arrested a man suspected of child molestation. When he'd opened the door to the holding cell every prisoner there had looked at the man with such cold loathing it made Jackson's blood almost stop in his veins. The guy hadn't lasted the night—Jackson found him the next morning beaten to a pulp. He'd choked on his own vomit with three socks rammed in his mouth.

The workers in the room were looking at Will Kaylor exactly the same way. Jackson felt the nerves in the back of his neck start tingling. He released a slow, quiet breath and surreptitiously unbuttoned the holster strap over his revolver.

"Hello," said Will flatly.

The men made no reply. Eyes looked back and forth from Will to Jackson.

"Well," said Darlene with false brightness, "would one of you like to give me a hand in the kitchen?"

Rusty and another man said they'd love to and followed her in, but not before giving Will one last angry glance.

As the remaining men started to whisper among themselves, Will touched Jackson's elbow and asked the sheriff to follow him upstairs.

Jackson excused himself and went after Will. They walked quickly up to Will's room at the end of the hall and closed the door.

Will turned on a small bedside lamp. "You know they really came here to see me, don't you?"

"I figured it was something like that."

"I was supposed to work the picket line today. My first day at work was the morning the strike started. Dad barely had a chance to show me the press before the walkout." His eyes filled with pleading. "Please believe I loved my dad and I appreciated what he tried to do for me, but I . . . didn't want to end up like him. He was so goddamn tired and unhappy all the time. I just . . . didn't want to let that happen to me."

Jackson put his hand on Will's shoulder. "Your dad told me once that he hoped you'd do better than he had. I really don't think he'd blame you, so don't go blaming yourself."

"But those guys downstairs blame me. As far as they're concerned I should have been the one who died today." He crossed to the window and pulled back the curtain. The factory in the distance shimmered with an eerie phosphorescence that seemed both peaceful and mocking.

"Have you ever been in the lobby of the bank downtown?" asked Will. "All those windows facing every direction? Have you noticed that you can't see any part of the factory from there, not even the smokestacks? I worked for a while last summer as a caddy at the Moundbuilders Country Club. They used to give us a free lunch. The factory's only five miles away but you can't see it from anywhere on the club grounds, even using binoculars."

"You're not making any sense."

"It's almost as if the people who don't want to know about it can't see it." He turned around and pulled the curtain farther back. "Can you see the factory, Sheriff?"

"Yeah."

"My room faces north, all right?"

"Okay . . . ?"

Will dropped the curtain and crossed to open the door, gesturing for Jackson to follow him to the other end of the hall. They entered Herb and Darlene's room. Will pointed at the curtains.

"Their window faces the exact opposite direction of mine. Pull back the curtain."

Confused, Jackson did as Will asked.

—and found himself facing a view of the factory. The angle was slightly different, but it was undeniably the factory.

"That's impossible," he whispered. "The damn thing's north and this window—"

"Dad showed it to me the night before I started at the plant. If you go downstairs and look out the back door, you'll still be able to see it. Look out any door or window facing any direction in this house and you'll see the plant."

Jackson let the curtain fall back.

Will shrugged his shoulders in defeat. "I don't know why I'm showing you this, telling you these things. I doubt you even understand."

Jackson faced him. "I know exactly how you feel, Will. My dad was killed at the plant when I was seventeen. Up until the day he died he'd been priming me to go work the line. I didn't want to, God knows, I saw what it did to him, how it sucked his life away. He was dead long before the . . . accident. I watched it happen bit by bit, the way his spirit just ground to a halt in a series of sputtering little agonies. I hated that place, even used to have these dreams where the machines came alive and chased me. The morning he was killed my mom started in on me to go get a job there. I didn't know what to do. But I got lucky and was drafted. Even Vietnam was preferable to that place. Mom died while I was over there. As terrible as it sounds, for as much as I loved her I was almost relieved that she was dead because it meant she wouldn't hound me about taking my father's place at the plant."

"Why did you stay here?"

"I wish I knew." Jackson absentmindedly scratched at

an area near the center of his back, thinking about the marks he'd found there when he was a child, and pulled his hand away. "Maybe it was my way of defying that place. I kept remembering the passage from Revelations that the priest read at Dad's funeral: 'Yea, sayeth the spirit, that they may rest from their labours, and their works do follow them.' Well, *I* wasn't going to follow and I was damned if that place was gonna drill into my conscience and follow me. For so many years I'd listened to Dad talk about it like it was an actual living thing that I came to think of it that way, so I guess part of me decided to stay here just to spite it, to drive past it every day and think, 'You didn't get me, motherfucker!' At least that way I can . . . I dunno, make my dad's death count for something." He exhaled, smiled, and put his hand on Will's shoulder. "Those men can't force you to do anything you don't want to, not while *I'm* wearing this badge, anyway."

"Thanks, Sheriff. Dad always said you were one of the good guys."

"So was he. So're all the workers."

Will stared down at his trembling hands. "You know the funny thing? I keep thinking about being . . . a virgin. I've never even *kissed* a girl. I've been trapped here all my life, waiting to follow in my dad's footsteps, watching him and Mom waste away, not able to do a goddamn thing about it. I spend half my time feeling like shit and the other half mad that I feel that way. I look in mirrors and think I'm seeing a picture of my dad. I think of everything he and Mom have missed out on and I just . . . surrender, y'know? Because I love them. And I don't know if I'm my own man or just the sum of my family's parts."

Jackson started out of the room. "You stay here. I'm gonna go send those men on their way."

Will rose from the bed. "Sheriff?"

"Yeah?"

"Thanks for telling me about your dad. It helped me to decide. I'm gonna go with them."

"Jesus, Will, you just said that—"

"—I said that I *didn't* want to go—but I've been thinking about what Dad said, about looking out for obligations before thinking about your own happiness, and he was right. And just like you, I gotta make my dad's death count for something."

Jackson stared at him. "You sure about this?"

"Yes. It's the first thing I have been sure of. It's about time."

The boy was now resigned.

The son would become the father.

"All right," said Jackson, swallowing back his rage and disgust.

"I'd . . . I'd really appreciate it if you'd come along, Sheriff."

"Why's that?"

"I think you and I have something in common. I think we both never understood what our fathers went through, and I think we've both always wanted to know."

Jackson glanced out the window, at the factory. "I could never imagine what he must've . . . felt like, day after day. I could never—" He blinked, looked away. "Yeah. I'd like to come along."

They went downstairs. Will asked his mother to please help him pack his lunch pail.

The other men seemed pleased.

Jackson shook his head, offered his sympathy to Darlene once again, and left with Will and the others.

7

—someday you'll understand, boy, that a man becomes something more than part of his machine and
his machine becomes something more than just the
other half of a tool. They marry in a way no two people
could ever know. They become each other's God. They
become a greater Machine. And the Machine makes all
things possible. It feeds you, clothes you, puts the roof
over your head, and shows you all the mercy that the
world never will.

The Machine is family.

It is purpose.

It is love.

So take its lever and feel the devotion.

There you go, just like that.

8

The parking lot was deserted, save for cars driven by the midnight-shift workers.

They milled about outside the doors to the basement production cell, waiting for Jackson and Will.

As they approached the group Will gently took Jackson by the arm and said, "I think it'd be nice if you didn't stop coming around for cards Saturday nights."

"Wouldn't miss it for the world."

They stood among the other workers. Barrel-chested Rusty smiled at Will, nodded at Jackson, and said, "We got to make sure."

"I figured," said Jackson.

"Sure of what?" asked Will.

And Rusty replied: "You never actually started working with the press, did you?"

Will sighed and shook his head. "No. The strike was called right after I clocked in." Without another word, he took off his jacket, then unbuttoned and removed his shirt, turning around.

Rusty pulled a flashlight from his back pocket and shone the beam on Will's back.

Several round scarlike marks speckled the young man's back, starting between his shoulder blades and continuing toward the base of his spine. Some were less than an eighth of an inch in diameter but others looked to be three times that size, pushing inward like the pink indentations left in the skin after a scab has been peeled off.

"Damn," said Rusty. "Shift's gotta start on time."

"Don't you think I know that?" snapped Will. "Dad used to talk about how . . . oh, hell." He took a deep breath. "Better get on with it."

Rusty pulled a small black handbook from his pocket, then turned toward the other men. "We're here tonight to welcome a new brother into our union— Will Kaylor, son of Herb. Herb was a decent man, a good friend, and one of the finest machinists it's ever been my privilege to work beside. I hope that all of us will treat his son with the same respect we gave to his father."

The workers nodded in approval.

Rusty flipped through the pages of his tattered union handbook until he found what he was looking for. "Sheriff," he said, offering the book to Jackson, "would you do us the honor of reading the union prayer here in the front where I marked it?"

"It would be . . . a privilege," replied Jackson, taking the book.

Will was marched to a nearby wall, then pressed face- and chest-first against it, his bare back exposed to the night.

"Just clench your teeth together," whispered Rusty to Will. "Close your eyes, and hold your breath. It don't hurt as much as you think."

The other shift workers were opening their lunch pails and toolboxes, removing Philips-head screwdrivers.

Jackson would not allow himself to turn away. His father had gone through this, as had his father before him. Jackson had been spared, but that did not ease his conscience. He wanted to know.

He *had* to know.

Rusty looked toward Jackson and gave a short, sharp nod of his head, and Jackson began to read: " 'Almighty God, we, your workers, beseech Thee to guide us, that we may do the work which Thou givest us to do, in truth, in beauty, and righteousness, with singleness of heart as Thy servants and to the benefit of our fellow men.' "

The workers gathered around Will, each choosing a scar and then, one by one, in orderly succession, plunging their screwdriver into it.

" 'Though we are not poets, Lord, or visionaries, or prophets, or great-minded leaders of men, we ask that you accept our humble labour of our hands as proof of our love for You, and for our families.' "

Blood spurted from each wound and gouted down Will's back, spattering against the asphalt.

His scream began somewhere in the center of the earth, forcing its way up through layers of molten rock and centuries of pain, shuddered through his legs and groin, lodged in his throat for only a moment before erupting from his throat as the howl of the shift whistle, growing in volume to deafen the very ears of God.

Jackson had to shout to be heard over the din. " 'We thank Thee for Thy blessing as we, Your humble workers, welcome a new brother into our ranks. May You watch over and protect him as You have always watched over and protected us. Who can be our adversary, if You are on our side? You did not even spare Your own Son, but gave him up for the sake of us all.' "

" 'And must not that gift be accompanied by the gift of all else?' " responded the workers in unison.

" '. . . So we offer our gift of all else, Lord, we offer our labours for the glory of Thy name, Amen.' "

"Amen," echoed the workers, backing away.

"Amen," said Will, dropping to his knees, then vomiting and whimpering.

Jackson closed the union handbook and came forward, tears in his eyes, and began to cradle Will in his arms; the boy shook his head and rose unsteadily to his feet, then began staggering toward the slowly opening basement doors—

(here is my son
does he have the makings of a factory man?)

—squeaking, screeching, loud clanking, heavy machinery dragging across a cement floor—

—the doors opened farther—

—something long, metallic, and triple-jointed pushed through, folding around the edge. A glint as more metal thrust out and folded, seizing the door—

—throwing sparks, the mechanical hand raked down, gripped the handle, and pulled the door wide open.

. . . doors open and the OldWorker is cast away . . .

Something crumpled and manlike was tossed out over their heads and landed with a soft *whumph!* in the snow.

Will turned toward Jackson. "A man works his whole life away, and what does it mean?"

Jackson and the workers stared into the shimmering electric gaze beyond the iron doors.

"Welcome, my son," whispered Jackson—

—in a voice very much like his own father's—

"Welcome to the Machine."

. . . as the production line begins again . . .

9

You'll be a worker just like me, that's the way of it.

Work the line, wear the smell; the son following in his father's footsteps.

Something like this, well . . . it makes a man's life seem worthwhile.

I always knew you'd do me proud.

I love you, Dad. I hope this makes up for a lot of things.

I love you too, son.

Best get to work.

That's a good boy. . . .

SARAH PINBOROUGH

The quiet New England town of Tower Hill sits perched on high cliffs, removed from the outside world. At its heart lie a small college…and a very old church. There are secrets buried in Tower Hill, artifacts hidden centuries ago and long forgotten. But they are about to be unearthed….

A charismatic new priest has come to Tower Hill. A handsome new professor is teaching at the college. And a nightmare has settled over the town. A girl is found dead and mutilated—by her own hand. Another has slashed her face with scissors. Have the residents of Tower Hill all gone mad? Or has something worse…something unholy…taken over?

TOWER HILL

ISBN 13: 978-0-8439-6052-5

MORE TERRIFYING THAN EVER....

RICHARD LAYMON'S

THE WOODS ARE DARK

The RESTORED, UNCUT Edition, In Print for the FIRST TIME!

Neala and her friend Sherri only wanted to do a little hiking through the woods. Little did they know they would soon be shackled to a dead tree, waiting for Them to arrive. The Dills family thought the small hotel in the quiet town seemed quaint and harmless enough. Until they, too, found themselves shackled to trees in the middle of the night, while They approached, hungry for human flesh....

ISBN 13: 978-0-8439-5750-1

JACK
KETCHUM

Burned again. Men never treated Dora well. This latest cheated on her and dumped her. The last decent guy she knew was her old high school boyfriend, Jim. He'd said that he loved her. Maybe he did. So with the help of Flame Finders, Dora's tracked him down. Turns out he's married with two kids. But Dora isn't about to let that stand in her way…

OLD FLAMES

Includes the novella,
RIGHT TO LIFE

ISBN 13: 978-0-8439-5999-4

GRAHAM MASTERTON

A new and powerful crime alliance holds Los Angeles in a grip of terror. Anyone who opposes them suffers a horrible fate…but not by human hands. Bizarre accidents, sudden illnesses, inexplicable and gruesome deaths, all eliminate the alliance's enemies and render the crime bosses unstoppable. Every deadly step of the way, their constant companions are four mysterious women, four shadowy figures who wield more power than the crime bosses could ever dream of. But at the heart of the nightmare lies the final puzzle, the secret of…

THE
5TH WITCH

ISBN 13: 978-0-8439-5790-7

NATE KENYON

"A voice reminiscent of Stephen King in the days of *'Salem's Lot*. One of the strongest debut novels to come along in years."
——*Cemetery Dance*

A man on the run from his past. A woman taken against her will. A young man consumed by rage...and a small town tainted by darkness. In White Falls, a horrifying secret is about to be uncovered. The town seems pleasant enough on the surface. But something evil has taken root in White Falls—something that has waited centuries for the right time to awaken. Soon no one is safe from the madness that spreads from neighbor to neighbor. The darkness is growing. Blood is calling to blood. And through it all...the dead are watching.

BLOODSTONE

ISBN 13: 978-0-8439-6020-4

BRYAN SMITH

It was known as the House of Blood. It sat at the entrance to a netherworld of unimaginable torture and terror. Very few who entered its front door lived to ever again see the outside world. But a few did survive. They thought they had found a way to destroy the house of horrors…but they were wrong. A new house has arisen. A new mistress now wields its unholy power—and she wants revenge. She will not rest until those who dared to challenge her and her former master are made to pay with their very souls.

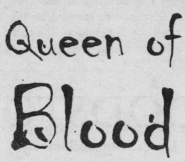

Queen of Blood

ISBN 13: 978-0-8439-6061-7

To order a book or to request a catalog call:
1-800-481-9191
This book is also available at your local bookstore, or you can check out our Web site **www.dorchesterpub.com** where you can look up your favorite authors, read excerpts, or glance at our discussion forum to see what people have to say about your favorite books.

✂ # ❐ **YES!**

Sign me up for the Leisure Horror Book Club and send my
FREE BOOKS! If I choose to stay in the club, I will pay only
$8.50* each month, a savings of $7.48!

NAME: _____

ADDRESS: _____

TELEPHONE: _____

EMAIL: _____

❐ I want to pay by credit card.

❐ VISA   ❐ MasterCard   ❐ DISCOVER

ACCOUNT #: _____

EXPIRATION DATE: _____

SIGNATURE: _____

Mail this page along with $2.00 shipping and handling to:
Leisure Horror Book Club
PO Box 6640
Wayne, PA 19087
Or fax (must include credit card information) to:
610-995-9274
You can also sign up online at **www.dorchesterpub.com**.
*Plus $2.00 for shipping. Offer open to residents of the U.S. and Canada only. Canadian
residents please call 1-800-481-9191 for pricing information.
If under 18, a parent or guardian must sign. Terms, prices and conditions subject to
change. Subscription subject to acceptance. Dorchester Publishing reserves the right to
reject any order or cancel any subscription.